# FROM
# A
# DISTANT
# STAR

# ALSO BY KAREN MCQUESTION

## FOR ADULTS

*A Scattered Life*
*Easily Amused*
*The Long Way Home*
*Hello Love*

## FOR YOUNG ADULTS

*Favorite*
*Life on Hold*
*Edgewood* (Book One of the Edgewood Series)
*Wanderlust* (Book Two of the Edgewood Series)
*Absolution* (Book Three of the Edgewood Series)

## FOR CHILDREN

*Celia and the Fairies*
*Secrets of the Magic Ring*

KAREN McQUESTION

# FROM A DISTANT STAR

SKYSCAPE

**SKYSCAPE**

Published by Skyscape, New York

www.apub.com

Amazon, the Amazon logo, and Skyscape are trademarks of Amazon.com, Inc., or its affiliates.

ISBN-13: 9781477830178 (hardcover)
ISBN-10: 1477830170 (hardcover)
ISBN-13: 9781477830161 (paperback)
ISBN-10: 1477830162 (paperback)
eISBN: 9781477880166

Cover design by Shasti O'Leary Soudant

Printed in the United States of America

*For Terry Goodman*
*This one's for you*

# CHAPTER ONE

*"Nowhere to go but out,*
*Nowhere to come but back."*
—"The Pessimist," Benjamin Franklin King

A piercing light flashed across the sky and plunged to the earth, landing in a farmer's field. The old dog, Mack, who had been peeing against the side of the barn, saw the disc-shaped object crash and bounce, skidding thirty feet and throwing dirt as it went. A high-pitched humming and faint glow came off the object, arousing his curiosity, and he trotted out to take a look. Getting closer, he approached cautiously, nose to the ground. The object was the size and shape of his water bowl, iridescent in color, and topped with a shiny dome.

Mack circled around, sniffing while he inched forward, his eyes glowing from the reflection of the object's light. As he watched, the top popped open with a gentle hiss, leaving a snout-sized gap. At the same time, the lights on the object dimmed, then went off entirely. Utterly fascinating.

The old dog was sure his boy, Lucas, would want to know about this. It had been a longstanding tradition that Mack brought back anything of interest from his explorations, something that never failed to delight the boy. He always got an enthusiastic rub behind the ears for his trouble, and sometimes a treat, but as curious as Mack was, he was also wary of this thing. It didn't smell like anything he'd ever encountered before. Under different circumstances, he'd have marked the spot and brought Lucas back later during a walk, but the boy hadn't gotten out of bed in a long time and the dog knew the other people in the house wouldn't help. All of them, except the girl, acted as if Mack were a nuisance. Sometimes he even had to remind them to fill his food bowl.

The night sky was bright with stars and a nearly full moon, and as his eyes adjusted, he brought his nose closer for a good whiff. Metallic, almost like blood but not quite. And there was something else too, something that he couldn't quite place. So very odd. Of all the millions of smells he knew, this wasn't one of them. He knew the scent of humans, Lucas being his favorite. The boy's sweat after working in the fields or coming home from ball practice signaled his arrival before he even came into view. Later, when things changed and Lucas had less energy for their walks, the boy's smell became tinged with a medicinal odor that seeped out of his pores and clung to his clothing and hair. The relationship between the dog and his boy changed too, with Lucas having barely enough energy to pet him, and the others shooing Mack out of the room at every turn. And now Lucas slept around the clock. It just wasn't right.

Mack heard the creak of the screen door opening right before the woman's voice rang out. "Mack? Where are you? Get back here now!" Her tone was impatient and he knew if he didn't return to the house soon, she'd lock the door and he'd be stuck outside until morning. He yipped a quick response before quickly sticking his nose into the opening at the top of the disc-shaped object in order to commit the smell to his olfactory memory. This time he caught a different odor: something alarming, something *alive*. At the very second his brain grasped this fact, a shapeless something flew out of the craft, latched onto his nose, and wiggled upward until it covered his eyes. The sensation was stronger than a breeze, almost like a splash of water to the face, but not exactly like that either. He stepped back, blinked, and shook his head trying to get the thing off him, but it was stuck, covering his eyes and making his vision murky. Panic-stricken, he panted and trembled, feeling it seep through the membranes to the back of his eyes. A split second later, he felt nothing. It was gone. He whined to himself, a sound of relief.

"Mack! I mean it!" Her voice pierced the night air. It was the sound of aggravation and bone-weary tiredness, but the dog only heard the finality of it. He barked to let her know he was on his way, then turned and raced back to the house.

# CHAPTER TWO

"Emma, it's getting late." I looked up to see Mrs. Walker in the doorway with her arms crossed, doing her best impression of a stern parent. "Were you planning on staying all night *again*?"

Really? She had to ask? After all this time, she still didn't get it. If my own mother didn't mind me being here night and day, what was Mrs. Walker's problem? "Yes," I said, looking down at Lucas, lying still in the bed next to me. I wasn't going to leave him. Not now. Not ever.

"Okay," she said, giving in and turning around. I heard her in the kitchen, setting up the coffeemaker for the next day, then emptying the dishwasher. Lucas's hospital bed had been set up in the dining room, right in the middle of the house. Lucas's parents had no idea how much I'd heard of their private conversations, their many discussions concerning me and Lucas and his so-called "impending death." I knew they didn't want me here in their home. They resented my imposition on their family. But they didn't have the heart to keep me away.

During the school year, Mrs. Walker had made a good case for me to spend some time away. I had school to attend in the morning, homework to do in the evening. I'd already dropped out of all my extracurriculars, but I didn't want to miss school. When Lucas got better, he'd be finishing high school. I was a year behind him originally, but with all the time he'd taken off for the treatment of his cancer, he'd have a lot to make up. If all went well, we'd wind up graduating together. During the year, I had reluctantly left his side to go to classes and tried to concentrate on my subjects, but it was nearly impossible. My grades should have taken a hit, but I think my teachers felt sorry for me, the girlfriend of Lucas, the guy bravely battling cancer, so they gave me grades I didn't quite deserve. All the teachers loved Lucas. He was the golden boy of Westridge High: blond curly hair, football star, honor student, great personality, always smiling. It was a small country high school and everyone knew him. Everyone liked him too. All the guys were his buddies. All the girls wanted him for their boyfriend. But none of those other girls could have him. He was mine.

And I was his. I was his savior, the one he hung on for. He'd said as much, back when he was still speaking, and even now that he was comatose, I could tell he knew I was there, right by his side. I talked to him and stroked his hair, and when Mr. and Mrs. Walker and Lucas's brother, Eric, weren't around, I did more than that, kissing him and caressing his skin, hoping somehow to reach him. Hoping he'd find the emotional thread that linked us so I could pull him away from the next world and back into this one.

When Lucas and I had started dating at the end of my sophomore year, it was pretty clear I wasn't his parents' first choice for their son. It didn't matter that I was an honors student and used my best manners; they were still stuck on the fact that my mother and I lived in a trailer park off the highway. That, and the fact that I am, and always have been, completely fatherless. The first dinner at their house, Mrs. Walker had asked, "What does your dad do, Emma?"

Lucas shot his mother a disapproving look, but I was ready with my standard response. I shrugged and said, "I don't know. I've never met him."

My mom had told me that my father had been an international student at the university where she'd once worked as an administrative assistant. They'd had a fling for a few weeks and then he was gone, back to where he came from. Mom was vague about his country of origin, but judging from my coal-black eyes, olive skin, and dark hair, it seemed likely he was Middle Eastern. My mom wasn't much for long-term relationships. She'd always had boyfriends, but none of them were keepers. One had shown me how to hot-wire a car and the best way to roll smokes. That guy was named Owen. He didn't last long before Mom found out about his outstanding warrants and kicked him to the curb. Her taste in men was questionable, but at least they never lived with us.

So the Walkers looked down on me. Once I overheard Lucas's mother say, "She follows him around like a duckling, like she'd be lost without him." Lucas wanted to confront her about this, but I talked him out of it. That was back when I still thought I could win them over. But it never happened. Lucas and I had been together for over a year and the entire time they hoped we would break up, but we didn't.

I didn't think too much of them either, for two reasons. First of all, for as many problems as my mom had, she was the perfect mother as far as I was concerned because she didn't try to take credit for everything I did. Sometimes I'd hand her my report card or show her a paper I wrote and she'd practically cry with joy. "Brilliant," she'd say, hugging me. "You are absolutely brilliant. I'm so impressed."

Not like Lucas's dad, Mr. Walker, who took credit for everything Lucas did, bragging, "He takes after me." Or worse yet, smugly telling Lucas, "See, I told you if you studied, you'd get an A." And then he always had to add, "Now don't get complacent. You still have to keep this up for the rest of the semester, you know."

So that was the first reason I wasn't a fan of Lucas's parents. The second reason is that they gave up on him so easily. Sure, he had cancer, but big deal, people got cancer and beat it all the time. It was a shock for everyone when he was diagnosed, but Lucas was athletic and strong. All you had to do was look at him and you knew he'd survive. He *was* life. Lucas could run like the wind. I'd seen him lift a ninety-pound calf like it was nothing. It was unthinkable that he'd die. I just knew this was a bump in the road. Something to beat. We had plans, the two of us, and dying of stupid cancer wasn't part of them.

But both of his parents gave up on him right from the start. They always thought the worst, selling his car when he got too sick to go to school. As if he'd never drive again.

His mother couldn't look at Lucas without getting teary eyed. And Mr. Walker was devastated to learn the treatment would leave Lucas sterile, as if passing on the family genes meant anything at a time like this. Mr. and Mrs. Walker had hushed conversations about statistics, and treatment plans, and numbers. Always the numbers. They'd say, "The numbers don't look good. They're not in the range." Their negativity was everywhere, seeping from room to room, poisoning the air. Later on, they started talking about funerals and how they didn't want him to suffer any longer, and I had to put my hands over Lucas's ears to keep him from hearing. The last member of the family, Lucas's fourteen-year-old brother, Eric, started to avoid everyone, including me and Lucas. When he wasn't doing chores or going to school, he was out in the barn, tinkering with old cars in his workshop. He holed up in there like he hoped to come out someday and find everything fine again.

I was the only one dealing with this in a sane way. The only one. After Lucas went into a coma, even the visiting nurses tried to undermine me. They'd point out how much weight he'd lost, how his skin tone had changed, and how shallow his breathing was. One of them, a tall woman named Nancy, put her hand on my shoulder and talked to me like I was a first grader. "See how sunken his eyes are?" she said. "And how nonresponsive he is?"

She pinched his wrist and Lucas did nothing but lie still like he was playing dead. "I've done hospice care for a long time, honey. This is the beginning of the end." She went on to say he might have as much as a week, but that if we were lucky, he'd slip away sooner than that. "Poor baby has suffered enough." She told me they were doing something called palliative care. He had a catheter for his pee and a patch for pain relief and that was all. "Not much urine," she said, showing me the bag. "And what there is, is dark in color. His body is shutting down."

I didn't bother to respond to her, but after she left, I whispered in Lucas's ear, "Don't listen to her. You're going to get better. We'll show her." Once he went into the coma and couldn't eat or drink on his own, I dribbled water into his mouth and wiped a wet sponge over his parched lips. Screw Nancy and her wise proclamations. She didn't know a thing about Lucas. After he made his miraculous recovery, I'd tell him all about Nancy—her ridiculous scrubs covered in cartoon panda bears, how she called everyone "honey," and the way she always bustled in humming some nameless tune, acting like she knew it all.

Because I had a few things up my sleeve that I hadn't told anyone about. Mainly that I was calling in outside forces. First of all, I'd been praying like no one on the face of planet Earth had ever prayed before. I'd never been one for prayer, but when things got serious, I put it into overdrive, imagining God on the other end thinking, *hmmm . . . Emma doesn't usually pray. This must be serious.* I could almost feel God making a plan for everything to work out just fine.

So that was the first thing.

The second thing I'd done was visit Mrs. Kokesh right after school let out for summer vacation a few days earlier. She lived as far from the center of town as the Walkers did, but in the other direction. With my backpack strapped on, I rode my bike to her house. By the time I arrived, I was out of breath, my legs like jelly. Her two-story house was falling down, white paint peeling, porch sagging. Moss growing on the roof. The place was reportedly haunted. Mrs. Kokesh sold produce from a stand by the road during the growing season, which generally didn't start until late June in this part of central Wisconsin, but mysteriously, her vegetables were always ready before everyone else's.

She also did magic, for a price. I'd heard the stories for years. Tales of dying pets brought to health. Love potions that really worked. Magic candles that affected everyone who breathed in the smoke. A spell that ended a drought. But things backfired too, and if she didn't agree with your motives, you might get what she thought you needed instead of what you asked for, and some of it was pretty nasty. That was the story anyway. I didn't know anyone who'd actually gone to her, but the stories, they went round and round. I saw her once at the gas station filling up her ancient Buick, and she just looked like an old lady to me, all hunched over and wearing lots of layers of clothing. It was her disguise, they said. She looked like a harmless old lady, but really she was very powerful.

I made the decision to visit right after Lucas went into the coma and Nancy said he was as good as gone. I still had my faith, but things were looking really bad; even I could see that. All the stories I'd heard at school had made me a little afraid of Mrs. Kokesh, but after biking all that way, there was no way I was turning back. I got off my bike and let it drop to the ground, then went up the steps to the porch and knocked on the door. She answered like I had an appointment, greeting me by name and ushering me inside. She wore a shapeless, brown dress with a droopy fabric belt. "How do you know my name?" I asked.

"Small town," she said, shuffling past a staircase and down a dimly lit hallway. "Pretty girl like you stands out. Especially when you're with the Walker boy. Him with his blond hair, you so dark."

"You know Lucas?" I'd followed her into the kitchen where she gestured for me to take a seat. I pulled out a chair and set my backpack on the floor next to my feet.

She nodded and got a glass from the cabinet and a pitcher of lemonade from the fridge. "I know everyone in this nothing town, but he is especially memorable. I've had more than a few girls come with him in mind, asking for love spells." She set the glass of lemonade in front of me. "One said she'd loved Lucas since the third grade."

I wrapped my fingers around the cold glass, but didn't drink. "Did you do it? The love spell?"

"Ha!" Mrs. Kokesh said. "What do you take me for? This magic stuff is nothing to fool around with. It can't be wasted on high school crushes." She crooked one scolding finger toward me and leaned across the table. Up close, I could see every wrinkle on her face, the lines crosshatched like badly drawn artwork.

"So your magic is real. It works?" I said.

"Of course it works, but it's serious stuff. Not to be trifled with." Behind her, a gray tabby cat jumped up onto the kitchen counter, sniffing at the open pitcher of lemonade.

"Your cat?" I pointed and she turned to look. "Is he supposed to be up there?"

"He's okay," she said, shrugging. "Just curious."

I tightened my grip on the strap of my backpack. It held all the money I had in the world. A lifetime of babysitting cash, Christmas gifts, and last year's strawberry-picking money. "I came today because of Lucas."

"You want him cured." She raised one eyebrow. "You're in love with him and you want the cancer gone."

"Yes." I couldn't believe my luck. Here I'd been afraid to come and she'd welcomed me right in. I didn't even have to ask. She knew immediately what I wanted and said it like it was no big deal.

"Can you do it?" I asked.

She tilted her head to one side, regarding me carefully. I held her gaze, keeping very still, afraid to break her concentration. Right now it seemed like I had a shot and I didn't want to blow it. Behind her, the cat wandered to the end of the counter; I heard a soft thud as he landed on the floor. She tapped her fingers on the table for what seemed like the longest time, and finally she said, "There is a potion that can be used to save a person's life."

I exhaled in relief. "So you'll do it?"

"I can do it, of course, but I'm seeing that something else is going on that might be a problem."

"What do you mean?" I asked.

Mrs. Kokesh shook her head. "I'm not sure. It is out of my area. I've never seen anything like this before." She smiled. "All of the universe is connected, you know. Every living being is part of the cosmic fabric and all of the energy is intertwined. I'm feeling something impending with your boy. A disturbance in the force, isn't that what they call it?" She cackled as if she'd told a joke.

"I guess," I said slowly, unsure of what she was saying.

"Okay, I'll tell you what." She slammed her hand on the table. "What the hell. I'll do it. I have to warn you, though, he may not come back the way you want him to."

"What do you mean?"

"He might not be the Lucas you know and love."

"Like, what would be different?" I asked.

"You're asking me? Ha! I have no idea," she said. "People who've been near death, they come back different. Sometimes more serious, sometimes more careful. Or he might be more spiritual and want to become a priest." She raised her eyebrows. "Are you prepared for that?"

I could tell she was messing with me now. I said, "Lucas would never become a priest. The Walkers aren't even Catholic."

Mrs. Kokesh shrugged. "Just an example. Don't get so bent out of shape. People change even under the best circumstances. And when you pull them back from death's door, well, that's no small thing. Maybe he'll be not so smart or not so strong. His brain has probably been oxygen deprived, so who knows what's happened there. This potion has its limits. You still want to do it?"

"Yes," I said. I'd take Lucas back any way I could get him. I unzipped my backpack and took out everything I'd heard she might need: a photo of Lucas, a lock of his hair, and a small vial with a rubber stopper containing a bit of his saliva. I took them out and lined them up on the table.

"You came prepared," she said, nodding in approval. She held the vial up to the light. "His spit?"

"Yes."

"Good." Mrs. Kokesh stood up abruptly, the legs of her chair scraping against the grooved linoleum. "Give me your phone number and I'll call you tomorrow when I have the potion ready." She grabbed my full glass of lemonade and poured it into the sink.

I stood up, zipping my backpack. "You can't do it now? I can wait."

"It's not like making cupcakes," she said gruffly. "You don't just whip these things up. I'll call you tomorrow as soon as it's done."

I pulled some paper out of my backpack, wrote down my name and cell number, then slid it across the table. Without even looking at it, she folded it and stuck it in the front pocket of her baggy dress.

"Okay then," she said, taking my arm and pulling me out of the kitchen. "Off you go."

Before I knew it, she'd guided me down the long hallway and pushed me out the front door. Once I was on the porch, the door slammed shut abruptly behind me. She never even said good-bye.

"Thanks," I called out, picking up my bike. "I'll see you tomorrow."

The next day, I biked back as soon as she called. Mrs. Kokesh was ready for me, sitting on the top step of the front porch with a paper bag on her lap. When I approached, she handed the bag to me. "As promised," she said, her voice grim. "But I have to warn you, I have a bad feeling about this."

I opened the bag and saw that it contained an empty pickle relish jar, the label still on it. "I don't get it." I gave her a confused look. "What is this?"

"The potion is at the bottom," she said. "There's not much, but you don't need much."

I held it up to the light. Sure enough, a small puddle of clear liquid coated the bottom of the jar. For some reason, I'd been thinking it would be blood red. This looked like nothing. Like she was selling me water. I tilted it back and forth and watched it slosh from side to side. "What do I do with it?"

"Spread it over his eyes and put it on his lips," she said. "Then press your lips to his and seal it with a kiss."

I tried to get a read on her expression. "Really? Or are you kidding?"

"I never kid about magic." An orange cat came around the corner of the house and jumped up next to her. She absentmindedly stroked his head. "The eyes are the windows to the soul. The lips are the doorway to the body. You need both."

"Do I say anything after I do it?"

"What would you say?"

"I don't know."

"You don't have to say anything." Mrs. Kokesh cleared her throat, aggravated. "Just wipe it over his eyes and lips, then kiss him," she repeated impatiently. "Why does everyone want to make it more complicated than it is? You can follow directions, can't you?"

"Yes," I answered, and then remembered something. "You said you had a bad feeling?"

Mrs. Kokesh nodded. "Something's not right about this whole situation. I don't know what it is, but I'm getting a sense things may go haywire."

My hopes, once so high, were getting lower by the minute. After all her talk, it sounded like this might not even work. "But I can still try it, right?"

"Of course. Wait, I'm seeing something odd now." Her nose wrinkled as she concentrated. "I'm seeing you in the belly of the whale. You and Lucas both."

"The belly of the whale? Like Jonah in the Bible?"

"Not quite." She shook her head. "It's gone now. I can't tell you what it means. Just be careful."

"I will." I mean, I wasn't planning on *not* being careful. I dug into my backpack and took out my money. "How much do I owe you?" I asked.

"No charge." She stood up, brushing off the front of her dress. "I wish you the best of luck, Emma. You're gonna need it." She went into the house and the orange cat followed her, scurrying in just before the screen door clattered shut.

That had been earlier today. Ever since, I'd been waiting to be alone with Lucas, but someone was constantly hovering. First the visiting nurse came (not Nancy, thankfully) with more morbid talk, and then both of Lucas's parents hung around on and off all evening. I'd taken to sitting in the recliner off to one side of the room, but as soon as we were alone, I always moved and sat on the bed right next to him. Eventually, I knew, they'd go upstairs to bed. Lately, Mrs. Walker seemed to not sleep much at all, coming down several times a night to check on Lucas, and offering to relieve me so I could go home.

As much as I disliked Mrs. Walker, I kind of respected her too. She stayed up later than anyone else, checking on Lucas during the night, and getting up at dawn to join her husband out in the barn. Mr. Walker had a job during the school year, but over the summer, both of them were all about the farm. They'd hired an extra man to help out so they could be with Lucas throughout the day, but still, Mrs. Walker had to be exhausted. I couldn't wait for her to finish up and make the trek up the stairs, but first she let the dog out, and then she busied herself in the kitchen. When she finished emptying the dishwasher, I heard her wiping off the kitchen counters, scrubbing at a stubborn spot and sighing. From past experience, I knew this would be the last of it. Next she'd open the back door to call Mack back inside, lock up for the night, and head for bed.

But before that could happen, we heard a noise from outside: a huge thud followed by an echoing ricochet. I lifted my head trying to figure out what it was. Fireworks? A shot gun? No, it was more muffled than that. Almost like something vibrating. Mrs. Walker stuck her head in the doorway. "Did you hear that, Emma?"

"Yeah, I did. It sounds like it was near the barn."

"What was it?" Her forehead furrowed.

"I don't know," I said, shaking my head. "It was almost like something hit the ground."

"I hope that dog didn't get into anything." She left and I heard her open the back door and call out, "Mack? Where are you? Get back here now!" Mack barked in return and she waited a couple seconds before hollering for him again. Her voice was harsh, and I knew if he didn't come quickly, she'd leave him out for the night. Once or twice, I'd let him in even after she told me not to. He had to pay the price for not listening, she said. But I was too tender-hearted to leave him outside. He was Lucas's dog.

Luckily, Mack came back inside before Mrs. Walker gave up on him. I heard her scold him for not coming right when she'd called. Before long, he wandered in by me, taking refuge on the floor between Lucas's bed and my recliner. I reached down to pat his head. Mrs. Walker came in to give me one last set of instructions. "If anything changes with Lucas, come and get me," she said. "Right away."

"Yes, of course."

"And don't you let that dog up on the bed," she said. "I found dog hair on the blanket yesterday." Her eyes narrowed at me like an accusation.

"It must have been on someone's clothing when they leaned over the bed," I offered.

She softened. "Well, maybe. Good-night, Emma."

"Good-night, Mrs. Walker."

She left to go upstairs. When I heard the water running in the bathroom above me, I prayed to God again, this time promising anything if he'd bring Lucas back. After Mrs. Walker padded down the hallway to her bedroom, I lifted Mack onto the bed, where he nestled into the space between Lucas and the railing, resting his head on Lucas's shoulder. He knew the drill, the right way to lie so he wouldn't hurt Lucas. Mack was a mutt, all black with a white spot on his belly. The only thing we could tell for sure was that he must be part border collie. Lucas said that the border collie part was what made Mack so smart.

I stroked Lucas's cheek. "Hang in there, Lucas. It's all going to be better soon." He didn't bear much resemblance to the boy who'd stolen my heart the very first time he smiled my way. I could still picture him leaning against his locker, talking to the head cheerleader, Madison Walinski. She was talking frenetically, flipping her hair back, and doing her fake laugh. Her usual self-absorbed routine. Lucas was nodding like he was listening, but anyone could see from the trapped look on his face that he was just being polite. When he glanced my way, we locked eyes and an understanding passed between us—sympathy from me, resignation from him. He flashed me a smile and it was like the heavens opened up and cast a beam of light my way. Such a beautiful boy. Impossibly beautiful. From that moment on, I wanted him. And then, I got him. And that, I thought, was the end of the story. My own personal happy ending, which turned out not to be so happy when cancer interfered.

The chemo had taken away his beautiful curls and only a bit of fuzz had grown back. The lack of hair made his face look even thinner, like skin stretched over a skull. His hands and feet were always cold now and almost bluish. It didn't matter what he looked like, though. I loved Lucas more than I'd ever loved anyone in my life. I couldn't live without him.

I found the relish jar in my backpack and unscrewed the lid, then tilted it and dipped two fingers into the potion. *Please, God, let this work.* Mack whined like he knew something was up. He lifted his head to watch as I wiped the potion onto Lucas's eyes. The movement of my fingers pushed Lucas's eyelids up a little, and they stayed open a crack. Was I supposed to actually put the liquid *in* his eyes? I wasn't sure. I added a little more, carefully moistening the open space below his lids. Then I dabbed the rest on his lips. Curious, Mack worked his way forward on the bed so that his muzzle was right alongside Lucas's face.

"Yeah, Mack," I said. "I know this is weird. Don't worry. I'm not hurting him." I screwed the lid back on the jar before leaning over to kiss Lucas on the lips, then pulled back nervously to see what would happen. Lucas still laid flat on his back, his hands exactly where they'd been positioned by the nurse after she'd turned him. His breathing was still shallow and there was no expression on his face. I watched carefully and then gave him another kiss. "I love you, Lucas." Absolutely nothing had changed.

For some reason, I'd been thinking the potion would work immediately. It didn't have to be a total cure. I would have settled for a twitch or a smile. Anything that told me he'd made the turn away from death and back to me. Disappointment overwhelmed me and I felt my eyes fill with tears. The kiss had left a bit of the slippery potion on my lips and I went to grab a tissue out of my backpack. Mack whined a little bit while I cleaned up my face. "It's okay, boy," I said. I still had some liquid left in the bottom of the jar. "We'll try again later."

# CHAPTER THREE

When the main ship was hit, the scout knew he was going to die if he didn't act quickly.

The mission had started off well enough. All of the scouts knew their jobs and followed standard protocol. His small craft was one of twenty attached to the underside of a much larger circular ship, the *Seeker*. They traveled through space that way, the scouts in their crafts, secured around the bottom rim, along for the ride.

The mission was the same each time. Together they traveled from their galaxy to other worlds. Once they reached position over the surface of the targeted planet, the *Seeker* would give the order for them to disengage. At that point, they'd drop down and hover over the planet's outer crust to acquire data: assessing the ground for mineral content, and sending out pulses that would survey the inhabitants in the surrounding area to see how highly evolved they were. They'd been visiting some of the planets for many lifetimes, each time monitoring how advanced the citizens had become, how prone to aggression they were, how quickly they were evolving to the higher path. The scouts kept a low profile, avoiding areas that were densely populated, and purposely timing their visits for the least visibility.

This planet, the one they called Earth, was a curious one. A certain percentage of the inhabitants were so highly evolved some of the elders thought they could be contacted directly and invited to join the coalition. But the evolved inhabitants were few, and didn't seem to hold any power over the masses, who were, by all accounts, brutal. If they couldn't be trusted to treat each other well, how receptive would they be to outsiders from another world?

This scout didn't care either way. He was new to the job and took pride in doing such important work. Back home, his physical body lay dormant, waiting for his return, a shell without a spirit. Many years earlier, the elders had discovered that, with atmospheric variances from planet to planet, it was easier to separate their consciousness from their body and send just that part along, rather than try to physically adapt each time. Each scout's consciousness fit within a tiny craft, which required less space and fuel, but their intellect and other senses were still there, which was all that was needed. The mother ship powered their minicraft, but navigation fell to them. They maneuvered using their thoughts and intent, following a prearranged route, but able to deviate if need be.

When the main ship broke through the atmosphere and reached the targeted position, all twenty of the scouts in the smaller crafts waited for the drop-down signal, ready to cover their assigned areas. The scout had been to Earth before, the last time scanning an arid environment. A "desert," the inhabitants called it. Although not as abundant in life forms, it had a certain stark beauty. The landscape on this mission was very different. He'd been told they'd encounter different forms of foliage, as well as creatures big and small, but probably not the most highly evolved inhabitants. If they did encounter one of these "people" (as they were known in the local language), they were to leave the area immediately.

If everything went according to plan, all twenty scouts would return to the original ship at a prearranged time, latching onto their spot against the ship until they reached the next location. Most of them had done this type of mission many times before. It was all very routine.

At least, that was the plan.

When a missile came at the main ship after it entered the atmosphere, the new scout was the only one who disengaged. He did it in a panic, violating the rule that said only to detach on command. While the *Seeker* and the other nineteen crafts still attached exploded above him, his small craft spun away, emergency illuminators snapping on as he hurtled downward at a dizzying speed. When he finally hit the ground, it was at an angle, sending his craft skidding and bouncing violently before coming to a stop. He'd lost control and hadn't even gotten his bearings when the top of the craft opened, its seal damaged by the impact. The illuminators hissed and then crackled. They brightened before dimming, and then went dark completely.

Being grounded and cut off from the power supply was the worst possible thing that could happen to a scout. The scout's ability to communicate was limited to the main ship, the *Seeker*, and he relied on it to repower his craft after each mission. As disoriented as he was, he tried to weigh his options. His craft was damaged, the main ship obliterated, leaving him without a way to communicate with his home planet. Worse yet, he'd been left grounded: a consciousness without a body. In this state, he was an energy field known as bio-plasma: a collection of memory, emotions, and thought processes. But he wasn't whole. There was no way to go home. And he wouldn't last long if he couldn't transfer to a new living vessel. Death was certain.

When the creature approached, the scout didn't even try to assess the life form. He saw an opportunity, one he knew he might not have later, and he took it. The second the creature came close enough, the scout exited his craft and latched onto this being. His life depended on finding a new host and he couldn't afford to be picky.

He shimmied in through the moist membranes of the viewing portals, an optimal way to be absorbed and take over. The creature resisted, but was too disoriented to do much. Within seconds, the scout was inside. Initially, the scout let the creature keep control of the body while he got his bearings. When the creature's ears picked up a sound signal—"Mack? Where are you? Get back here now!"—and responded by moving across the terrain to a structure, the scout recognized it as a summoning. His host, he now knew, was the subordinate of the one creating the noise.

The creature trotted inside and the scout took note of the earthlings' habitat—the way the space was divided and cluttered with objects fashioned from deceased plants and mined ore. He watched as two of the "people" communicated back and forth using audible sounds, and afterward, he had the physical sensation of being lifted onto an object where a third inhabitant lay inert. The scout could tell that the creature he inhabited had an affection for the people and especially this one, the young one who—the scout could immediately sense—was near death, the cells in his body having gone rogue and destroyed his health. Why would they allow his body to deteriorate to such a degree when the problem was so easy to fix? Clearly, this society was not very advanced at all.

He watched as the other inhabitant applied a substance to the eyes and mouth of the unhealthy being. A death ritual? Or maybe it was somehow supposed to help soothe and bring relief? The being leaned over and pressed faces with the sick one and the scout understood that this must be a good-bye. Death was near, in the air and all around. If he could make the leap before this ill organism died, the body would be a perfect container for him.

His chance came soon enough. When the creature inched closer and his nose aligned with the sick one's newly moistened

orifices, the scout used all his energy to leave the subordinate creature, departing through the eyes and entering the new body the
same way.

# CHAPTER FOUR

For the past three nights, I'd stayed by Lucas's side, sleeping only a little bit here and there. The lack of sleep caught up to me, though. That night, after unsuccessfully applying the potion to Lucas's eyes and lips, and sealing it with a kiss, a wave of fatigue hit me so hard it nearly knocked me over. I turned off the small lamp on the side table and went back to the recliner, thinking I just needed fifteen minutes to doze. Two hours later, I woke up to the sound of Mrs. Walker shrieking when she caught sight of the dog snuggled up next to Lucas. "What do you think you're doing? Get out of there," she yelled.

My eyes flicked open as Mack jumped off the bed and took off, tail between his legs. From the light of the kitchen and the nightlight in the corner, I could see Mrs. Walker's face contorted in anger. "What did I say, Emma? Didn't I tell you to keep that dog off the bed?" She wasn't even trying to keep her voice down, that's how mad she was.

I rubbed my eyes. "I'm sorry, he must of . . ." And then I stopped, because there was no way I could pretend Mack did it on his own. He was an old dog, and not prone to jumping on the furniture. He even took his time climbing the stairs. Besides that, he was such a sweet dog I didn't want him to get in trouble for something I did. "I'm sorry." I tried to look repentant as I faced her angry stare. Finally, I had to look away.

"Of course you're sorry," she said. "For all the good that does."

"I won't do it again. I just thought it would bring Lucas some comfort."

"You don't get it, do you?" she said, leaning down to whisper angrily in my face. "Lucas is beyond comfort."

"That's not true," I protested.

She kept on like she hadn't even heard me. "He's dying, Emma. I'm losing my son and you being here is making it worse. You're stealing precious moments from Eric and me and his father. We're his family." I caught the emphasis on the word "family." To her, it was everything. "Lucas is my firstborn. At the funeral, you'll be crying and everyone will feel sorry for you. Poor sweet Emma, they'll say, they were so in love. She never left his side." Now her tone was mocking. "But you know what? You have the rest of your life. Soon enough, you'll have a new boyfriend, and eventually your memories of Lucas will fade. Your life will go on and on. Meanwhile, I will always be a mother who has lost a child. The pain will always be fresh for me."

"I'm sorry," I said again. I wanted to say more. I wanted to protest that Lucas was irreplaceable for me too, that she'd underestimated us and our love. We had a bond way beyond that of the typical high school relationship. I adored Lucas, and no one else would ever come close. I wanted to explain to her how it really was, but I'd just woken up from a very deep sleep and the words got stuck between my brain and mouth.

She stood up and pointed to the doorway. "I think you need to go sleep on the couch in the living room and in the morning, you can go home. You won't be staying overnight anymore. I should be the one sleeping in the recliner, staying with him. You can come for no more than an hour each day, just like every other visitor."

"Oh no, please don't do that." I got up from the chair to make my case. "I won't let Mack near him anymore, I swear. And I can just sit on the floor. In the corner, out of the way. You won't even know I'm here. Just don't make me go. I can't be away from him."

"Oh, for crying out loud." She threw up her hands. "It's no use, Emma. I've already made up my mind. I can't deal with your drama on top of everything else. I'm tired. I'm so tired." She walked past me, her slippers shuffling against the hardwood floor, and settled into the chair, covering her face with her hands. That's when the unthinkable happened. Mrs. Walker began to cry, silently at first, her body shaking and then heaving, and then she began sobbing, gulping air and wailing, ugly cries that tore at my heart. I'd thought she was made of steel, but in that second, I saw I'd been wrong.

I only hesitated for a second before going over to give her a hug. She let me, or maybe it was more that she didn't stop me. I wrapped my arms around her shoulders and she leaned into me, still crying, her fingers covering her eyes. I didn't say anything because I didn't know what to say. I understood her anguish. We both loved Lucas. We had that much in common. After a few minutes, I felt her body relax, and her wails subsided to whimpers. "Do you want a Kleenex?" I finally asked.

"Yes, please."

I left her side and found the tissues in my backpack, then handed her a few. One didn't seem like it would be enough.

"We should probably keep a box down here," she said, first wiping her eyes, then blowing her nose. "We used to have one."

I nodded. I remembered seeing it on the side table next to Lucas's bed, but it wasn't there now.

She said, "I know you think I hate you, Emma, but I don't." For a split second, I thought we were going to have a bonding moment, but then she continued. "I don't hate you; I resent you. I wish I didn't, but that's the truth of the matter. My son is dying and there you are trying to take over, as if his father and I aren't capable of taking care of him. And you always seem to be in the way. Every time I turn around, there you are."

I took in a sharp breath. If this was an apology, it was the worst one ever. "I know it's difficult for you," I said.

"For such a small person, it's amazing how you're always in the way," she said, as if I didn't catch it the first time around.

"I just want to be near Lucas. I didn't know I was bothering you."

She locked eyes with me. "You think I'm this horrible person, but I'm not. I'm a mother. Any mother would feel this way. Someday you'll understand."

"Maybe so," I said, not wanting to argue. She wasn't even trying to understand my point of view. I stood with the back of my legs against the bed, one hand resting in the spot where Mack had been. "I didn't know I was getting in the way. I promise I'll try not to." Standing over Mrs. Walker, me fully dressed while she wore a flimsy nightgown and fabric slippers, her hair mussed, face swollen and red, I felt a slight advantage. She'd spoken in anger, but I knew her pride would keep her from taking back what she'd said. I'd have to take the lead. If I offered a compromise, I had a feeling she'd be more willing to let me stay. I said, "I'll go now and sleep on the couch, and in the morning I'll go home to shower and change clothes. When I come back, I promise not to sit in the recliner. I understand your point. That should be for family. From now on, I'll stay out of the way, and I won't say a word unless you want me to."

Our eyes met, and I held still, watching as she considered. "No," she said after what seemed like a long silence. "I'm not negotiating with you, Emma." She still had the tissue crumpled up in her hand. Only a few minutes ago, I'd hugged her and felt like I'd broken through her defenses, but now the tone of her voice told me otherwise. "I stand by my original decision. Go in the living room and get some sleep. I'll wake you up in the morning so you can go home. When you want to visit, you will need to call first. We'll let you know if it's convenient. And if you're not here when . . ." Her voice trailed off for a second and then she pulled herself together. "If you're not here when Lucas passes, you'll be one of the first to be called."

"But . . ."

"You're not family, Emma, and I won't pretend you are. Now go into the living room and lay on the couch. I don't want to tell you again."

Her voice rose with each sentence, until the last one was nearly a shout. It was enough to hold anyone's attention, but I barely heard it because I felt something brush against my hand, the one that rested on the bed behind me. I turned to look and saw that Lucas's fingers were touching my wrist. His eyes were wide open, darting from side to side like he couldn't control them, and his head twitched slightly, like someone reacting to an ice cream headache.

"Did you hear me, Emma?"

"I heard you," I said, not turning back to her. "But it's Lucas." My voice cracked with happiness. "He's awake."

# CHAPTER FIVE

Mrs. Walker got up out of the chair and pushed me aside. "Lucas? Honey, it's Mom." She stroked his head and he glanced all around the room like he wasn't sure where to look. I thought he caught my eye for a split second, and I grinned, suddenly giddy with joy. Mrs. Walker turned toward me, breaking the mood. "Emma," she said. "Make yourself useful. Turn on the light. And go get him some water and a straw."

I flipped on the dining room chandelier over Lucas's bed. The sudden brightness caused him to blink, so I lowered the light using the dimmer switch. Mrs. Walker made cooing sounds like he was an infant, and adjusted his bedding, tucking the blankets in around his sides. I went into the kitchen and got a plastic cup out of the cabinet, then filled it partway with cold, filtered water. I went to the drawer that had the box of bendy straws. Before the coma, getting Lucas food and water had been something I did on a regular basis. I'd thought I was being helpful. I didn't know I had just been in the way.

I brought the cup back and Mrs. Walker took it out of my hand and set it on the side table. "Stay right here and watch him," she said, pointing to a spot on the floor. "I have to get Eric and Steve." She scurried off excitedly, her slippers flapping through the house. I heard her on the landing, calling, "Steve! Eric! Come quick!"

When they didn't come right away, she ran up the steps to rouse them in person.

Meanwhile, Lucas was becoming more alert. His eyes were still open, but moved around less. They'd settled on me, something I took as a good sign. I left my assigned spot and went to touch his face. "Hi, baby." I waited for recognition to light up his eyes, but he was so dazed, it never came. His lips moved, but nothing came out and that's when I noticed how chapped his lips were. "I'm going to give you some water, okay?"

I held the cup below his chin and angled it to put the straw between his lips. "Go ahead," I urged. "It's just water." No reaction. Maybe he was too weak to drink. I put my finger on the end of the straw and held it, then released the water into his slightly opened mouth. Overhead, I heard the scrabbling of Eric and his dad getting out of bed. Soon the whole family would be here and I'd be shoved off to the side. A thin stream of water dribbled out of the side of Lucas's mouth and down his chin, but he swallowed the rest, his Adam's apple moving as it went down his throat. "More water?" I asked, holding the cup out.

He stared at the cup and then repeated, "Water." He broke the word into two distinct syllables like he was saying it for the first time.

I put the straw back in the cup and again put it up to his mouth. This time his lips clamped around it and he drew in, sucking water like his life depended on it. I heard the family coming down the stairs, their bare feet pounding against the carpeted treads. I took the cup away from Lucas and put it back on the table where Mrs. Walker had set it. I couldn't imagine she'd be mad that I gave him water, but who knew with her?

When the family came into the room, I respectfully stepped back, but my eyes never left Lucas. Already his color was better. Even in the few minutes since his mother had gone upstairs, he seemed calmer. More himself.

Mr. Walker came through the doorway first and went right to Lucas's side, leaning over to talk to him. Mrs. Walker and Eric came around to the other side, and again I had to move to get out of the way. "Lucas," said Mr. Walker. "It's me, Dad." He paused and then continued. "We're all here. Me and Mom and Eric." He glanced up and smiled at me. "And Emma too. We love you." He cleared his throat. I could tell he was getting choked up. "Eric?" he said, looking across the bed. "Do you have something to say to your brother?"

Eric had a scared look in his eyes, and I had a sudden realization that his continuous avoidance of Lucas had come down to this—he didn't want to lose his brother. They weren't super close, but they got along okay, considering they were three and a half years apart. When Lucas had been healthy, they'd stood up for each other, both at school and at home with their parents. That was no small thing in that house, believe me. Whenever Mr. and Mrs. Walker starting telling Eric how he should apply himself and get a 4.0 grade point average like his brother, Lucas would jump in and defend him. He'd point out all of Eric's strengths—the detailed architectural plans he drew for fun, the way he could fix anything—the dishwasher, farm equipment, the toaster, cars. If it had moving parts, Eric could figure out what was wrong with it. He was only fourteen and already he'd fixed up three junker cars and sold them for profit.

"I'm good at memorizing," Lucas would say, "but Eric has the mind of an engineer. He's a genius that way." Still, his parents didn't get it. In their eyes, Eric was just a shadow of his brother. Eric had the disadvantage of being quiet with dark, bushy hair, and glasses, while Lucas was outgoing, athletic, and blond. Lucas won the genetic lottery for the obvious traits, while Eric's were mostly hidden. Unfair, but that's how it was in a lot of families.

Now Eric stepped forward, his hand hesitantly patting Lucas's arm. "Hi, Lucas," he said. "It's me, Eric." Lucas's eyes widened and Eric broke into a grin. He turned to his parents. "He knows me."

Lucas's arm rose off the bed, reaching toward the cup on the side table. "Water," he said, with a croak, and the entire family beamed like he'd done something amazing. Eric grabbed it and put the straw between his lips. When Lucas gulped the water, Eric said, "Wow, dude, you're really thirsty." He looked up at his parents. "I guess he was dehydrated."

"That's enough," Mrs. Walker said, reaching over to take the cup away. "Remember what we talked about." She turned to me and said, "I talked to one of the hospice nurses the other day and she said this might happen. Sometimes patients rally and the family is given the gift of having them back for a short while. She said sometimes it lasts minutes and sometimes it goes for hours, but that we shouldn't get our hopes up and mistake it for a recovery." She took a step in my direction and whispered. "She said it always happens right near the end." Behind her, I saw Eric's expression change, his eyes filling with tears.

Mr. Walker patted Lucas's arm. "It's okay, son. Everything's okay."

I didn't tell Mrs. Walker she was wrong, that I knew this wasn't the end. The potion I'd gotten from Mrs. Kokesh had worked and this was only the beginning.

I didn't care what Mrs. Walker thought. I knew the truth. I was getting Lucas back.

# CHAPTER SIX

The scout knew what it was like to have a body, of course. On his home planet, his own body laid waiting for him. Upon returning from his missions, slipping into his corporeal form always felt like coming home—comfortable, warm, fluid in motion.

But this body? It was awkward, with gawky limbs and joints with such limited motion it was a wonder these earthlings could function at all. The two viewing ports had to be aimed just right in order to work properly. Every movement took incredible effort. No wonder the inhabitants of this planet were so hostile.

When the beings gathered all around him, their audible speaking felt like an assault. He didn't know which way to aim his vision or how he should react. When the kindhearted being gave him what she called "water," he instinctively knew that the body craved this substance, that it was necessary for existence. If that was the case, why was this body so depleted of water? It was hard to make sense of so many things.

He instinctively knew that the audible communication was a reaction to him awakening. All around him, he felt tempered happiness, except for the kindhearted being who seemed certain his awakening was permanent. The scout processed as much as he could. The identity of his body was, he thought, "Lucas." He was fairly certain of this, so it was puzzling that the biggest one called him "son." Could it be that the inhabitants on this planet were known by multiple names? He had so much to learn if he was to impersonate Lucas.

The scout needed the Lucas body to become healthy and strong. It was his only hope for finding a way back home.

# CHAPTER SEVEN

Lucas didn't die that night or the next morning either, and at first, Mrs. Walker held onto her story. She said he was rallying, his body pulling up all its energy for a final good-bye. One last hurrah before he slipped away. The one good thing was that she'd forgotten I'd been banished from the sick room. Mack didn't do as well. Ever since she'd caught him up on the bed, Mrs. Walker wasn't letting him anywhere near Lucas.

On my own, I'd decided to go home the next morning. I took a shower and ate, then set the timer on my phone and allowed myself the luxury of a two-hour nap. Now that I knew Lucas was fine, I wasn't so stressed about leaving his side.

When I returned, I walked in on a nurse and Lucas's parents having a conference in the kitchen. Mrs. Walker's lips pressed together in a thin line when she spotted me coming through the back door without calling first, but she didn't say anything and I walked right by, going straight to Lucas. Next to his bed, Eric sat in the recliner, his hands clasped together. His eyes were on Lucas, who was sleeping.

"Hi, Emma," Eric said. He looked happy to see me.

"Hi, Eric. What did I miss?" I slipped my backpack off my shoulder and let it rest on the floor, then sat on the edge of Lucas's bed, watching the rise and fall of his chest. His breathing was deeper now, which had to be a good sign. More oxygen going to his lungs.

"Nothing much," Eric said. "Everything's about the same as when you were here. He'll be super awake for a while and then fall asleep."

"He didn't ask for me?"

"No. He hasn't said anything except 'water.'"

I shrugged. "Give him time. He's been through a lot. He's not going to recover just like that."

Eric gave me a startled look. "Emma, didn't you hear what my mom said? She said this is part of the process. He's not recovering. It's the beginning of the end." And then he repeated what the hospice nurse had told his mom—how patients sometimes rally right at the end and how the family should cherish the gift, but not make it out to be more than it was.

"Yeah, I heard her," I said, and even though I wanted to let Eric in on my secret, I didn't take it any further. As sad as Eric was now, that's how overjoyed he was going to be when he realized his brother really was going to live. All I had to do was wait. Soon enough, he'd know the truth.

Silently, we watched Lucas sleep—Eric thinking his brother was sinking closer to death, and me knowing he was recharging for his entrance back into life. In the background, I heard the adults at the kitchen table, talking about Lucas as if he would be gone in a few hours. At one point, my name came up and I strained to listen. It sounded like the nurse was making a case for letting me stay. She said that it would bring me closure and that my presence might help Eric too. After that, the nurse talked about who they should call when the time came, and how the death certificate would be issued. Mrs. Walker began sobbing then and Eric, hearing his mother, started to cry too. I handed him a tissue and he accepted it, dabbing at his eyes and trying to blink back the tears.

When we heard the nurse leave, Mr. and Mrs. Walker both came into the room, bringing kitchen chairs to sit on. I got off the bed and stood out of the way, in the corner. Mrs. Walker led the family in a prayer, all three of them linking hands over Lucas. I bowed my head respectfully, thinking that prayer never hurt, although this particular one was all about Lucas being released from pain and asking God to receive and guide him.

And then we all waited, the three of them sitting while I stood and leaned in the corner, hoping that Lucas's parents agreed with the nurse and wouldn't send me away. At one point, Mrs. Walker whispered in Lucas's ear that it was okay if he had to go. She said, "Your dad and I understand if you have to leave us. You have our permission to go toward the light." But even then, he hung on. We sat and sat, all of us quiet. It was almost boring, watching Lucas sleep, and I became hyperaware of everything in the room: a random fly that buzzed in from the kitchen and then out again, the sound of a car outside driving past the house, the smell of the pot roast Mrs. Walker had set up in the slow cooker.

When Lucas's eyes opened an hour later, all of us were pulled out of our stupor. "Look, he's awake!" Eric said excitedly.

"Hi, buddy," Mr. Walker said.

Lucas's head swiveled to the side table. "Water," he said, his arm flailing in that direction. When Eric brought the straw to his mouth, he gulped thirstily. That was when I noticed the urine in the catheter bag hanging off the side of the bed. Instead of the dark color we'd been seeing for the last few days, the liquid was as light as Mountain Dew. Mr. Walker was the one sitting closest to me, so when I caught his eye, I pointed and brought it to his attention.

He did a double take and leaned over, peering down at it, before showing his wife. "What do you make of this?" he asked her.

Her brow furrowed, and she didn't answer for a moment. Then slowly she said, "I don't know. There has to be a medical reason. Maybe things change near the end?"

She was still in denial. After that, Lucas's parents discussed the fact that he'd only said one word—water—and decided it was a reflex, some part of his brain that hadn't shut down yet. One final word. But that theory was blown to hell as the hours went by and we saw more improvements. Lucas still seemed groggy, but he stayed awake longer each time and then he started turning his head when someone said his name. He held the cup himself eventually and handed it back when he was done. At one point, he tried to sit up, but had some trouble, so Mr. Walker adjusted the hospital bed to give him a boost. Now that Lucas was sitting upright, the mood in the room lifted. Somehow all of them had suddenly become hopeful. The only thing Lucas wasn't doing was saying anything more than one word, but he followed our conversation by turning his head to look at each person as we spoke. He had an intense look on his face, one I recognized. When we used to do homework together, Lucas had always had a certain expression I associated with him concentrating hard, like when he was solving a difficult math problem, and that was how he looked now. He was fighting his way back.

It was difficult for me to have all of them in the room when all I wanted was to be alone with him. If they hadn't been there, I would have crawled in next to him and explained everything that had happened. I would have kissed his lips, hoping to wake him up like in a fairy tale. Maybe even applied the potion one more time to accelerate the healing process. But they were his family and I was just the girlfriend, the one who always seemed to be underfoot, so I kept quiet and stood out of the way, watching the miracle unfold, knowing I was responsible for bringing Lucas back, but also knowing I had to keep it to myself. That was okay, though. It was worth it.

That day ended and another morning came and Lucas only got better. Mr. Walker headed out to the barn, and Eric drifted in and out. Only Mrs. Walker and I were glued to his side. Someone had dropped off homemade chocolate pudding a day earlier, and Mrs. Walker decided to try spoon-feeding some to Lucas. When he greedily ate a whole bowl in about thirty seconds flat, she wiped his mouth with a napkin and allowed herself a smile. "Emma, could you put this in the sink and run some water in it?" she said, handing me the empty bowl.

"Water, Emma," Lucas said, making us both freeze.

Mrs. Walker gave me a hard look and reached for the cup herself. "Go on. I'll give him the water."

My heart soared at the sound of Lucas saying my name. I grinned all the way to the kitchen and even stayed and rinsed off all the dishes in the sink and loaded the dishwasher. Lucas had said my name. *Take that, Mrs. Walker.* She could say I was in the way, but Lucas wanted me there. Out of all the people in the world, I was the one he'd called by name.

At some point, Eric brought his laptop in to watch a movie. When Lucas seemed interested in the sound, Eric moved the side table around and set up the laptop there so his brother could see it too. All afternoon Eric and Lucas watched continuously: first, an old western, then *Mean Girls* (little did I know it was one of Eric's favorite movies), and then reruns of some of their favorite shows from when they were kids. Later, they watched some funny video clips. Lucas focused on the screen with an incredible intensity, like he was going to be tested on it later or something. At one point, Mrs. Walker said, "Eric, don't you think this is enough? Lucas must be getting tired."

I waited for Eric to shut it off, but he just shrugged and said, "No, he likes it. You like it, don't you, Lucas?" As if to prompt him, Eric nodded and in response, Lucas's head bobbed up and down in the same way.

Lucas seemed to be back, but he still wasn't interacting much, besides a few nods and saying two words (one of which was my name!). Mrs. Kokesh's warning about possible brain damage crossed my mind, but I didn't let it bother me. I had said I wanted Lucas back no matter how it ended up and I meant it.

In the afternoon, he started eating and drinking on his own, which I took as a good sign. I watched Mr. and Mrs. Walker exchange looks of amazement as he devoured a ham and cheese sandwich, and I nearly clapped when he finished the last crumb and wiped his mouth with a napkin. He was making progress, even if it was slow. It was unreasonable to expect much more at this point. I'd pulled him back from the brink of death. His recovery, I reasoned, wasn't going to be instantaneous. I wished he'd show more interest in me than the laptop, but I figured we'd have the rest of our lives to be together. All in good time. Right now, I was willing to let Eric have him. The poor kid had been living in fear of his brother's impending death for months and months; he was due for something good. I would have loved to have Lucas all to myself, but I wasn't completely selfish.

When the doorbell rang that evening, we all knew it was Nancy, the visiting nurse, arriving at her scheduled time. Mr. Walker went to let her in and Mrs. Walker followed, leaving me and Eric and Lucas alone in the dining room. I listened as Nancy bustled in as usual, depositing her laptop on the kitchen table while asking how the previous day had gone. I could picture the way she stood, hand on hip, always the authority. Lucas's parents were telling her about the recent, unexpected developments. Their voices were subdued, but I edged closer to the doorway and caught some of what they were saying.

Nancy never missed an opportunity to say she'd been a hospice nurse for sixteen years and she was telling them now that she'd seen *everything*. No two patients were alike, but there were definite patterns. And then she started talking about how some patients rally (oh, how I was beginning to hate that word) and how family members and other loved ones project their hope for a recovery and sometimes see more than is really there. "My job is really hard

sometimes," Nancy said. "Besides providing medical care, I sometimes find families rely on me for emotional support too. They see
a little thing and make more of it than it is and then I have to be the
one to bring them down to earth."

She was so full of herself, and until recently, I seemed to be the
only one who noticed this fact. But now Mrs. Walker was growing
wise to her. "I understand all of that, Nancy, but believe me, that's
not what's happening. You have to see him," she said sternly. "He
ate a sandwich and a full bowl of pudding. He spent all afternoon
watching movies with his brother. His urine is *yellow.*"

"Oh." From the tone of Nancy's voice, I could tell she was taken
aback, but she recovered quickly. "Well, let's take a look, shall we?"
she said brightly.

As I heard their approaching footsteps, I scurried away from
the door, taking my place back in the corner. Eric had pulled his
chair closer to the bed and set the laptop on Lucas's legs. Both guys
were so engrossed in what they were watching that, when their
parents and Nancy entered, they didn't even look up, but my gaze
was fixed on the doorway, waiting for Nancy's reaction. She stared
at Lucas with a stunned, wide-eyed expression. Her mouth hung
open, and she stopped in her tracks, blocking Mr. and Mrs. Walker
behind her. I decided to break the spell.

"Hi, Nancy," I said.

She ignored me, but my voice got the attention of both Eric
and Lucas, who looked up to see who I was talking to. Nancy,
meanwhile, seemed to have recovered from her shock.

"Hi, Lucas," she said, her voice chipper, walking closer to the
bed.

"Hi, Nancy," Lucas said, his inflections matching mine exactly.

Mrs. Walker nudged her husband, whose eyes widened. Eric
reacted too, flashing a grin in my direction, like we were members
of a secret club. All of us stayed silent while Nancy went into nurse
mode, checking Lucas's heart rate and blood pressure, and staring

into his eyes with a tiny flashlight. She lifted up the catheter bag and stared at the urine for a few seconds before setting it down again. Finally, she spoke.

"How do you feel, Lucas?" she asked, her hand on his shoulder.

The words that made up his reply came out haltingly, but they were words and they were spoken in the right order and it was an answer. The right answer. Lucas said, "I feel better."

I wanted to hug him and, at the same time, I felt like cheering. And his family looked like they felt the same way.

"Are you experiencing any pain?" she asked, her tone confused, but also kindly. My opinion of Nancy went up a notch. She was still a know-it-all, but I could tell now that she actually did care.

Lucas shook his head. "No pain. I would like—" he said, his eyes gazing at the ceiling as if trying to think of a word. The whole room waited in suspense until he said, "—to stand and walk. Can I stand and walk?"

Nancy's hand flew to her forehead, like she felt a sudden headache coming on. "I don't know if that's such a good idea, Lucas. I think I should call Dr. Griffin and see what he says." Dr. Griffin was the name of Lucas's oncologist. Not my favorite guy, probably because he'd given my boyfriend a death sentence. Nancy said, almost to herself, "Yeah, I think I should make some calls. Just sit tight." She motioned to the bed with the flat of her hand. "I'll be right back." She left the room with a flustered flap of her arms and Mr. and Mrs. Walker followed behind, murmuring excitedly to each other.

# CHAPTER EIGHT

After they'd left, I said, "So you feel better, Lucas?"

He lifted his chin and nodded. "Much better. Can I stand and walk?"

Eric stood up. "I say we let him." He came around to my side of the bed, and pulled back the blanket and sheets.

I wasn't sure this was a good idea. "Maybe we should wait and see what Dr. Griffin says?" I asked, not moving.

"Oh, screw Dr. Griffin. What does he know? He's been wrong about everything else." Eric's smile widened into a grin. "You get on one side, Emma, I'll get on the other." Eric unhooked the catheter bag and held onto it while assisting Lucas with his free hand.

I followed his lead and helped guide Lucas's legs over the edge of the bed. All Lucas had on was one of those thin hospital gowns that opened in the back. Normally, it didn't make a difference because he was covered up in bed, but now I could see more and I was shocked by how pale and skinny his lower legs were. His kneecaps were so knobby they almost looked malformed. This was not Lucas's body. The Lucas I knew was bulky and strong. I remembered resting my head on his chest and feeling the solid rise and fall of his breathing and the beating of his heart. Now I could feel his bones through his arms. Such a change. I consoled myself by thinking he'd have time to gain weight and get back in shape before school started again in the fall.

Taking a cue from Eric, Lucas scooted sideways on the bed, allowing me to take his other arm. He eased off the bed and onto his feet, standing straight and tall. Lucas smiled, not the easy, toothy smile I knew, but a satisfied stretch of thin lips. It was the first smile I'd seen from him in a long time. It felt good to see him on his feet, and even better to feel him right next to me, even if it meant he was holding on to me for support.

"Good going, Lucas!" Eric exclaimed. "Now just put one foot in front of the other."

Eric and I knew we couldn't risk being seen, so we walked Lucas slowly around the bed to the other side of the room, and paused at the window, which had been covered by blinds since the hospital bed had taken up residence in the dining room. Sunlight glinted in between the slats, hinting at the beautiful summer day outside.

"Can I see it?" Lucas asked, his head wobbling forward to indicate the window.

I pulled on the cord and the blinds flew up, giving us a view of the barn and the fields beyond. To my eyes, the world had gotten prettier in the last forty-eight hours.

"Oh," Lucas said, his voice tinged with surprise.

"What?" Eric asked, giving me a sideways glance.

When Lucas didn't answer, I said, "It looks different from here, doesn't it?"

"Different from here," he agreed.

On a working farm, there was never any time to admire the view. Lucas and his family were always coming and going to the barn with a purpose. All of them worked hard, and in between taking care of the cows and everything else that needed to be done, Lucas had school and sports and going out with friends. And me. Stopping to stare out the dining room window would never have fit into Lucas's old schedule, but here it was, the farm laid out before us and nothing better to do but stop and take it all in: the big trees on one side that would be covered with apples in the fall; the silo where the feed for the cows was stored; the original barn, now used by Eric as a workshop; and on the other side of the yard, the new barn with its gleaming metal roof.

"It's beautiful," I said to no one in particular. "Don't you think?"

Eric shrugged. "Kinda, I guess," he said.

We were walking Lucas back to the other side of the bed when the doorbell rang again. It wasn't Nancy this time; she was still on the phone. I heard Mrs. Walker open the front door. A few moments later, she let someone in. I caught a man's voice saying something I couldn't quite make out. Could the doctor be here already?

The voices got louder and now I heard a woman join in, saying something about how she hated to intrude, that it would just be a few questions and then they'd be on their way.

Like kids who were about to get caught with our hands in the cookie jar, Eric and I hurried to get Lucas back to where he was supposed to be. We had just gotten him back in place, blankets arranged and catheter bag hung on its hook, when Mrs. Walker appeared in the doorway.

"This is Emma," she said, stepping aside. "The one I told you about. The friend of my son Lucas. She was here that night."

Behind her stood a man and woman, both about my mom's age. Each of them wore office attire—dark pressed pants and light colored button-down shirts. The woman had a soft-sided briefcase slung over one shoulder; the man had an iPad tucked under his arm.

Mrs. Walker continued. "My son Lucas was comatose at the time. And my other son, Eric, the one with the dark hair, was upstairs sleeping when we heard the noise."

But the woman was only interested in me. "Hi, Emma," she said, her mouth widening into a friendly grin. She extended her hand to me. "We have a lot in common. My middle name is Emma." Like that meant we would be instant friends.

I reluctantly shook her hand. "Hi," I said. I darted a glance toward Mrs. Walker. "What's going on?"

Mrs. Walker said, "These people are from the—" And then she stopped, trying to remember.

My new friend filled in her pause. "I'm Mariah Wilson and this is Todd Goodman. We're with a federal agency, the NTSB, the National Transportation Safety Board, investigating an incident that happened two nights ago involving an accidental collision. We believe some pieces of the aircraft may have landed in the area. We're just here to ask a few questions."

"Wow," I said. "What kind of collision? An airplane crash?"

"We're just here to ask a few questions," she repeated. "And then we'll be on our way."

Mrs. Walker said, "Why don't we take this into the living room and let Lucas rest? Eric, stay with your brother." She beckoned with one finger. "Emma, come along."

I dutifully followed her into the next room, walking past Nancy, who was talking to Mr. Walker.

Mrs. Walker said to the agents, "You really caught us at a bad time. My son is very ill and the nurse is following up on an unexpected change in his health."

"What kind of change?" Todd asked.

Mrs. Walker said, "He's gotten better."

All four of us trooped into the living room and I took a seat in the chair that was normally Mr. Walker's, a dark-colored recliner Lucas loved to describe as "cow-pie brown."

The agents sat side by side on the couch, while Mrs. Walker stood next to me, her hand protectively on my shoulder.

"Now, Emma," agent Mariah said, leaning forward eagerly. "Two nights ago, Wednesday, can you tell me if you heard anything out of the ordinary?"

"I was sitting by Lucas and there was a noise outside."

"What time did this occur?" she asked.

"I don't know." I looked up at Mrs. Walker. "Eleven, maybe?" She nodded.

"Can you describe the noise?" Mariah asked. Next to her, Todd was jotting down notes on his iPad.

"A thud, followed by an echoing sound. It was kind of muffled."

"Was it loud?" she asked.

"Well, loud enough," I said. "Both of us heard it. Mrs. Walker was in the kitchen and I was in the dining room."

She went on to ask how long the noise lasted and what direction the sound came from and I answered both questions, and then she asked if I had noticed anything else unusual that evening. Anything at all.

"No." I shook my head. "Nothing out of the ordinary."

"And you haven't noticed anything unusual outside—any foreign objects or signs that the ground had been disturbed?"

"No."

"We told you that already," Mrs. Walker said. "We didn't find any part of an airplane, believe me, or I would have told you."

"I know," Mariah said, "but we like to check with everyone in the household. Sometimes people notice something, but don't mention it to others in the family."

"Emma is not a member of the family. She's a visitor," Mrs. Walker said, folding her arms in front of her.

"I understand," Mariah said soothingly. "Sorry. Okay, next question—your son, Lucas. You said he has cancer?"

"Yes."

"What kind of cancer?"

"What does it matter?"

Mariah smiled. "I know it seems ridiculous, but my supervisor would like us to be thorough, so I always include a few extra details in my report, just to make him happy."

"I'd rather not get into my son's health history," Mrs. Walker said. "It's a private matter. Put that in your report."

Todd spoke up. "What is Lucas's full name?"

Mrs. Walker said, "Lucas James Walker." She glanced over at Todd, who appeared to be typing Lucas's full name into his notes. "Why is any of this relevant?"

"And Lucas, you said, has unexpectedly gotten better."

Mrs. Walker's face stiffened. "Yes, that's right."

"When did this happen? Was it after you heard the noise, by any chance?"

Then Mrs. Walker did something completely out of character. She lied. "No, this is something we noticed earlier in the week, and he's been improving by the day. The doctor said it's rare, but it happens."

"Oh." Mariah didn't have anything to say to that.

"Now if that's all, I'll see you to the door and you can be on your way," Mrs. Walker said firmly. This was the Mrs. Walker I knew. A force to be reckoned with.

Mariah ignored Mrs. Walker and addressed me directly. "I just need your full name for my report, Emma, and that will wrap things up."

I looked to Mrs. Walker, who nodded her approval. I said, "Emma Garson."

"G-A-R-S-O-N?" I nodded and she asked, "Middle initial?"

"L. It's Leigh. Emma Leigh Garson."

The two agents stood. "One more thing," Todd said. "We'd like to take a look around the property, if you wouldn't mind."

"A look around?" Mrs. Walker said, her face showing how clearly she disliked this turn of events.

"If that's okay," Todd said, smiling widely. "We just want to walk out around the barn and see if we can determine what caused the noise. If it's a piece of an aircraft, it belongs to our agency and it needs to be recovered and assessed."

"And you have to do it right now?"

"Yes, ma'am," Mariah said. "It's time sensitive and we are here now. If we take care of it now, we won't have to come back and bother you again."

Mrs. Walker hesitated and then she said, "All right. But our dog is outside and he doesn't like strangers. Emma, could you go out and get Mack and bring him inside?" She addressed the agents. "Just hang on. As soon as Mack is inside, it will be fine."

I followed her instructions without answering, getting up and heading to the back door. I heard Todd say, "She seems like a lovely girl. Your son's girlfriend?"

Mrs. Walker's terse response: "She's a friend of the family." That was a new one. Me, a friend of the entire family? Very curious.

Something about these two agents didn't seem quite right and I wasn't the only one who thought so. Mrs. Walker had picked up on it too. She had been guarded when they asked about Lucas and she insinuated that they wouldn't be safe outside if the dog was there. Not true. Mack wasn't fond of strangers, but he wasn't a biter. More likely, he would just bark continuously. So what was the deal? Was Mrs. Walker worried these people might hurt the dog? Unlikely, I thought, but better safe than sorry.

Stepping down the back porch steps and into the yard, I called out, "Mack!" and headed toward the barn. During the day, Mack did double duty as pet and work dog, keeping wild animals away from the livestock. We didn't get mountain lions in this area, like they sometimes did up north, but coyotes and foxes were not uncommon and even gophers, cute as they were, could burrow and do a lot of damage if kept unchecked. Out in the country, the presence of a dog, even a friendly one, served as an added security system. "Mack!"

I heard a bark on the other side of the barn and followed the sound. As I got closer, Mack bounded out from behind the building, his tail wagging. He rushed up to greet me, and I rubbed behind his ears. "Why are you making me track you down, Mack? Can't you just come when I call you?" I turned toward the house, thinking he'd follow, but instead, he took off again, this time heading for the field that ran along the edge of the property.

"Come here, Mack!" I yelled, but he didn't acknowledge the command, and all I could do was watch helplessly as his back end disappeared into the tall grasses of the field. I sighed. Mrs. Walker was going to be annoyed if I took too long, and if I explained that it was Mack's fault, he might be punished and become an outside dog for the duration of the week.

I took off after him, chasing him into the field of rocks and weeds. I was really annoyed now. It would have been so much easier if Mack had just listened to me in the first place. He'd always been an obedient dog, but Lucas's illness had changed him, just like it had changed the rest of us. When your world goes wonky, all the rules get thrown out the door.

Even though it wasn't that far, I was out of breath when I caught up to him. As soon as I got close, I grabbed his collar, determined to drag him if necessary. Anything to get him back to the house. But that moment, Mack looked up at me and whined, then pawed at an object on the ground. "What is it?" I wondered aloud, leaning over to take a look. It was circular, the size and shape of the metal covers they put over plates of food in the hospital. Mack nosed in closer too, and now both of us cast a shadow over the thing. I couldn't quite get a handle on what it was made of and I couldn't say exactly what color it was either. I'd seen tropical fish this color: a silvery greenish-blue that changed hue depending on the angle. I walked around it, watching as it changed color, sometimes looking shimmery as the edges melted into the grass, other times almost camouflaged as it reflected the grass around it. If Mack hadn't shown me, I might have walked right past it. The top of the object was circular and open, one side still attached, like the lid of a ketchup bottle. I couldn't see anything inside, and I wasn't about to stick my hand in to find out for sure.

Mack nudged it with his paw and I noticed that it sat at the end of a trail of flattened grass that went back several feet. I let go of Mack's collar and followed the furrow, noting how it made a line that stopped and started like the thing had bounced before skidding to a halt and that's when I knew. This was what Mrs. Walker and I had heard hit the ground the other night. In a second, my mind made all the connections and I was able to put together what had happened. This thing, whatever it was, had fallen from the sky at an angle, making the first boom. The echoing noises we'd heard came from the ricochet as it bounced and skidded along the ground. I'd been wrong in saying it sounded like it was behind the barn, but I wasn't too far off. It had actually come down in the field next to it.

This is what the agents inside were looking for. Mariah and Todd. What agency did they say they were with? I strained my brain, trying to remember, but the most I could recall was that it was the National Something Safety Board. They were looking for pieces from a collision, they said, but that, I sensed, was a lie. This was no piece of aircraft. It didn't have the jagged edges of something that had been torn apart. It wasn't a piece of something; it was something all by itself. But what? I wasn't an expert, but I'd been on this earth for seventeen years and I didn't recognize the material it was made from. Nothing looked like this. Mack barked, breaking into my thoughts, and a second later, Mrs. Walker yelled from the back door.

"Emma? What's the hold up?"

I yelled back. "Sorry, Mrs. Walker! I'll be there in a second."

She was impatient, I could tell, wanting to get these people out of her house so she could talk to the nurse and find out what the doctor said, and she also wanted to spend more time with Lucas, now that he was conscious and seemingly better. I understood, but I also needed more time. Mack circled the object and looked up at me. If I could read his mind I was betting I'd discover we were thinking the same thing. We had to hide this object. Hide it to make sure the agents wouldn't find it. I needed more time to study it. Maybe Mrs. Kokesh would know what it was and the connection between this thing dropping from the sky and her potion and Lucas getting better. What had she said? *A disturbance in the force?* Yes, that was it. *Star Wars* really got that one right.

I picked up the object, half expecting it to shock me or start vibrating or something, but it felt as solid and inflexible as Mack's food dish. With the toe of my shoe, I scuffed up the flattened grass until it wasn't as noticeable. Then I hurried off, Mack following me as I darted behind the new barn to the old barn.

The old barn was original to the property, over a hundred years old. It was tiny compared to the new barn, only about as big as a three-car garage. The sides were weather beaten but the structure was solid and the roof sound. Eric used it for whatever projects he was currently tinkering with. There were always car carcasses and engine parts inside. Anything Eric thought he might need in the future. He was a genius at bringing dead machines to life, but it all looked like junk to me.

I went around the back and pushed up the wooden bar that kept the door latched shut. The door in front was large enough to drive a tractor through, but this back door was for people, and I was able to quickly open it and slip inside. It was dark, and I didn't want to wait for my eyes to adjust, so I fumbled around, finally setting the object on the floor behind the door. No one would stumble onto it and no one would look behind the door. It would be safe there until I returned later. I left the barn as quickly as I could and Mack trotted alongside as I headed back to the house.

# CHAPTER NINE

"Well, it's about time," Mrs. Walker said, as I came back with Mack at my side.

"I'm sorry. He was chasing a squirrel and wouldn't listen. I had to go hunt him down." This time I didn't mind shifting the blame to Mack. I needed an explanation and this one was plausible. Still, I felt kind of bad when she roughly grabbed his collar and escorted him to the basement door. Mack dutifully clomped down the stairs, banished to the dungeon of the house where he'd stay until Mrs. Walker felt like releasing him.

The two agents stood in the kitchen, far enough from the back window that I was sure they hadn't seen me follow Mack to the field and move the object. Todd, in fact, had his attention on the iPad, while Mariah was eavesdropping on what Nurse Nancy was telling Mr. Walker.

"Dr. Griffin doesn't want to move him to the hospital just yet, but he did order lab work," Nancy said. "I'll be taking urine and blood samples with me today and dropping them off at the hospital."

"Do you really have to draw blood?" Mr. Walker asked. He put his arm around his wife's shoulders when she returned from disposing of Mack. "Poor kid has been through so much already."

"Doctor's orders," Nancy said, like the doctor's word was law. "But don't worry. I'm very skilled at blood draws. I'll make it quick."

I seemed to be the only one who remembered about the agents standing in the kitchen. I didn't like the way Mariah openly stared while listening to their conversation. This was about Lucas and it was none of her business.

I interrupted by asking, "Is it okay for the agents to go outside now that Mack is in?"

My question pulled them out of their discussion. Mrs. Walker's head swiveled in their direction, looking like she just remembered they were there. "Oh yes, go on out," she said.

Agent Mariah nodded, then pulled what looked like an ear bud from the underside of her shirt. A thin wire trailed down underneath. She moved her mouth closer and said, "The homeowner has given permission for a search of the property. Do a complete sweep starting from the back of the house."

Mr. Walker looked startled. "I thought the two of you were going to be the ones looking."

"Oh no, sir," Mariah said. "We're hardly dressed for field work." She smiled. "Our team does this on a routine basis. They know what to look for and they'll work quickly and leave your property undisturbed."

Even as she spoke, we could see dozens of people, mostly men but a few women too, all of them in dark-colored clothing, coming up the driveway. A few of them held long-handled equipment in front of them as they walked. Metal detectors? I wasn't sure.

"Who are all these people? Where did they come from?" Mrs. Walker asked, her voice incredulous. I wondered the same thing. They had to have been parked down the road, waiting for the signal.

"This group is part of our NTSB search team. They're professionals, experts at recovering aviation wreckage." Todd looked up from his iPad to talk. "With so many working together, we can cover more ground. That means we'll be on our way and out of your hair in no time. We appreciate your cooperation." His speech sounded scripted.

"Well, I guess it'll be okay," Mrs. Walker said. "As long as it's just outside and they don't go into the barns. I mean, you wouldn't have a reason to go in the outbuildings, would you, if you're looking for airplane parts?"

Mariah didn't answer, but spoke again into her communication device. "Team members, listen carefully. You are not to go inside any of the buildings. We do not have clearance for anything indoors. The barns are off-limits. Repeat, search the property, but do not go inside any of the buildings."

Todd said, "Thank you, Mr. and Mrs. Walker and Emma. We'll be heading outside now to oversee the operation and then we'll be leaving shortly." He reached out his hand and Mr. Walker shook it.

Mrs. Walker saw them to the door, and watched as the pair walked back toward the others. "The operation?" she said. "First they made it sound like the two of them were just going to take a quick look, and suddenly this is a big deal with fifty people searching with equipment. It makes you wonder exactly what they're looking for. You'd think we'd have heard about a plane collision."

Mr. Walker shrugged. "Our tax dollars at work."

Then Nancy announced that she really had to do the blood draw right away if she was going to drop off the samples before her next scheduled patient visit. We followed her into the dining room where Lucas and Eric were watching an episode of *Cosmos* on the laptop. Nancy opened her medical kit on the end of the bed.

"What's going on?" Eric asked, pausing the show.

Lucas's eyes followed me as I took my new spot in the corner and I gave him a grin.

Mrs. Walker ignored Eric and spoke directly to Lucas. "Lucas, honey, Nancy needs to take some blood before she goes."

Nancy was all business at this point, taking Lucas's arm and swabbing it with an alcohol wipe. The antiseptic smell filled the small room. He looked startled, but didn't pull away. Outside, I heard the voices of the team calling out to each other as they swept the field. Would they notice the furrow? Maybe not, since the field was so big and I'd done what I could to stir things up. But even if they did see it, anything could have caused it—a farm implement, an animal, a wheelbarrow. I was pretty sure it wouldn't arouse suspicion, but I did have another worry. Had any of those people seen me move the object they were now hunting for? I didn't think so, but I couldn't be completely sure. Trying not to look nervous, I wiped my sweaty palms on my shorts and focused on Lucas instead of my fears.

While Nancy cleaned her hands with sanitizer, she spoke to Lucas in that baby tone she used for anyone under the age of thirty. "Now, Lucas, I'm going to be drawing four vials of blood, but I'll only need to do one poke. It will pinch for an instant and that will be it. And don't worry about me taking your blood. Your body will make more." She smiled broadly.

"I know this," Lucas said and his family beamed at his response. I was glad he was getting better, but his speech was so odd. It was his voice and the same words he might have used before, but the intonation was like a Russian immigrant doing an impression of an American accent.

I kept thinking about how Mrs. Kokesh had said Lucas might come back different and I felt a pang of regret. I thought he might move more slowly or be not as quick-witted, but this was something else entirely. It was like he was learning to be Lucas all over again. How long would it take before he was completely himself again? I had said I'd be okay with anything, but the truth was, I wanted him how he used to be. I wanted us like we used to be. I imagined us parked in his car, his hands on either side of my face looking at me like he just couldn't believe his good luck. I remembered the smell of him as he came in from the fields slick with sweat and teasing me by holding out his arms for a big hug, me squealing and telling him to go take a shower. And after that, the long, luxurious kisses, the kind I wished would never end. We were constantly looking for ways to be alone. I knew the contours of his body and the feel of his skin, and even now the thought of him made my pulse race. Over time, we'd become more and more intimate. We were just a breath away from having sex when he became sick and then there was the diagnosis and the treatment. And the medicine to treat the side effects of the treatment. And it just got worse from there. We'd been through a lot, but now that it was going in the other direction, we'd have a second chance at a lifetime of happiness.

Nancy wrapped a rubber tourniquet around Lucas's arm and flicked at his vein with her fingernail. He watched, fascinated, as she quickly slipped the needle in and blood flowed out. She filled four vials, and then expertly covered the needle with a square of gauze before pulling it out. "Lucas, could you hold the gauze in place, please?" Nancy asked.

Lucas didn't move, so I stepped forward and placed two fingers over the pad. Nancy unwrapped a Band-Aid and nodded to me to let go, then removed the gauze and used it to cover the puncture mark. "There you are," she said. "Good as new."

"Now I can stand and walk?" Lucas said. "I can leave the bed?" He looked from Nancy to his parents.

"It's up to your mom and dad," Nancy said. "If you feel up to it, and have someone nearby for support, I think it would be fine."

"I'm better."

"I know you *feel* better," Nancy said. "And that's definitely a good thing, but we'll know more once we get the test results."

Mr. Walker edged over to the window and lifted the blinds to see what the team was doing outside. I saw a slight frown cross his face, but I was distracted by Lucas who had pulled back his covers, exposing the catheter tube and everything else. "I want this out," he said. "It's not needed."

"Lucas!" Mrs. Walker hurried over and moved the blanket to cover him up. "Not in front of Emma."

But Lucas was yanking at the tube now, determined to remove it. Mr. Walker rushed away from the window and both he and Nancy had to restrain Lucas's hands.

"It's not needed," Lucas said again, looking miserable. "Take it out."

"Can you take it out?" Mr. Walker asked.

Nancy hesitated. "The doctor didn't say—"

"Oh, for God's sake, just take it out." Eric's voice rang out loud and clear, commanding the attention of everyone in the room. I'd almost forgotten he was there, but now he stepped forward, looming over all the adults, who were leaning over the hospital bed. "Lucas can get up and walk to the bathroom on his own now. He doesn't need it."

Startled, Mrs. Walker's eyes grew wide. "Eric!" she said and that one word said it all—that he was being disrespectful and speaking out of turn. That this was not his decision.

But Eric didn't budge. "What's the big deal? He doesn't need it, so just take it out. If you leave it in, he's just going to yank on it anyway."

Mr. Walker cleared his throat. "I think Eric's right. Would you take it out, Nancy? You can put in your records that it was at our request. His mother and I will take responsibility."

So it was decided that Lucas would be freed from the pee tube. Eric and I were asked to leave the room, which was fine by me. Much as I loved Lucas, this was not an image I wanted to commit to memory. I wandered into the kitchen and looked out the window of the back door. Eric had the same idea, and soon we were shoulder to shoulder.

He said, "You know, I searched the news while you were talking to those people in the other room, and I came up with nothing. What did she say—there was an aircraft collision? You'd think it would be a big deal if they have all these people searching."

"That's what they'd like us to believe."

"You don't believe it?" He took a step back to take in my expression. "How come?"

"Something about their story doesn't add up," I said, and leaned in to whisper. "I think there's more to it than they're saying." It was on the tip of my tongue to tell him more, to confide in him about the object I'd found in the field, but I held back. Not just yet.

"Yeah, something's off about this," he agreed. "It's probably one of those top-secret military things. And if they don't want the public to know, there's no way we're ever going to find out."

# CHAPTER TEN

That night, when no one was looking, Lucas pulled off his pain patch and left it on the side table next to his water cup. When his mother asked about it the next morning, he said he didn't need it anymore.

And that was just the beginning. Every day, he seemed better. His wispy hair seemed noticeably thicker from one day to the next. It was happening so fast it was like a dream. And every step of the way I proudly thought, *I did this. Me. If it had been left up to the Walkers and modern medicine, he'd be dead by now.*

By then, I'd already transferred the object I'd found in the field, moving it from Eric's barn to my bedroom closet at home. I was afraid one of the Walkers might find it, or worse yet, that the agents might return to do a more thorough search and confiscate it. I still didn't know what it was, this disc-shaped thing that fell from the sky. Something illegal that had been smuggled into the country? Or a secret military weapon in the testing stages? I was willing to believe anything at this point. The one thing I was becoming sure of was that the object and Lucas's recovery were somehow connected. It had to be the disturbance Mrs. Kokesh had mentioned. I wasn't sure how or why the two things were connected. It could be anything. Maybe the military was using this object for chemical warfare and the chemicals had a healing effect on Lucas's cancer, and the potion was a separate thing entirely. I decided that when all the commotion settled down, I would try to figure it out.

And there was commotion.

Word travels fast in a small community, and soon Lucas's friends, the ones who'd stopped coming around when they thought he was dying, came to visit the farm in droves. I think every member of the senior class came at some point that first week, so many converging on the farm at once that Mrs. Walker made them come inside in shifts. By that time, she'd allowed Lucas to get dressed in regular clothes, though he'd lost so much weight he had to borrow Eric's jeans. He still wasn't very talkative, but his speech seemed less halting and he could hold a conversation. The guys on the football team asked if he'd be playing next year since he'd be a senior again and he smiled his new, thin-lipped smile and said, "I'll have to see how it goes." They clapped him on the back and told jokes and he grinned at all the right times and I breathed a sigh of relief. He was almost back to normal.

For days, I yearned to talk to him alone, but there was always someone around. I wanted to ask what he remembered about the night I put the potion on his lips and kissed him. Did he hear me when he was in the coma? Did he know how close he'd been to death?

The visiting nurses still came, but less frequently, and on day four of the miraculous recovery, Lucas went back to the hospital for more tests. When Eric said he wanted to stay home and work, Mrs. Walker let me come in his place, so it was me and Lucas in the backseat of the car with his parents up front. The hospital was an hour away, so while the adults were talking about traffic and road construction and alternate routes, I took the opportunity to reach for Lucas's hand resting on the seat between us. He looked startled at my touch and then looked down at our interlocked fingers like he was trying to figure out where I started and he ended. I smiled at him and he smiled back and I felt our old connection come through. I mouthed the words "I love you" and waited for him to do the same, but it didn't happen. Instead, he just furrowed his brow and turned his attention to the front of the car. Like he had no idea what this lip moving thing was all about. As if we hadn't mouthed those words to each other a hundred thousand times. I was crushed and confused.

That was the first weird thing.

The second weird thing happened after we'd returned from the hospital later in the day. The tests had been run and even though the technicians couldn't tell us what they saw, off the record, every one of them indicated that the results were mind-bogglingly good. We arrived back at the Walkers' house happy, so happy, because Lucas's parents and I just knew that when we heard the final results from the oncologist, it would be good news. Mack, who'd been kept outdoors and away from Lucas for the last few days, came bounding up to the car when we pulled into the gravel drive. I got out on my side and he jumped up on me, as if he knew we'd just gotten the best news of our lives. I rubbed behind his ears and patted his side, exclaiming over him.

"Good dog, you are such a good dog, Mack," I crooned. He barked and jumped, like a crazy, happy dog, loving every bit of the attention I was giving him. But that all changed when Lucas and his mom walked around from the other side of the car.

At the sight of Lucas, Mack bared his teeth and growled. It was a deep-throated growl, a warning of an attack to come. A chill went up my spine at Lucas's reaction, which was no reaction at all. He kept walking toward the house like he didn't know that Mack's growl was abnormal or alarming.

"Mack!" Mrs. Walker scolded. "What are you doing? You know Lucas."

Mr. Walker held Mack's collar and commanded him to sit, and the dog did, reluctantly dropping to his haunches.

Mrs. Walker called out, "Lucas, come back here. Let Mack smell your hand." Lucas turned and walked back, seeming unsure what this was all about.

"Put your hand out," Mrs. Walker said, demonstrating.

Mack stayed seated, but all the while he strained at the collar, growling and showing his teeth in a way I'd never seen before. It made my breath catch in my chest. A few minutes before, I'd have sworn that Mack was gentle as a lamb, incapable of turning on his owners, but now I wasn't so sure.

"That's enough, Mack," Mr. Walker said, a firm grip on the collar. "It's just Lucas. You know Lucas."

Lucas followed his mother's direction, extending his hand toward Mack's snout, and the dog lunged for him, teeth snapping just a fraction of an inch from Lucas's fingers. Alarmed, Lucas stepped back and Mr. Walker yanked the dog away.

Mrs. Walker's hand flew up to her mouth. "What's wrong with him?" she asked, looking at Mack who'd now stopped growling, although he still looked unsettled. "Why is he acting this way?"

"I don't know," Mr. Walker said. "Maybe Lucas smells different because of the tests?"

I stared at Lucas. He didn't look troubled at all that his beloved dog wanted to chomp off his hand, and I knew it wasn't just that Lucas smelled different from the tests at the hospital. He'd had all those tests before and Mack had never acted that way.

The way Mack was reacting now was a different thing completely. He was acting like Lucas was a stranger, an invader encroaching on home turf. Someone who meant to do the family harm. I remembered Lucas's lack of response when I mouthed "I love you." That was the first weird thing. And now Mack, the closest thing Lucas had to a guardian angel on Earth, was acting like he was an intruder. That was the second weird thing. Each one by itself might mean nothing. But together, they added up.

I thought about Mrs. Kokesh's warning that the Lucas who came back from death might not be the same Lucas I knew and loved. She'd been right, unfortunately, and it was worse than I could have imagined. I hated to go back and face her again, but she might be able to help. Maybe she could help me reach the Lucas within, the real Lucas. He had to be there, somewhere underneath the surface. I didn't know how to reach him, but I had to try. And if Mrs. Kokesh couldn't find him, no one could.

# CHAPTER ELEVEN

It took two weeks for me to get permission from Lucas's parents to take him out of the house so we could be alone. By then, the doctors had proclaimed there was no sign of cancer anywhere in his body.

The oncologist, Dr. Griffin, said, "We don't use the word 'cure' for this type of situation, but I feel comfortable saying Lucas Walker is in remission. On behalf of the staff of St. James Hospital, we couldn't be more pleased with the outcome of Lucas's treatment here."

I can tell you what he'd said verbatim, because this was a quote from an interview with our local news anchor, Melanie Fox, from the channel 8 news. Lucas's story was a six-minute segment. They showed him pretending to do chores around the farm, and they interviewed his parents as they sat stiffly on the couch, Mr. Walker with his arm around his wife's shoulder. Eric only made a cameo appearance, and I didn't even make the cut at all. They spliced in some old footage of Lucas playing football before his diagnosis and somehow came up with a photo of him in the hospital bed looking like he was two degrees away from death. My best guess is that they got that picture from Devin Bombeck, this tool from the football team who took photos of everybody all the time, even when you told him not to.

I watched the clip over and over again, noting the dramatic music and the contrasting before and after shots, the way they cut the conversation with Lucas's parents to just a short bit of Mrs. Walker saying it was a miracle. The thing that interested me the most, though, was the press conference held by Dr. Griffin on the front steps of the hospital. Lucas's case was suddenly a big deal, not just locally, but worldwide. Other hospitals wanted to know what protocol they used to get such incredible results, and Dr. Griffin made himself out to be a hero. So I watched the clip, and was so annoyed at how he took all the credit that I barely noticed the way the camera scanned the crowd at the bottom of the steps. Most of the people in the audience were local reporters and staff from the hospital, but there were a few random bystanders as well. I didn't pay much attention the first time around, but the second time I watched the clip, I did a face palm because who did I see in the crowd? Mariah and Todd, the friendly safety agents, dressed in normal clothes, trying to blend in. I paused the video and made the image bigger, which only made it more pixilated, but there was no doubt it was them. Why were they at Lucas's doctor's press conference? It didn't make sense.

Other kids on Facebook had talked about the agents questioning people from the surrounding farms, asking if they'd seen or heard anything the night we heard the boom, but no one had, and right after that, the news of Lucas's recovery overshadowed everything else and the agents were forgotten.

Every day, Lucas seemed healthier and stronger. His hair grew in so that there weren't any thin patches anymore and he got the color back in his cheeks. He spoke in a more normal tone of voice and responded in a way that made sense. He fooled everyone—his family, his friends, the doctors. Everyone but me and Mack.

The end of the second week, I asked his parents' permission to take Lucas out on Saturday evening. "Just out for a burger at Scotty's," I said. Scotty's was the local burger joint, frequented mostly by teenagers and young families. "And then to a baseball game at the high school. All the guys really want him to be there." Lies. It was all lies. The best lies I could come up with on short notice.

Mrs. Walker exchanged a skeptical look with her husband. "I don't know. Lucas is just getting over being sick. I hate to take a chance." She said it like he had a bad case of the flu and she was afraid he'd relapse. "Can't you just watch a movie here? I can heat up a pizza for you, and we have root beer. It's the kind Lucas likes."

"It's just that everyone was looking forward to seeing him at the game. And he's been cooped up at home for so long." Through all of this, Lucas said nothing, another oddity. Usually he could charm his mother into agreeing to anything. She had a soft spot for her older boy.

"I know, Emma, but what if something happens?"

"Nothing's going to happen." I sensed I was losing ground here, but I wasn't going to go down without giving it my best shot. "We won't be far, and I'll have my cell phone," I said. "If he seems too tired or doesn't feel well, we'll come back early, right Lucas?"

"Right," he said. "We'll come back early."

"And how are you planning on getting there?" Mrs. Walker frowned. "Lucas isn't going to be driving our car, I can tell you that much."

"My mom said I can use her car. It's very reliable. And it has all the latest safety features," I added hurriedly. "She doesn't want me to stay out late either. I told her I'd be back by ten at the latest." Neither of Lucas's parents said a word, so I made an adjustment. "Or we could be back by nine-thirty, if that's better."

"It's just that he's only been well for such a short time," Mrs. Walker said.

Mr. Walker turned to his wife and said, "What if Eric goes with them? Would that make you feel better?" I didn't want Eric to go with us, but if that was the only way it was going to happen, it was better than nothing.

Eric yelled from the next room. "I don't want to go on their date. Let them go alone. What's the big deal?"

I silently thought, *thank you, Eric,* but it turned out that his objections and my wishes didn't matter. Mr. and Mrs. Walker decided that the only way they'd allow Lucas and me to go out for the evening was if Eric came along. And so, with me at the wheel, Lucas in the front passenger seat, and Eric in the back, the three of us drove away from the farm at five-thirty on Saturday evening.

"This seat belt isn't staying closed," Eric called out as we barreled down the highway.

"It's broken." I tossed my answer over my shoulder. "Try the other one."

"So much for all the latest safety features," he grumbled. "I can't believe they made me go with you guys. Such a waste of my time."

I was nearly to Mrs. Kokesh's when Eric figured out something was off.

"Hey," he said, his head swiveling to look behind us. "You missed the turn off to Scotty's."

"We're not going to Scotty's," I said. "Or at least not right now. If we have time, we'll stop afterward."

"Afterward?"

"I have to talk to Mrs. Kokesh about Lucas."

"Mrs. Kokesh!" I glanced in the mirror to see Eric abruptly sitting up in the back seat. "What's going on, Emma?" Even Lucas seemed interested, turning my way with a questioning look.

"I used her help to cure Lucas, but something went wrong," I said, gripping the steering wheel. "Something went terribly wrong. I have to talk to her and I want her to see him."

"What went wrong?" Lucas asked.

I glanced in the rearview mirror and saw Eric waiting for my answer. I spoke to Lucas.

"You're not the same," I said. "You know that, right? You're try-ing, I can tell, but there's something missing. Something is really wrong."

"Give the guy a break," Eric said. "He's been cut open, radi-ated, medicated, gone through chemotherapy, been in a coma, and everything else. He's doing pretty good, considering. You're mak-ing a big deal out of nothing."

"No." I shook my head. "You're wrong. Even taking all that into consideration, he's still not the same Lucas." I knew Lucas. I knew every cell in his body. Every thought in his head, every emotion in his heart. Our souls had once been intertwined, but I wasn't feeling it anymore. "I'm not imagining things. I'm telling you I know the difference." I glanced over and saw Lucas's beautiful, expressionless face looking straight at me. "You're not the same, are you Lucas?"

Lucas didn't answer, just turned his head to look out the win-dow. Eric said, "Well, now you've made him feel bad. Stop being so mean, Emma." He sighed heavily.

"It's not just me," I argued. "Mack sees it too, and you know what they say about how dogs can sense things people can't."

"Yeah," Eric said, "but Mack also drinks out of the toilet, so I wouldn't go by that." We rode in silence for a moment, the only car on the highway. "I can't believe you went to Mrs. Kokesh."

"You think it was a bad idea? Because it's witchcraft?"

"No, because I wish I had thought of it myself."

Smiling, I pulled into the drive leading up to Mrs. Kokesh's house. Once the car was parked, I grabbed my canvas bag and the three of us got out and walked up the steps. A white cat lounging on the porch saw us and took off like a shot. Mrs. Kokesh was home, I was sure of it. The main door was open and I could see through the screen door into the hallway. I banged on the door with the side of my fist. "Hello? Anyone home?" I pounded again.

"Maybe she's not here," Eric said.

"She's here," I said.

A second later, Mrs. Kokesh's voice came booming from the top of the stairs. "Hold your horses! I can only go so fast." She shuffled down, taking each step one at a time, as if her feet hurt. Like before, she'd dressed for colder weather, wearing a man's cardigan over a faded floral-print dress. The flip-flops on her feet were her only concession to summer. "You again, Emma?" she said, swinging open the door. "I shoulda known you'd be back."

She gestured for us to come in and we all trooped down the hall. Lucas walked along as if this whole outing was normal, but Eric made a gesture to me like *what's going on?* which I just ignored. Soon enough, he'd know everything I knew.

When we reached the kitchen, I took a seat, not even waiting for an invitation. I kept my large bag ready on my lap. The guys stood awkwardly until Mrs. Kokesh threw up her hands and said, "You might as well sit and be comfortable." Once everyone was gathered around the table, she said, "So, you got a complaint, Emma? Everything not hunky-dory in your world?"

"There's a problem," I said.

She threw back her head and laughed. "There's always a problem, honey. The problem is that you people expect too much. I'm seeing Lucas here, and he looks like he's not dying anymore, so I'd say I held up my end of the bargain. I saw on the news that people are saying it's a miracle. It doesn't get any better than that."

"It was a miracle and I'm grateful to have Lucas back," I said. "It's just—"

"I'm not giving you your money back," she said, cackling. Then to Lucas and Eric, she said, "I saw this coming. I warned her and did it for free. Now she's complaining."

"I'm not complaining. I just need your help again."

"Help? What do I look like, the help desk?" She slammed the palm of her hand on the table. "No one in this nothing town has the time of day for me until they have a problem. Then they're like, 'Mrs. Kokesh, you're my only hope. You have to help me.'" She put her hands together like she was praying. "That's how it starts out. Then I help them and when things don't go exactly the way they want, it's all my fault. Well, I'm telling you, missy, I'm tired of taking the blame. I give and I give and I give, and what do I get? Nothing!" She spat out the word. "You people come traipsing up my porch begging and pleading, and I do the best I can but it's never enough. I'm tired of it. I get no credit and no gratitude."

"I give you complete credit," I said. "And I am grateful."

"But?" she cried out, and turned to Eric. "There's always a but, believe me."

Eric said, "Could you let Emma finish? I want to hear what she has to say."

"I know what she has to say," Mrs. Kokesh said, leaning back with folded arms. "I've seen it all before. I've heard it all before."

I reached into my bag, pulled out the object Mack had found in the field, and set it on the table. "Have you ever seen something like this before?"

# CHAPTER TWELVE

Mrs. Kokesh leaned forward, her eyes narrowing in confusion. "What the hell is that?"

I'd had the object for two weeks, first stashing it in the old barn, and then in the closet in my bedroom. I'd looked at it countless times, studying it from every angle, and I still didn't have an answer for her. I shook my head.

"Some kind of container? I don't really know. I was hoping you could tell me."

The object was as big around as a large pie plate and maybe four inches tall. Nothing remarkable about the size and shape. It was the color and material that made me gaze in wonder every time I looked at it. Shimmery and beautiful, like carnival glass or a hologram, but not really like either of those things either. Familiar and yet unlike anything I'd ever seen before. It was cool to the touch all the time, regardless of the outside temperature. It reminded me of when scientists discover a new species of animal, like that crystal frog they found in Peru with skin so translucent you could see its heart beating through its chest. Impossible, yet there it was.

Mrs. Kokesh reached for it, then stopped. "May I?"

"Of course." I pushed it across the table so she could examine it. "The same night I used your potion to cure Lucas, this thing crash-landed at their farm, back behind the house. At least, I think that's what happened." I sighed. "Lucas's mom and I heard a big noise, like something hitting the ground, and then it sounded like it skidded. I found it in the field, two days later. Some government agents came to their house, saying they were looking for some wreckage from an aircraft collision. Mrs. Walker sent me out to bring the dog in before she let them search the property and Mack led me right to this."

"Fascinating." Mrs. Kokesh turned it, looking at it from every side, and then lifted it over her head to see the bottom. "The agents—did you tell them you found this?"

"No, I hid it in the barn before they came out."

"Good girl!" she said approvingly.

"The weird thing is that the agents were at the press conference Lucas's doctor held to talk about his recovery. Why would they be there if they were just investigating an aircraft collision?" I asked.

Mrs. Kokesh said, "I don't know."

"So you've had this the whole time?" Eric said. "How come you didn't tell us about it? It was on our property."

"You can have it if you want," I said. "I didn't steal it. I was just keeping it safe until I figured things out."

"But you didn't even mention it. And you took it home with you," Eric said, a whine in his voice. Sometimes he seemed so mature; other times he was every bit a fourteen-year-old. "You could have told me. I can keep a secret."

I continued: "So this thing, whatever it is, came down, but I didn't know about it that night because I didn't go outside. Then I used the potion on Lucas, and the next day he started to get better."

"You're welcome," Mrs. Kokesh said sarcastically. "Glad I could help."

"Thanks to you, Lucas got better," I said, clarifying. "And it really was a miracle. But the complication is this thing here." I pointed. "And that Lucas isn't himself, really. I don't feel the connection we used to have." I glanced at Lucas, who sat there impassively, like we were talking about someone else.

"I warned you about that," she said.

"I know. I get that, but it's not that he's a little different. It's like he's a different person. The dog growls at him like he's a complete stranger, and Lucas acts like he doesn't know me anymore."

Eric jumped in. "He knows you. Don't be stupid, of course he knows you. Lucas," he said, nudging his brother's arm. "Who is that?" He pointed to me. "What's her name?"

But Lucas didn't answer. He was too busy staring intently at the mystery object. Mrs. Kokesh noticed this too, and picked up the object and set it in front of him.

"You haven't had much to say, Lucas," she said. "What's on your mind?"

Lucas touched the object tentatively and flipped the top back and forth. Open. Closed. Open. Closed. I'd done that myself a dozen times, and I'd also stuck a comb into the opening, and when that seemed okay, my hand, but the inside was dry and empty. Whatever it had once housed wasn't in there anymore. A funny look crossed Lucas's face. He almost looked like he was about to cry.

"What is it, Lucas?" I asked.

"It looks different from here," he said, his eyebrows coming together.

"You've seen this before?" I was confused. He'd been in a coma when it had landed, and it hadn't been anywhere near him since. He couldn't have seen it. I felt something warm and furry brush against my ankle and hoped it was one of Mrs. Kokesh's cats. I wasn't going to take my eyes away from Lucas for even one second to check. "Where did you see it?"

No response. He just kept staring at it, and finally he picked it up and examined it the way Mrs. Kokesh had, from every angle, top to bottom.

"Lucas," Mrs. Kokesh said sharply. "We can't help you unless you tell us the truth. You can trust us. Where did you see it before?"

With one finger, he pushed it back to her. "I was mistaken. I've never seen it before."

"Well," Mrs. Kokesh said, clearly miffed, "so much for that. Let's come at this from another direction. Lucas, do you feel different from before? Like you've transformed into someone else?"

"No," he said, his voice strong. "I am the same."

"Emma says you're different," she said.

Lucas cleared his throat and turned to me. "Your concern is noted and appreciated."

"Lucas." I reached over and grabbed his arm. "What happened to you? And what is this thing? Do you know?" I looked for a reaction, but his face was expressionless. A mask. I'd have given anything to see him be himself again, even if it meant he would be angry or depressed. Anything would be an improvement over this nothing.

"Emma is the reason you're alive, you know," Mrs. Kokesh said.

Lucas nodded. "It's important to know who to blame."

What was *that* supposed to mean? I wanted to shake him, but instead I just sat and searched his face, hoping to see signs that he was messing with us. If that wasn't it, I would have settled for finding out he was temporarily insane. Anything to explain why Lucas was acting so weird.

Eric leaned into the table now and spoke directly to his brother. "We've been through a lot with your cancer. The doctors told us you were dying."

"Given the choice, I'd rather be living than dying," Lucas said.

"Lucas," I said. "Do you remember everything that happened before? Remember when we drove out to the quarry that one night?"

I thought if I talked about something significant, it would jog his memory. The summer night at the quarry stood out, because

Lucas and I had ignored the "No Trespassing" signs, climbed over the fence, and stripped down to our underwear to swim under the stars. It had been a sticky, humid night and sinking into the water with Lucas right next to me felt daring and exciting. In the dark, our bodies pressed together in the cool water, it had been hard to know where I ended and he began. More would have happened if it hadn't been for the poorly timed appearance of a portly security guard with a powerful flashlight. When the guard had yelled at us from the other side of the water, we'd scrambled out, grabbed our clothes, and took off before he could catch up to us. We'd laughed all the way to the car, pulling on clothes as we went. By the time we'd gotten to the fence, we were fully clothed, although Lucas's shirt was on inside-out. Just thinking about our getaway could make me smile even now. But Lucas acted like the word "quarry" didn't bring up any memories at all.

"What happened at the quarry?" Eric asked.

Lucas's head bobbed up and down. "I remember everything, Emma."

"I know you've said that, but can you tell me something specific?"

"I'm tired," Lucas said. I'd noticed he used that excuse a lot lately.

"All you have to do is give me one example," I said, exasperated. "One thing that tells me you remember our history." But Lucas only shook his head.

"This is getting us nowhere," Mrs. Kokesh said. "If Lucas knows something, he's choosing not to share it with us." She glared in his direction before casting a sympathetic eye toward me. "I'm sorry, Emma. I can't change him and make him love you more."

"That's not what I'm asking—"

She held a hand up to silence me. "But since you think this object and Lucas are connected, let me investigate. I have some

books. I'll do some research. My best guess is that this thing, whatever it is, comes from another world."

"Another world? Like another planet?" Eric asked.

Her head tilted to one side. "Maybe. Or from another dimension. But definitely not from around here. Let me do some reading
and some testing and I'll get back to you."

"If it *is* from another dimension, what does that have to do
with Lucas?" Eric said.

Mrs. Kokesh shrugged. "That's what we need to find out. I have
to say, this has been a most interesting visit. Usually people come
to me asking for revenge or money or love." She ran her finger
around the rim of the object. "Can I keep this for now?"

"No," Lucas said firmly.

I glanced at him, startled. He'd gone with the flow for the last
two weeks, staying quiet as can be, not expressing a preference for
any foods, obeying his mother without question, agreeing with
everything people said. Now he was going to object?

"I think it would be okay if we left it with Mrs. Kokesh for a
day or two," I said.

"No." Lucas pushed his chair back and stood, picked up the
object, and put it under his arm. "Time to go," he said.

"I agree. I think we need to go," Eric said, getting up and following Lucas out of the room.

"I guess we're leaving," I said to Mrs. Kokesh, gesturing to the
doorway.

She nodded. "Be careful, Emma. I don't know what you've gotten yourself into, but everything tells me it's dangerous."

"I will."

"Hang on just a minute," she said, getting up and rummaging
through the drawer next to the sink. "I have something you might
need." She pulled out various items—Scotch tape, a calculator, a
deck of cards, the plastic tabs from grocery store bread, a bag of
rubber bands—and one by one, she placed them on the counter.

Meanwhile, all I could think was that Eric and Lucas had left without me. As if reading my mind, she said, "They aren't going to get too far. You drove, right?"

"Yeah, I drove." Just as I suspected. She'd watched us arrive from an upstairs window.

"Aha!" Mrs. Kokesh said, jubilantly. "Here it is. All the way in the back. I knew it was in there, but for a second I thought I wasn't gonna find it." She turned around and held out a small leather case, zippered on two sides. "A gift from me. You might need it."

"What is it?" I took it from her and as soon as I had it in my hand, I could tell what it was by its weight and shape. "A gun?"

"Think of it as your ace in the hole," she said. "It's not very big, but it'll do the job."

"I don't think I'll be needing a gun," I said.

She shrugged. "Better to have it and not need it than need it and not have it. And I have a feeling you're going to need it."

I unzipped the case and took it out, holding it carefully between two fingers. She explained that it was loaded and showed me that the safety catch was on.

"I don't know about this," I said. "I've never shot a gun before."

"It's not that difficult." Mrs. Kokesh said, tapping her chin. "Once the safety catch is moved to the off position"—she paused to show me how to slide the button to one side—"you just pull the trigger."

"But isn't that dangerous?"

She rolled her eyes, like I was a complete idiot. "Yes. That would be the point, Emma."

"Oh, okay," I said. "Thanks, I guess."

From outside Eric's voice rang out: "Emma, hurry up!"

"Yeah, I have to go," I said. "Bye." And I went down the hall so fast I almost tripped over a cat.

# CHAPTER THIRTEEN

"What the hell, you guys?" I said as soon as I got past the front porch. Eric and Lucas stood next to the locked car. Lucas had the found object cradled against his body like it was a football. "You couldn't have waited for me?"

"It's not like we could leave without you," Eric pointed out as I unlocked the doors. After everyone got in, I pulled out of the driveway so fast that we left a trail of gravel dust behind. What a letdown. I'd thought Mrs. Kokesh could tell me what was wrong with Lucas, but it turned out she had her limits, just like everyone else.

We went to Scotty's so that my lie to the Walkers wouldn't be a total lie after all. I convinced Lucas the object would be safer in the trunk of the car and he reluctantly allowed me to tuck it in next to the spare tire. By now, Lucas was even more of a local celebrity than he'd been in the first place, and I dreaded having to talk to other kids from our school, but as it turned out, the only ones we encountered were a group of five sophomore girls sitting in a corner booth and giggling continuously. When they were leaving, they stopped at our table and told Lucas they were glad he was better. "You're going to be back at school this fall, right?" said one of them, a red-haired girl wearing a sheer tank top and really short shorts. She snapped her gum and rested a hand on Lucas's shoulder as she spoke to him. I didn't know her name, but mentally I named her Bambi McSlutsky.

Lucas nodded agreeably. "Sure," he said. Just then, the waitress brought our food, so they left, which was good timing because I was ready to swat Bambi and her annoying friends. Even though Lucas now had the personality of a droid, he'd regained his good looks and was so beautiful that girls flew to him like bees to nectar. But they couldn't have him because I'd claimed him first. He was my nectar. My forever boy.

Right from the start, Lucas and I were so sure we'd wind up together that I decided to document our dating years for all eternity. Sophomore year, my English teacher told us to be careful of anything we did online, including emails. He had a theory that everything, even things we deleted, could be accessed in the future. "It's all still out there," Mr. Anderson said, "and someday your great-grandchildren will be able to pull up everything you ever did online, videos on YouTube, emails, anonymous comments on message boards. The good, the bad, and the ugly." He rubbed his hands together and chortled with glee. "They'll get true insights into who you are, so make sure that what you put out there is what you want future generations to know." If he thought he was scaring us, he was wrong, at least for me. I liked the idea of our future children and grandchildren and great-grandchildren knowing about our love story, so every week I started sending Lucas emails that talked about places we went and things we did together. I signed every email "Love, Emma <3." My name, surrounded by my love for him.

I even kept the emails going through Lucas's cancer treatment, but the day he told me the treatment rendered him unable to father a baby, I lost interest and stopped. My love for Lucas hadn't changed, but knowing there weren't going to be future generations made my email project seem pointless. Still, the emails were out there, a forever record of the two of us.

After we were done eating, all three of us agreed to skip the baseball game and go straight home. Eric had no interest in sports, Lucas had no opinion either way, and for me, the thought of having to sit in the bleachers and talk to all of Lucas's fans was depressing as hell. Better to tell Mr. and Mrs. Walker that because Lucas seemed tired, we decided to cut the evening short. I'd get credit for using good sense and they'd be more likely to let us go out the next time.

When we walked out to the car, Eric said, "Lucas, you sit in back. I want to talk to Emma."

This new Lucas never questioned anything and he didn't object this time either, but got in the back and put his seat belt on. I missed the old Lucas, the one who would have said, "Like hell you're sitting upfront with my girlfriend!" I imagined the two of them tussling over me, Lucas putting Eric in a headlock. I had once had a boyfriend, the love of my life, but now all that was left of him was a shell.

"What did you want to talk about?" I asked, once we were heading down the road.

"Just a minute." Eric fiddled with the radio until the music only came through the back speakers. The car was so old that the sound quality was terrible, but if Lucas minded at all, he didn't say so. Eric faced forward, his words coming out of the side of his mouth. "Remember what you said to Mrs. Kokesh about Lucas being a different person?"

"Yeah, of course I remember. It was only like an hour ago."

"I think you're right."

"About what?" I glanced his way, but his face didn't tell me anything. Clearly, he didn't want Lucas to hear what we were talking about.

"I think you're right. He is a different person," he said. "I didn't see it at first. He just seemed slower, like he was waking up from the coma. Even on the drive over I thought you were overreacting.

Making too much of it. You know, like girls do." Hastily, he added, "No offense."

"None taken." I flipped on my turn signal and veered right onto the highway. "So what changed your mind?"

"Movie quotes."

"Excuse me?"

Eric leaned over and spoke through gritted teeth. "You know how Lucas has been making odd comments? He says things that sort of fit what we're talking about, but not really? I didn't think too much of it, until we were at the witch's house. Then he said three things that came right from *The Outlaw from San Antonio*."

"The outlaw from what?" I glanced in the rearview mirror to see Lucas staring out the side window like a little kid.

"*The Outlaw from San Antonio*. It's an old western. My favorite, even if it is pretty cheesy. I've seen it like a hundred times. But Lucas never liked cowboy movies so he only saw it for the first time after he woke up from his coma."

I remembered Eric bringing his laptop into Lucas's sick room and the two of them watching a western. I couldn't have come up with the name of the movie for any amount of money, though. It wasn't the kind of thing Lucas and I would normally be interested in.

He continued. "He quoted from it three times tonight. When he said, 'Your concern is noted and appreciated.' And then when he said, 'It's important to know who to blame.' That's straight from the movie."

"Maybe it's a coincidence?" I asked, glancing at the rearview mirror to see Lucas looking out the window. "The movie was still on his mind, probably."

"Yeah, well how about when he said, 'Given the choice, I'd rather be living than dying'? A direct quote from the movie." His eyes got large. "When he said that, I just about fell over. That was when I knew for sure. Normally, Lucas would never talk like that."

"So what conclusion are you drawing here?" I asked quietly.

"I don't know, but it's like he's not Lucas. It's like he's trying to be Lucas, but he's having some trouble getting it right so he's copying what we say and picking up lines from TV and movies."

My mind reeled. As much as I'd been the one to say Lucas wasn't himself, I hadn't thought he was literally a different person. "So what are you saying? He's possessed by a demon or what?" Now I was speaking through clenched teeth, although there was no indication that Lucas was listening or even cared about what we were talking about.

"I don't know," Eric admitted. "All I know is he's not acting like my brother." He jabbed a thumb in the direction of the backseat.

And he thought girls were melodramatic. I said, "Maybe he has amnesia and he's relearning how to be himself. Or maybe he had a stroke or some kind of brain explosion or something and it completely changed his personality." I'd heard of this happening. People who had strokes and had to relearn how to read, or woke up from comas only able to remember recent events but nothing from the past. I'd read about one woman in England who was knocked unconscious and woke up speaking with a French accent. All these things came about as a result of mixed-up, crazy brain injuries. Sometimes even the doctors didn't understand why they happened. There had to be a sensible explanation.

Eric said, "Yeah, but then how do you explain that he knew about the thing you found in the field?"

I shrugged. "He was mistaken. Confused." Our voices were getting louder, but if Lucas knew we were talking about him, he didn't show it.

"No. He definitely recognized it. This is what I think—something else is inside of Lucas and that something is wearing him like a costume, making him walk and talk and eat and everything else."

I had to remind myself that Eric was fourteen and watched a lot of the Syfy channel. "Okay," I said, humoring him. "Let's just say you're right. What do you want to do about it?"

"I don't know." He shrugged. "It's up to you, I think. You were the one who brought him back in the first place."

The rest of the way home, I drove without speaking, the music filling the void. I tried to make sense of what had happened: a magic potion, a fallen object from another world or dimension, a dying boy brought back by true love's kiss. The stuff of storybooks or movies. But now Eric was suggesting that what I'd done out of love had resulted in something sinister. What if he was right? *Oh, Lucas, what did I do? And how can I fix it?*

When we were just down the road from the farmhouse, Eric turned around and explained to Lucas that he had to hide the object in the barn. "We can't let our parents see it or they'll turn it over to the authorities and those agents will be back."

"Someone will take it?" Lucas said.

"Yes." Eric nodded emphatically. "I'll keep it for you and you can see it whenever you want."

Lucas thought for a moment and then said, "Okay."

When we got to the Walkers', I pulled the car around back, threw it into park, and popped the trunk. Eric jumped out and disappeared into the barn with my discovery. When Mrs. Walker came through the back door, the three of us were walking toward the house.

"What's going on?" she asked, suspicious. It was hard to get anything past her.

"I found a hubcap on the road for my collection," Eric said. "I just stuck it in with my stuff."

"No, I mean why are you back so soon? Is Lucas okay?" She rushed down the steps and put a hand on Lucas's forehead, the international sign of mother-caring.

"He's fine," I assured her. "After we ate at Scotty's, he looked a little tired, so we decided to skip the ball game."

But she wasn't done fussing. "Do you want to go to bed, Lucas? Or just rest on the couch? I could get you something to drink." She turned to me. "I want to make sure he stays hydrated."

"Something to drink," he said, and for the first time I really noticed what Eric had mentioned. Like a beginner trying to speak a foreign language, Lucas was repeating what we said rather than coming up with his own words.

"Lemonade?" Mrs. Walker said brightly. "I just made a fresh pitcher."

"That sounds good," I said. "Can I have a glass too?"

"Of course, Emma." Our early return seemed to have softened her attitude toward me. "Why don't you kids wait on the front porch and I'll bring out the drinks?"

"I'm good, Mom," Eric said, brushing past us and heading toward the house. "I've got some stuff to do."

Mrs. Walker sighed as she watched her younger son bound up the steps and go inside. Eric found interacting with people draining. I knew he was going to his room to be alone where he could recharge. "Thanks for taking Eric with you," she said. "I wish he would get out more but he seems happy just staying home and building things with his junk pile."

"We didn't mind," I said. "Eric's cool."

"That's nice of you to say," she said.

"No, I mean it."

But Mrs. Walker didn't look convinced. It gave me a new perspective on what it must be like to be Eric. Poor kid. Someday, he might carve an impressive niche in the world, but for now he was just Lucas Walker's awkward little brother.

Mrs. Walker went into the house, while Lucas and I walked around to the front and sat down on the wicker love seat on their front porch. The Walkers had planters with red geraniums on either side of the flagstone path and an American flag proudly waving from one of the porch columns. Their house was picture perfect. When Mrs. Walker came out with a tray holding iced glasses and set them on the wicker table in front of us, it was like a scene out of a lemonade commercial.

"Anything else?" she asked. "I can get some cheese and crackers. Or raisins?"

"I'm good, thanks," I said.

"Good, thanks," Lucas parroted.

"Okay, well, I'll let you kids have some privacy," she said, brushing her hands on the front of her shirt. "When the mosquitoes start biting, that will be your cue to come in." She went into the house and shut the door behind her.

Her mosquito comment told me that she expected us to come inside when it got dark. As soon as the sun went down, the mosquitoes came out in full force. The sun was sinking, so I'd have to act quickly. For the first time in a long time, I had a chance to talk to Lucas uninterrupted and I was going to use that time to get to the bottom of this.

I handed him a glass of lemonade and took one for myself, taking a sip before I asked, "How's the lemonade, Lucas?"

He looked at the glass and then at me. "Good."

"I've always thought that lemons are the sweetest fruit, don't you think?"

Lucas stared at the glass as if the answer might be somewhere within the liquid. "It's good."

"And so sweet. Don't you think it's sweet?" I prodded. "Because lemons are sweet?"

There was a long pause like he was trying to decipher what I was saying. Finally, he said, "Yes, lemons are sweet."

My heart sank. He was even worse off than I'd thought. I spoke slowly, not knowing how much he understood. "Lucas, baby, I was just testing you. Lemons aren't sweet at all. They're sour, really sour. You have to add sugar to lemonade or you wouldn't be able to drink it at all. You know that, right?"

"Oh," he said. "Lemons are sour?"

"Yes." I took the glass out of his hand and set it next to mine on the table, then put my hands on either side of his face. I got so close our noses were nearly touching and I could see the flecks of gold in his green eyes. He had trouble holding my gaze, but I wasn't going to let him off the hook. I pulled his face closer and put my lips on his for the first time since I'd used Mrs. Kokesh's potion. We usually avoided PDA at the Walker house because Lucas's mom disapproved and you never knew when she might come barging in, but I no longer cared. I pressed against him and parted my lips, closing my eyes and exploring his mouth with my tongue. Tentatively, he responded, but it wasn't Lucas. He was acting too timid. Unsure. It felt all wrong. I opened my eyes to stare into his wide eyes.

"Talk to me," I said letting go of him. "Why are you so different?"

He shifted uncomfortably and looked off in the distance. "I don't understand."

"Don't say that," I said. "I missed you so much when you were sick and now that you're back, I feel like you're pulling away from me. Don't do that, Lucas. I can't take it. This is killing me."

"I'm sorry." But he didn't sound all that sorry. They were just words.

The sun was beginning to sink over the horizon. I didn't have much more time. "Look," I said, "I want to help you, I really do. But if you won't talk to me, I might have to tell your parents that something is going on." I rubbed the back of my head. I could feel a headache coming on. "Or maybe those agents. If what happened to you has anything to do with the round, shiny thing, they might be able to help."

"No, don't do that . . ." He paused like he was trying to come up with something, but the silence that followed told me he was coming up short.

I held out one hand. "You tell me and maybe I can help. Or—" My other hand extended, I said, "Or you don't tell me and we involve lots of other people. I don't want to do that, but honestly, Lucas? I don't know what else to do."

I inched closer and reached up to cradle his face one more time. Mrs. Kokesh had said eyes were the windows to the soul and I wanted a good view. I had expected him to pull away, but he didn't; he just looked right back at me. If this wasn't Lucas, who was it? I didn't get the sense that this was a demon, or any kind of evil possession. This version of Lucas, whoever he was, looked like a scared toddler.

"You can trust me," I said. "I can help."

We locked eyes for what seemed like the longest time. Finally he said, "Okay. I will tell you."

# CHAPTER FOURTEEN

The scout tried to make sense of this planet and his place in it as Lucas Walker. First, he absorbed information from television and the Internet. He spent an entire day with Eric watching ridiculous things that the boy seemed to find entertaining, but as far as he could tell, none of it held much value for figuring out the human condition. Learning to read didn't take much time at all. The shapes that comprised their alphabet were primitive, comparatively speaking, and he deciphered the code quickly.

When Eric gave him Lucas's tablet, he put it to good use searching for articles that would help him figure out a way to communicate with his home planet. The greatest scientific minds of this world would be novices on his. Planet-to-planet communication, something that was commonplace and had been for generations, was nonexistent here. Some of the humans didn't even believe there was intelligent life on other planets. He found himself shaking his head, imitating the way Eric shook his when he thought something was particularly stupid.

When he came across the communications called emails, he read every one, paying special attention to those from Emma. He got insights into the girl's thoughts and feelings, and her wishes and dreams for the future. All of it was spelled out in the emails. She described activities she'd shared with Lucas and went over conversations they'd already had. Presumably, Lucas would know about all this, so why did she bother to write about it and transmit it to him? So very curious. And another curious thing: Every email ended with "Love, Emma <3." He understood that letters made words and that numbers were assigned to a numeric value, but why would she put "<3" after her name? Did she consider herself to be less than three? And less than three *what*? He went over all kinds of possibilities, but none of them made sense, so he filed the question away for another day.

At times, he amused himself by translating from the telepathic language of his people to words in English. His planet, he decided, would be called Tranquility, for its calm, orderly existence. His ship, the *Seeker*, for its exploratory nature. The two nurturing beings that created him were, of course, "Mother" and "Father," and all his many siblings "brothers and sisters." His role as scout was a "job." And his match, the one he'd sworn allegiance to? That would be his "girlfriend." Girlfriend. Such an odd word. Combining the gender with the role somehow elevated it in importance. Emma, he knew, adored Lucas and would even give up her life for him. Scout was not sure that his girlfriend, the one he now thought of as "Regina" in earth language, would do the same. She was smart and strong, but did not seem to favor him over any of the others, even though they'd been chosen to be the match of each other. Most of the time, she overrode his wishes and expressed displeasure with his shy and hesitant ways. He always felt that, just by his very nature, he was a disappointment. Perhaps, though, he was overthinking the whole situation.

# CHAPTER FIFTEEN

After Lucas agreed to confide in me, he didn't waste any time. He stood up and extended his hand, a small smile stretching across his face. For a split second, he seemed like my Lucas again. I grabbed his hand and he led me off the porch and around the side of the house. I followed, having to walk quickly to keep up. I asked, "Where are we going?"

"I will show you," he said without turning back.

I thought of our lemonade glasses sitting on the wicker table and how Mrs. Walker would be checking on us in a few minutes only to find us gone. How long before she came looking for us?

We kept going, past the garage, toward the barn. I realized, seeing him take the lead, that even with his recent weight loss, he was still bigger and stronger than me. If he wanted to harm me, taking me away from the house would be the perfect plan. What if this was just Lucas with a scrambled brain? Maybe the drugs had changed him or maybe it was the lack of oxygen to his brain. Perhaps my confrontation had forced some kind of breakdown. I'd overreacted, I thought. I should have waited to see how things played out. I should have given him more time to recover.

His hand gripped tighter, squeezing my knuckles, as he pulled me around the side of the barn. The fields far beyond were ringed by a row of trees that blocked the view of the adjacent property.

My heart pounded from exertion and fear; if someone wanted to strangle me, this would be the perfect spot. I hated that I was even thinking this way about Lucas. The guy who loved me more than life itself. And I loved him just as much, but I didn't recognize the stranger he'd become.

He let go of my hand and thrust his arm upward, one finger pointing to the sky. "Look," he said, his voice quivering with excitement.

And in that second, I let go of the notion that my Lucas had somehow morphed into killer Lucas, a guy who would choke me until I stopped breathing, then fling my body out into the field. Standing next to him like this felt like old times. Like it was just us again. Me and Lucas, or at least a form of him that I could live with if I had to.

"What am I supposed to be looking at?" I asked.

"What do you see?"

The sun was a sliver of light over the horizon, just a glint in the trees off in the distance. Above, the sky blushed orange and pink.

"The sunset," I answered. "It's gorgeous." It always was. A dusky, blue backdrop interrupted by slashes of light and color. From night to night it was never quite the same, but somehow it was always familiar and beautiful. And it happened every single night. If you gave it some thought, you'd wonder why all of society didn't shut down to watch this. If we were smart, we'd be turning off our electronics, leaving our homes, and settling down on our porches and driveways just to take it in. Each night a different miracle in the sky. But no, most of us never even bothered to look out the window. While this gorgeous light show went on outside, we did the dishes and texted and argued and watched TV. We let all of those tedious, mundane, everyday things get in the way. "Tonight it's really pretty."

"No," he said emphatically. "Not the sun." His arm stretched in an arc above his head, like answering a question in class. He dropped his arm and asked, "Up. What else is up?"

I squinted. It wasn't quite dark enough to see much more than the sunset, but I knew the stars were out there. "Everything else. The stars and the moon and other planets." I struggled to think about what else really was out there. Astronomy wasn't my thing. I couldn't tell you the difference between a comet and a meteor. "But they're all far away."

"Not all is far," he said, shaking his head. "The moon is near. The sun is near." He raised one finger skyward. "My home is far."

"Your home?"

He nodded, and gave me a look like he was glad I understood, but I didn't.

"I don't get it. What do you mean your home is far?" We were just behind the barn, but still I pointed back the way we'd come. "Your house is right over there."

His face fell. "Lucas house is there," he said, jerking his head to indicate. Again his arm rose, and this time his index finger led the way, pointing to the sky. "My house is there."

I felt a chill go up my spine and I took a step away from him. There wasn't much light left, but I could see the contours of his face—the familiar face that I'd admired and caressed, photographed and sketched. But suddenly, it didn't feel so familiar anymore. I swallowed back a lump of unease. I had asked him to tell me; now I owed it to him to follow through in a calm manner.

"So you aren't Lucas then?"

"No," he said. "I'm sorry."

There were only three possibilities. Either there was nothing wrong with him and he was joking, trying to get a rise out of me. Or the person standing next to me *was* Lucas, but he had somehow developed a mental illness or brain injury and now believed he was someone else. The third possibility, the one I didn't want to acknowledge, was that he was telling the truth.

"So you came from another planet, and now you're inside my boyfriend?" I said, struggling to keep my voice steady.

"Yes."

"How did that happen?"

"I had an accident," he said. "The object you call the round, shiny thing?"

"Yes?"

"I was inside that. We were shot down."

I felt my heart skip a beat and then speed up. His voice sounded so sincere. He believed what he was saying, I was sure of that. "And then what happened?" I asked.

"The others in my group are dead," he said. "They stayed with the ship. I did not. I left when it happened."

"So you were actually *inside* the round, shiny thing?" I said slowly and he nodded. "Were there lots of you in there?"

"No, just me. The others had their own round, shiny things. And all of us were connected to a bigger ship."

"But why? Why would you come to Earth?"

"We are like . . . explorers?" he said. "We visit and record data, and that is all."

"Lucas, if you're messing with me, I'm going to be so mad." Even as I said it, I knew it was wishful thinking. I wanted him to laugh and say he'd just been fooling around. That he couldn't believe I fell for it. But Lucas, even with his great sense of humor, didn't make fun of people. That wasn't his way.

"I am sorry," he said. "But I had to go somewhere and Lucas was dying. I knew I could fix him, and in turn, he could save me."

The chill in my spine was proving to be permanent. He was talking complete nonsense, the kind of story that could get a person thrown in an insane asylum, but I could tell he thought he was telling the truth.

"Okay," I said, exhaling. "So, just say I believe you. We'll say that I believe you're an alien from another planet. A teeny tiny alien traveling in a spaceship the size of a birthday cake. You got shot down, and now all the other aliens you were with are dead. So you were shot down and you crashed in the Walkers' field and you magically just went into Lucas. So then where did Lucas go?"

He looked miserable and didn't say anything, just wrung his hands like an old person. My thoughts spun around and landed on the unthinkable. I choked out the next question. "Is he dead?"

"Oh no. Lucas is still alive, here in this body, but he is not able to move or talk. It is like he is sleeping." He nodded to himself, satisfied with his explanation. "A kind of sleep."

"Then wake him up." I heard my voice become harsh. "Get out of there and let me talk to him. I want Lucas back."

"Emma, please," he said. "Emma, I cannot do that. If I go out of Lucas, I will die."

"Okay, I have an idea. You go back in your round, shiny thing and go home, and leave Lucas alone."

"I wish I could." He was speaking more quietly now and I had to strain to hear him. "But it is broken and won't work."

A mosquito buzzed around my ear and I waved it away. "But they'll come looking for you, right? Your people will know that you're stuck here and they'll come back." My mind flipped through all the things pilots did when they were in trouble. Sent up flares and signaled for help. "You must have sent out a distress call or something. They heard it and they'll come back to pick you up. Right? Isn't that how it works?"

"No, my people will not be back. They think I am dead."

"But did you even *try* to contact them?"

He shook his head. "I could not. It happened too quickly."

"Can you contact them now?"

"I have no way to contact them," he said. "Emma, you must not tell anyone. You said you could help me."

"I know." Of course, when I said that, I had no idea what I was dealing with. I had to think this through. If Lucas was delusional and thought he'd become the host body for an alien, what would it take to bring him back? "What if you go inside someone else? Then will Lucas come back?"

"Maybe."

"So do it."

"No. I can't."

"You can't or you won't?"

His head wobbled from side to side and he didn't say a word. Finally, I couldn't take the silence anymore. I said, "If you traveled here from another planet, you must be more advanced than us, so why can't you figure out how to let me have Lucas back? Are you one of the stupid ones? Is that why they left you behind?"

He didn't flinch or move, just miserably took it like he thought he deserved my abuse, which made me even madder. Why wouldn't he even try to defend his position?

A voice pierced the night air, coming from the back of the house. Lucas's mom. "Lucas! Emma!" Only Mrs. Walker could manage to sound pissed off and worried all at the same time.

The Lucas imposter took off, running back toward the house and leaving me behind. I followed him. It had gotten pretty dark, so I made the trek partially from memory, the sound of Lucas's shoes slapping against the ground just ahead of me. The back porch light was on, and now I could see Mrs. Walker standing in the yard, hands on hips. She was an average-looking woman normally, but she turned ugly when she was annoyed and right now she was super ugly. As we approached, she said, "You had me scared out of my mind. I've been looking everywhere for you two."

"I'm sorry," I said, slightly out of breath. "We were looking at the stars." Next to me, Lucas had stopped in his tracks.

"There are stars in the front of the house too, you know," she said. "You can see them from the porch."

"I know, it's just that Lucas wanted to show me something." I almost bit my lip, regretting my explanation, because I knew she could start interrogating me about what Lucas wanted to show me and I had nothing ready to tell.

But that didn't happen. Instead, Mrs. Walker went up to Lucas and touched his face. "Lucas, you're crying? What happened?"

He was *crying*? Lucas never cried. When his grandfather died, he didn't shed a tear. Once, he broke his collarbone midway through a football game, but he kept playing and later on he said it barely hurt. Lucas's parents always bragged about how tough and brave he was. Even as a little kid, they said, Lucas never cried.

Was he crying now because of what I'd said? I'd been horrible to him, but somehow I thought this version of Lucas was immune to name calling and accusations. Did I hurt his feelings? Or was this is a physical reaction, Lucas who was trapped deep down inside crying because he couldn't reach me? But Lucas never cried. So that couldn't be it.

"Lucas?" Mrs. Walker lifted his chin to force him to look at her. "Why are you crying? What's wrong?" He shook his head but didn't say a word, so she turned her attention to me. "Emma? Is there something you'd like to tell me?"

"What? No, we were just talking."

"Did the two of you have a fight?"

"No!" I said. "I think Lucas is just tired, right Lucas?"

His head dropped forward. "I'm just tired," he said.

Mrs. Walker put a hand on his shoulder. "Let's get you inside and put you to bed." Her soft voice turned sharp when she added, "Emma, I think it's best if you go home now."

They went inside and left me standing there, a cloud of mosquitoes swirling around my head. Mrs. Walker was so quick to dismiss me, so fast to assume we'd had a teenage squabble. What if I'd warned her that her son thought he was possessed by an alien? I almost laughed when I thought about what her reaction would be. If he denied it, she would think I was crazy or lying. She didn't really like me to begin with; this would just seal the deal. But there was no way I could keep this to myself. I desperately needed to tell someone and hopefully, that someone would help me figure out what to do. I slapped at a mosquito and got into my mother's car to go home.

When I pulled out onto the road and glanced back at the house, I saw a light on in a second-story room and a figure silhouetted in the window. Eric. Watching, always watching. That kid didn't miss a thing. He was the smartest one in the house and the only one likely to believe me. Eric would be the one I could tell.

# CHAPTER SIXTEEN

The next morning, I slept late and waited until ten o'clock before getting on my bike and heading over to Lucas's house. Not getting there too early was deliberate on my part. I wanted to give Mrs. Walker a break from me.

After driving my mom's car the night before, biking seemed to take way too much time and effort. Pedaling, pedaling, pedaling. It never ended. If I had my own car, life would be so much easier, but as it stood I was lucky to be able to use Mom's once in a great while.

When I'd gotten home the night before, earlier than expected, my mother was watching TV, a bowl of popcorn on her lap. "Hey, baby," she called out, not even turning her head to confirm it was me. She always left the door unlocked until I came home. I often joked that someday instead of me coming in, it would be a serial killer, but she claimed to know the sound of my footsteps. She wasn't one to worry about anything. "I didn't expect you back before ten."

I settled down in a chair next to her. "Yeah, Lucas was tired, so we didn't go to the game."

Mom was wearing loose cotton pajama bottoms and a white cotton T-shirt, a definite sign she was in for the night. To be polite, she held the bowl out to me. The smell of hot buttered popcorn was tempting, but I wasn't hungry, so I shook my head.

"Something bothering you?" Mom asked, shutting off the TV and giving me a concerned look.

"No, not really. Well, maybe, a little bit."

"Hit me," she said, crossing her slipper-clad feet on the coffee table, like she was settling in to hear an interesting story.

"What if someone told you something that you found hard to believe? Well, almost impossible to believe? What do you do with that?"

"Is this someone Lucas?"

I nodded. "He's been so different since he recovered and when I ask him about it, his explanation is bizarre."

Her lips closed and she made what I thought of as her thoughtful face. "Hmmm . . . Is this something you can share with me?"

"No. I mean, I'd like to, but I promised to keep it between us."

"Oh, okay." Yet another great thing about my mother. She never pushed for more than I could give. "Well, I guess whatever he's saying is either true or it's not. Has he lied to you before?"

"No. Never." Lucas was honest to a fault. Always had been, as far as I knew. I said, "But what if what he's saying is because he's mixed up from all the medical treatment?"

"That could be, I guess. I mean, I'm not a doctor, but I suppose it happens." She popped a kernel into her mouth and the room was silent except for her soft crunching. I changed my mind about the popcorn, and got up to grab a handful. A moment later, Mom said, "Is what he's saying consistent, or does it keep changing?"

"So far, it's been consistent." Now I was the one chewing.

"And is this bizarre thing he's telling you plausible?"

"Maybe."

Mom shifted the bowl on her lap. "I guess your options are either to believe what he's telling you or not believe him. Sometimes a leap of faith is required. Listen to your gut, Emma. Your gut knows the answer."

"My gut is confused."

She laughed. "Then listen to your heart. And give him time. He nearly died of cancer and he's only been better a short while. Time is what you need."

The next day, I thought about our conversation while I was biking to the Walkers', down the country roads and past the strawberry fields, where I could have been earning spending money if I had put in an application early enough, but I didn't because I'd been preoccupied with Lucas's situation. The muscles in my legs ached. I was tired of biking. If I ever got a car, I would never ride a bike again.

When I arrived, I left my bike in the front yard and knocked politely on the front door. No one answered, so I let myself in, hoping that the first person I came across wouldn't be Mrs. Walker. But the house seemed empty. Mack, I knew, was outside. He'd gradually come to accept cancer-free Lucas and had stopped growling, but he still seemed wary of him, so Lucas's mother decided he was an outdoor dog, at least while the weather was nice. So Mack wouldn't be inside. But where was everyone else? Out in the barn? I raised my voice and called out, "Hello! Anyone home?"

"We're up here!" Eric's yell came from upstairs. "Come on up, Emma."

I didn't usually go upstairs. Actually, I wasn't *allowed* upstairs. Mrs. Walker equated bedrooms with sex, so she made it a rule that there would be no girls in the bedrooms, a rule I'd violated only once when Lucas and I were there alone. We'd made out pretty passionately on his bed, but that was as far as it went. I wasn't worried about breaking her rule now, though. With all that had happened with Lucas's recovery and the fact that Eric was there, it was probably okay. Probably.

I took the stairs two at a time, glad that Eric was around for a talk. When I got to the top, I found Eric and Lucas in Eric's room. Both of them were sitting on the floor, their backs against the wall, legs stretched in front of them. Eric had his laptop open and they were staring at the screen. When I walked in, they looked up.

"Hey, Emma," Eric said. "What took you so long? I thought you'd be here by now."

I dropped my bag on the floor and sat in Eric's desk chair. In the old days, I'd have nestled in next to Lucas, and he'd have wrapped his arms around me, pulling me so close our bodies would have melded tight against each other, but those days were over. "I wanted to give your mom a breather. She was annoyed with me last night." I looked at Lucas's face to see if he'd acknowledge the fact that he'd been crying or mention that the reason we'd left the porch was because he'd dragged me behind the barn, but his expression was blank.

"We need to talk," Eric said, lowering his voice. He waved a finger toward the doorway. "Everyone's outside, but you should close the door anyway."

I swung the door shut and settled back in the chair. Eric closed the laptop and said, "We've been talking." He gestured to Lucas. "He told me about his aircraft crash and how he needed a host body to survive so he latched on to Lucas. We've been brainstorming ways to fix this all morning."

"Really," I said, my breath catching in my chest. Eric spoke so matter-of-factly that it took me aback. "You believed that story?" I looked at Lucas, who had the good sense to look sheepish.

Eric said, "It's not just a story, Emma. It's what happened."

"I've been thinking about this all night," I said. "I can tell he believes it, but I just can't wrap my brain around it. His story is pretty out there."

"It is true," Lucas said with conviction.

"Well, I believe it," Eric said. "I knew right away he was telling the truth. It explains everything—why the agents were looking for wreckage and why they were interested in Lucas's recovery. And why Lucas's cancer is gone now."

And it also explained Mrs. Kokesh's feeling that there was a "disturbance in the force," I thought, then pushed the idea out of my mind. Thinking that Lucas was mentally ill was easier to fathom.

"We've been working on a plan." He put his hand on Lucas's shoulder. "Obviously, he can't stay here. And we want Lucas back."

I leaned forward, elbows on knees. "Maybe we should start from the beginning. Tell me what he told you because I don't think I got the whole story."

Eric got up and put the laptop on his desk, then sat on the edge of the bed. Lucas watched, then got up and sat next to him, copying the exact way he positioned his arms and legs. Eric said to Lucas, "Is it okay if I tell her what happened?" Lucas nodded in response.

And then Eric told me the whole thing. Very early that morning, after his parents had headed out to the barn, he'd heard crying from Lucas's room. Normally, in the summer, the whole family would be working from early on, but because of Lucas's cancer and recovery, he got a pass, and because Mrs. Walker didn't want Lucas to be alone, they took turns staying with him. This morning it was Eric's turn.

"At first, I couldn't figure out what that noise was," Eric said, "and then I followed it to Lucas's room. He was curled up in bed and really upset. That's when he told me."

Right from the start, Eric sensed Lucas was telling the truth. Eric believed that the object I'd found was a pod, a kind of shuttle attached to a larger spaceship that had carried him here from another planet. Apparently, the pod didn't hold the alien's actual body, though. What it contained was something more like his soul or his energy.

"His physical body is dormant back on his planet, waiting for him to return," Eric said, as if he were describing a cool scene in a movie. "And when Mack came up to sniff the pod, Scout jumped out and used Mack as a host."

"Who jumped out?" I asked.

"Scout," Eric said, pointing to Lucas. "That's what I'm calling him, because that was his job. He was a scout, part of a team that compiled data about other planets."

"What a minute." I held up my hand and turned my attention to Lucas. "What's your actual name? What did they call you on your planet?" I couldn't believe we were having this conversation, but as long as we were, I wanted some answers.

He smiled shyly, a look I'd never seen on Lucas's face. Lucas was all confidence and brash good humor. Being shy wasn't on his list of personality traits. "I can't say it in your language. We communicate differently than you do."

"Oh."

Eric continued. "Then, when Mack came into the house, Scout was along for the ride. He figured out he'd have a better chance of surviving if he had a human host, so when he saw Lucas and realized he was dying, he went out of Mack and into Lucas through the membranes in their eyes. After that, he cured the cancer, but then he was stuck." Eric's eyes grew wide. "So he had to learn the language and figure out who everybody was. That had to suck. Crazy how well he adapted."

"So you're okay with this whole thing?" I asked Eric. He seemed all right. In fact, he sounded almost happy about the fact that his brother was supposedly possessed by an alien—like it was a cool summer project. Like it was one of his junk piles in the barn he was going to put together and turn into something that worked.

"Of course I'm not okay with it," he said with an eye roll. "I mean, this is really bad for Lucas and for Scout. And us too, obviously."

I stood up and pointed toward the doorway. "Can I talk to you in private for a minute, Eric?" To be polite, I said to Lucas, "You don't mind, do you? Just for a minute."

Eric looked puzzled, but he followed me down the hall. When I was sure we were out of earshot, I said, "Do you think we can trust him?"

He shot a glance back to his room. "Who? Scout?"

"Yeah, Scout or Lucas or whatever you want to call him." I swallowed the lump in my throat that I knew would trigger tears if I didn't push it back.

"Emma, don't you believe him?"

Dammit, now the crying had begun. I wiped my eyes. "That's the problem. It's so crazy but I think I do believe him. And if it is true, how can we trust what he's saying?"

Eric put his hands on my shoulders and said, "Emma, we have to trust him."

I sighed. From little on we were told not to talk to strangers. Not to take candy, or help them look for their lost kittens, or get too close to their car. That's how kids got abducted and killed. Everyone knew that. And now a stranger had taken over his brother's body and Eric wasn't even alarmed.

"But we don't know what that thing inside of Lucas even is." I was trying to speak quietly and my words came out in a hiss. "Maybe he's killed Lucas, or is going to take over one of us next. How do we know?" Part of me still couldn't believe we were having this discussion. Lucas as a host body for an alien? I was in the middle of a horrible nightmare, one that felt real.

Eric's face softened. "You don't have to worry, Emma. None of that is gonna happen. Scout's just a kid, like us. This was his first job out of school and he feels like he screwed up by not following orders. He has a major case of survivor's guilt. You should have heard him crying this morning. It didn't even sound like regular crying. It was this primal, anguished sound. Man, it was like the worst thing ever. You know Lucas *never* cried. He was tough as hell. Not this guy. Scout, he's got tender feelings." He leaned in closer. "You know, he didn't even know what crying was. He was afraid he was doing something wrong, like peeing in your pants. Trust me, he's not dangerous. We have to help him or he'll never get home and we'll never see Lucas again."

I wouldn't have thought there was anything that Eric could say to make me feel better, but I had to admit this helped. Still, it wasn't what I wanted to hear. I took a deep breath. "This whole thing is unbelievable. I kind of want to go back and pretend nothing's wrong."

"Yeah, well that's not going to work. This is happening."

I leaned against the wall, shaking my head. "This is so messed up. I just want Lucas back the way he was."

"You and me both."

I sighed. "So what do we do about it?"

"Scout and I came up with a plan, and it involves you," Eric said. "Are you in?"

# CHAPTER SEVENTEEN

"Am I in?" I said. "I guess so. What's the plan?"

A minute later, all three of us were bounding down the stairs, headed outside to the old barn, the one Eric used as his workshop. Before he'd tell me the plan, Eric said he had to show me something. We managed to make it safely inside the barn with the door shut behind us without encountering anyone else. Eric flipped a light switch and the whole place came into view. What seemed like piles of junk in the dark still looked like piles of junk, but at least there was some order to all of it. A wooden workbench on the far wall was topped with pegboard covered with hanging tools. An enormous red metal chest of drawers next to it held still more tools. Lucas had told me once that Eric had more than a thousand dollars' worth of tools, all purchased with his own money. Off to one side was Eric's current project, a car covered with a large tarp.

"You know what's under here?" he said, striding over and whipping off the cover with a flourish, like a bullfighter with a cape.

"A car," I said, stating the obvious. A white car, with a big scrape on one side, but I'd seen worse. I walked around it and noticed that, unlike a lot of Eric's projects, everything seemed intact. It even had license plates, although they were expired.

"It's a Pontiac Grand Prix," he said, tapping on the hood. "It was ready for the scrap heap when I got it. A barn car." A barn car was what people around here called the nonworking automobiles that they kept in their barns, hoping to someday have the time or money to fix them up. When someday never came and they realized they needed the space, they'd offer the car free for the taking. When that happened, Eric and his dad would take their truck and tow the vehicle home. For the price of parts and the cost of his time and labor, Eric fixed them up and sold them. He'd done it a few times now and made a crapload of money.

"It's nice," I said peering inside. The upholstery was in good shape and the windshield wasn't cracked. It was decent, as barn cars went. Through the window, I saw Lucas leaning in to look from the other side, just like me, and I was touched at how hard he tried to fit in. "But old."

"It's not that old," Eric said. "If it was a kid, it would only be in fifth grade."

"Right," I said, doing the math and figuring that in car years, the Grand Prix was elderly.

"It was dead when I got it," Eric said. "Some idiot tried to drive it through standing water when the road flooded a few years ago. Killed it completely. But it purrs like a kitten now. Six cylinders and it only has sixty thousand miles. Probably the best car I've turned yet and I could make a big profit if I sold it." He reached into his pocket and pulled out a keychain, which he held out to me. "But I'm not going to sell it. I'm giving it to you."

"Me? Why would you give me a car?"

He still held the keys out, but when I didn't take them, he set them on the hood. "Because you're going to need it to carry out the plan. And when you come back with my brother, you're going to need a car next year. Seniors don't take the bus."

He was right about that. Seniors at our high school didn't take the bus. The ones who didn't have cars rode with those who did. Only friendless losers would be caught dead riding the school bus their senior year. Even as a junior, there was something of a stigma, so I always rode with Lucas on the days he went to school. When his cancer treatment kept him home, his friends were glad to give me a ride. But next year was another matter. One I hadn't even started to think about yet. A car would be a good thing to have, but no one just gave you a car, even a junky Pontiac Grand Prix, without some big strings attached. And only a complete moron would agree to something without knowing the details.

I crossed my arms. "So what's the plan?"

Eric leaned his butt against the car and crossed his arms the same way—to mock me, I thought. "You and Scout drive up to Ashland, up near Lake Superior. Just for a day. There's a private research facility right outside of the city called Erickson Ryder Incorporated. They must be working on something top secret, because they don't have a website or much of anything online. The one thing I did find was on a job search website where they said they were looking to hire scientists with an astrophysics background to do research on radio communications. They also said their work was strictly confidential."

"And why would we want to drive up there?"

"Because there's more to it than that." Eric's brown eyes flashed with excitement. "I did some more searching on this Erickson Ryder place and I found this message board with all these people talking off the record. Apparently, the company is an unofficial SETI site and they're doing all kinds of sneaky things."

"SETI? What's that?"

"SETI stands for Search for Extraterrestrial Intelligence. There are these places all over the world that monitor radio frequencies and what they're looking for are signs of transmissions from other planets. This one guy on this message board—he goes by the name Woodcarver—he's ranting all over the place about Erickson Ryder. He says they're not only receiving transmissions, but that they actually made contact and are inviting the aliens to visit Earth. This Woodcarver guy says he knows all this because one of his relatives has the inside track. And Woodcarver is mad as hell that they're doing this. He says Erickson Ryder is putting the whole planet at risk, that his grandfather was once abducted and tortured by aliens, and that instead of inviting them, we should be warning them to stay away."

"Woodcarver sounds like a wacko," I observed.

Eric shrugged. "It sounds better when you read it. He comes off as being fairly intelligent, and a lot of people on the message board believe him and look up to him."

"That just makes him king of the wackos."

He continued. "The last few messages Woodcarver posted were a month ago. First, he said he had proof that aliens were coming to the area and that he and his sister were going to be ready for them. They knew from the radio signals where they were going to land and they were ready to blow them back to where they came from. Revenge for what their grandfather went through. Then Woodcarver came back on the message board two days later and said he'd tracked the aliens' location, fired a missile, and destroyed a ship. The other posters on the message board cheered him on like you wouldn't believe. They think this guy is a hero."

"That is crazy," I said, but even as the words rolled off my tongue, I realized that it all fit. Everything that had happened: the time frame, the explosion, the reason why Scout's spaceship had been attacked. I cleared my throat before asking Eric the next question. "So we're supposed to go up to Erickson Ryder and then what?"

He said, "Then you'll have to play it by ear. Find someone who works there who seems trustworthy and tell them what happened and ask for their help."

"What makes you think they'll help?"

"Because it sounds like Erickson Ryder were the ones making friendly overtures. Scout said the reason his people picked this area is because they'd been receiving friendly signals from north of here. Scout said his people were systematically working their way closer and closer to see if they could close in on the signal before possibly making contact."

"He told you that?" I looked at Lucas/Scout, whose face looked like a blank slate. "He said they were systematically working their way closer and closer?"

"Not in so many words," Eric said. "But I got his meaning." I must have looked skeptical because he added, "Emma, you're being kind of mean. You try learning a new language in two weeks and see how you do."

"Okay," I said, exhaling. "I'm sorry. I didn't mean to be that way."

"So I'm thinking the signals had to be from Erickson Ryder," Eric said. "And if Scout's people received these signals from them before, they can get them again. All Erickson Ryder has to do is let them know he's stuck here and then they can make arrangements to come get him."

It sounded like one of those plans that are good in theory. You think nothing can go wrong, but something always does. "This Woodcarver guy might be full of it. How do you know for sure that the signals they picked up originated from this Erickson Ryder place?" I asked.

"Have you *been* to northern Wisconsin?" Eric asked. "There's not much of anything up there. What other place would have the capability to signal outer space?"

"But what if it's not them?" I asked. "Or what if they don't even let us through the door? We're going to sound crazy." Or maybe it was more that *I* was going to sound crazy. Lucas would just be the silent one standing next to the crazy girl. "I don't know about this."

Lucas stepped forward. "We can go and ask," he said. "Please?" And even though I knew he wasn't really Lucas, his voice, full of pain and pleading, was Lucas's like I'd never heard it before. And the sadness and desperation of it just cut right through me.

"But what if they're actually the people who shot the ship down? Instead of wanting to help us, they might want to kill us."

"We thought of that too," Eric said. "But based on what I know about SETI and all, it seems a lot more likely that Erickson Ryder would be the good guys and the hit on the spaceship came from Woodcarver's people."

"But you don't know for sure," I said.

Eric pushed his glasses up the bridge of his nose. "It's definitely a risk, but what choice do we have? Can you come up with anything better?"

"Maybe if we tell your parents they could—"

"Now who's talking crazy?" Eric said. "Can you imagine what my mom would say if you told her Lucas was inhabited by an alien from another planet? She'd get all of us committed."

"Okay, we wouldn't start with that. Maybe if we showed her his aircraft?" I suggested. "That's proof of something, right?" I had another thought. "Or maybe your dad might be more open." Of the two of them, he was nicer, anyway.

"No," Lucas said, emphatically shaking his head. "Do not tell."

"She might believe it, if all of us stick to the story." Both of them looked doubtful, so I tried another approach. "What if I talk to them first? Would you be okay with that?"

Eric shrugged. "I can't stop you, but for the record, I think it's a really bad idea."

"I'm going to go talk to them," I said, grabbing Lucas's hand. "They might not believe me, but they'll believe you." I saw him glance back as we left the barn and I followed his look to see Eric, who apparently wasn't budging. "Really?" I yelled back. "You aren't going to help me out here?"

"You're on your own, Emma," he called out. "I told you, it's a bad idea."

It took a few minutes to track down Mr. and Mrs. Walker. We eventually found them inside eating lunch, which I took as a good sign since they were already sitting down.

"There you are, Lucas!" Mrs. Walker said as we came into the kitchen. No mention of me, even though her son and I were physically connected and I was the one who brought him in. "Are you ready for some lunch? I can make you a liver sausage sandwich, your favorite."

"I would like that," he said. "Thank you." Eric was right about Scout; now that I was thinking of him as a non-earthling, I could see he'd picked up English pretty quickly.

"Emma?" she asked, getting up from the table. Aha! She *could* see me.

"No thanks," I said. "I had a late breakfast."

I waited until she came back with a sandwich and a glass of lemonade for Lucas. He nodded and picked up the sandwich, chewing leisurely, while periodically taking small sips from his glass. I watched as he did it and realized he was studying the way Mr. Walker was eating and following along. Mimicry at its best.

The kitchen table was bathed in indirect sunlight this time of day. It was warm today, but not too hot. The open windows brought in fresh air and I could hear birds singing and the occasional moo of one of the cows. No one spoke. Everyone was busy eating. It was almost a shame to interrupt this tranquil scene with upsetting news, but I had to get it in before they cleaned up and went back to work. There was no time for a leisurely lunch on a farm. It was just a chance to refuel.

I cleared my throat. "Lucas and I have something to tell you and it's kind of serious."

"Oh?" Mr. and Mrs. Walker exchanged an alarmed look.

Mrs. Walker pushed her plate away. "What is it?" She looked to her son, who was busy eating and was, I could see, not going to help me out here. She turned her gaze to me, a stricken look on her face. If it weren't for the fact that Lucas's treatment had rendered him sterile, she probably would have jumped to the conclusion that I was pregnant.

"Do you believe that there's intelligent life on other planets?"

Mrs. Walker frowned. "Other planets? What is this about?"

Her husband looked amused. "Just hang on, dear. I want to see where she's going with this. Okay, Emma, I'll play along." He nodded. "I think with a universe as vast as ours, it would be foolish to discount the idea of intelligent life on other planets, so yes, I would say I'm open-minded on the subject."

I took his reaction as a good sign and plowed ahead. "Remember that night that we heard the big thud outside? And then the next day, Lucas started to get better?"

Both of them nodded their heads, which was encouraging. Mr. Walker said, "Yes?"

I continued. "And then the government agents came to look for wreckage, but it was weird because there was nothing on the news about an aircraft collision?" Their faces were expectant. They were on board so far; I just needed to get the rest of the story out. Taking a deep breath, I said, "Well, it turns out all of that was connected. Something from another planet landed in the field next to the barn and it set off a chain reaction that caused Lucas to become cured, but now we have another problem."

"Oh, Emma!" Mrs. Walker scoffed.

"No wait, let me explain." I held up my hand. "The day the agents came, I found something outside, something I think they were looking for. It looked like a round, sort of metallic disc." I indicated the size with my hands. "I hid it in the barn. I wasn't sure why I didn't give it to them, but it's a good thing I didn't." Now I was hurrying to get it all. "Because it turns out that what I found was, like, a pod, a part of a spaceship from another planet. And the crew member who was in that pod crashed on the farm and went into Lucas's body, which was good because he cured the cancer, but now we need to get him out of Lucas's body and back home so we can get Lucas back." From the looks on their faces, I'd lost the room. "I'm not explaining it very well, I know, but it's true."

Their faces changed from incredulous to angry. They didn't believe me. "Emma, I don't know what your angle is, but I'm not enjoying it," Mrs. Walker said, grimacing. She stacked her plate on top of her husband's and gathered up the silverware.

"I know it sounds crazy. I didn't want to believe it either, but it's true. Right, Lucas?" I cast a look toward Lucas who was slowly chewing his liver sausage sandwich, no reaction at all. "Haven't you noticed how different he is? Almost like he's another person?"

Mrs. Walker got up from the table and put a loving hand on her son's shoulder. "Now you're just being cruel. Lucas has been working so hard to recover. I don't think he deserves this nonsense."

"I can prove it! I'll show you the pod-thing. Lucas, go out to the barn and get it from Eric."

Lucas stopped eating and said, "I don't know what you mean."

"The round, shiny thing. Your pod. Where is it?"

He turned to Mr. Walker. "Emma is joking, I think."

"Jokes are usually funny," Mrs. Walker said with disdain, leaving the room with her pile of dishes.

Mr. Walker said, "This isn't a good day for kidding around, Emma. We've got a lot of work to do."

"I'll show you," I said, pushing my chair back. I left the house, the screen door slamming behind me, and ran all the way to Eric's barn, where I found him crouched in front of the Pontiac Grand Prix, wiping one of the headlights with a cloth diaper. I rushed in and asked, "Where's Scout's pod?"

"Hidden where you won't find it," he said, not even looking up.

"Seriously, I need it to show to your parents."

"Seriously, I'm not giving it to you."

"Why not?" I glared at him, ready to pound it out of him if I had to. Without the pod as proof, his parents would think I was lying, or else that I had the most horrible sense of humor ever.

"Because it doesn't belong to you. It's Scout's and he doesn't want other people to see it. He took some kind of oath not to disclose his existence to the people of the planets they were visiting. He was supposed to kamikaze himself when the ship got hit, but he chickened out and now he feels like crap. So don't make it worse, Emma."

"Kamikaze himself?"

Eric's shoulders lifted into a shrug. "Yeah, they had some self-destruct thing they're supposed to do in emergencies."

"Why didn't you tell me this before?"

"I didn't want to say it in front of him. He feels bad enough already. The only reason he confided in us at all is that he was desperate. We have to respect what he's going through."

"I respect what he's going through. I'm trying to help!" I said, exasperated.

"I know," he said, finally standing up. "But you're going about it the wrong way. Telling more people is not going to solve this."

"You don't know that. It might."

"I do know that. It's not going to help, Emma. It will just make things worse." He said the words with such conviction that suddenly I believed it.

"But I don't know what else to do," I said softly.

"Man up, Emma. You're not a little kid. You don't have to go running to the grownups to solve your problems. You can do this." He came over and gave my shoulder an affectionate squeeze, something he'd never done before. I was struck by how mature he suddenly sounded—how mature he'd been about this whole thing. "I'll write out directions and program the GPS for you. I'll even write out some ideas for what you should tell the Erickson Ryder people."

"You're not coming with us?" Somehow, I'd pictured this as a group trip, which had been reassuring. Safety in numbers and all that.

"Are you kidding? I'm fourteen. There's no way my parents would be cool with that. They'd have an Amber Alert out before we barely made it down the road. But you two are a different story. They'll be pissed off, but there's not too much they can do about it. Lucas is eighteen, so legally he can do what he wants. We'll have him leave a note and I'll try to smooth things over with them after you go. And your mom is used to you being here all day and night, so this won't be any different." I must have looked doubtful because he added, "You can call me from the road anytime. It's just one day, Emma. A five-hour car ride each way. If you leave early in the morning, you guys will be home by nightfall."

"But what if the Erickson Ryder people can't help? Or what if they *won't* help or they don't believe us or they call the police on us? We aren't even sure they're the ones who sent the signal. Maybe we should call first." Despite my attempts to stay calm, my voice became shriller with every word.

"You're not going to call first," he said shaking his head. "No one is going to tell you anything over the phone."

I took a deep breath, trying to keep my fears at bay. "It's a long way to go when it might be for nothing. And what if—"

"And what if the whole world explodes before you even get there?" Eric said sarcastically, his fingers widening to act out an explosion.

"That might almost be a relief," I said.

"Man, you worry a lot," he said. "It's either going to be fine or it's not. Stressing about it is not gonna help. We'll hope for the best, and if the worst happens, you can just come home. But nothing is going to change unless we try."

I stood there looking at Eric, who seemed so sure of what to do. Easy for him to say since he'd be safe at home. Meanwhile I'd be the one driving all the way to Lake Superior and back in a day to try to talk to strange scientists about my possessed boyfriend. And yet, what choice did I have? If we did nothing, I would never get Lucas back. I took a deep breath, ready to dive in and commit.

"Okay," I said. "I'll do it."

# CHAPTER EIGHTEEN

The next day at four in the morning, we left on what I started thinking of as our trip to the unknown. Unknown for a lot of reasons. It was unknown if we'd make it all the way to Ashland in an old car. Unknown if we'd find the Erickson Ryder research facility once we got there. And the biggest unknown yet? If the Erickson Ryder people would have a clue what I was talking about and be willing and able to help us. I couldn't stop thinking that I might be driving ten hours today for absolutely nothing.

I'd talked to my mom the night before about taking a day trip with Lucas, just the two of us, and although she wasn't crazy about the idea of not getting permission from Lucas's parents, she said she understood. "We just need some time alone," I said. "It's been a crazy year."

She wrinkled her nose. "Does this have anything to do with the bizarre thing he told you about his recovery?"

"Actually, yes."

I waited to see if she'd ask for more details, but true to character, she let it go at that.

"Okay," Mom said, giving a nod. "Just stay safe, and call me throughout the day so I know you're still alive."

"I will." The next morning, after I took my shower, I tried to cover the dark circles under my eyes with concealer—"tried" being the operative word. I hadn't slept well and my eyes showed it. I did my best anyway, artfully dotting the concealer on and smoothing it out, then putting on eyeliner, mascara, and lip gloss. I almost put on my usual summer clothes—T-shirt and shorts—before remembering that I was going to try to convince a top-secret research facility I had proof of life on other planets, so I went for a more serious look. Gray-striped pants with a button-down shirt. That, and a ponytail, was my whole look. I turned from side to side as I faced the mirror. I still looked like a teenager, but at least I looked respectable.

Lucas would have loved this turn of events, I thought. He would have loved that he was saved from death by an alien invading his body and that I had to go all superhero, driving to scary parts unknown to talk to strangers about things I knew nothing about, in order to save him. That little detail would really have made him laugh. He would have loved how much this forced me out of my comfort zone. When we were together, Lucas always took charge, because I wanted him to. I let him drive, pick the movies, decide where we'd eat. Not that I didn't have an opinion, or that he wouldn't have done what I wanted if I had asked. The truth was that I just wanted to be part of his world. What we did wasn't important to me as long as we were together. That's how our relationship had always worked. But now everything had shifted to me, the weight was on my shoulders, and I sure wasn't feeling prepared.

I got my backpack ready with a change of clothes and a few other things, including Mrs. Kokesh's gun, then crept into my mother's room to say good-bye. She was sound asleep, of course, as any sane person would be at that time. In the light from the hallway, I could see her lying on her side, one arm flung over the spare pillow. She wasn't snoring, but her breathing was louder than usual. I leaned over to kiss her on the cheek.

"I'm going now," I whispered.

"Huh? What?" She lifted her head an inch off the pillow. "What's wrong?"

"Nothing's wrong," I said. "Lucas and I are heading out on our trip."

She settled back down. "Okay," she mumbled. "Have fun. Be good."

"I will." I made sure my note on the kitchen counter was prominently displayed by the coffeemaker so she wouldn't miss it. It covered everything we'd already talked about: the fact that Lucas and I would be gone until nightfall on a road trip, plus his cell phone number. Cell coverage in northern Wisconsin was spotty, but I didn't mention that because I didn't want to worry her. Plus, maybe we'd hit the spots that had coverage and it wouldn't be an issue at all.

It was still dark outside when Eric and Lucas pulled up in front of my place and Eric got out to let me slide behind the wheel. I found it ironic that the fourteen-year-old had to drive because the guy who'd traveled all the way from another galaxy didn't know how. Once inside, I handed my backpack over the seat to Eric, who stowed it on the floor next to him. "Did you have any trouble getting out of the house?" I asked.

"Nope." Eric grinned. "My folks slept through everything. Hopefully they won't wake up before their usual time."

I retraced his route back to the Walkers' to take Eric home, stopping a little ways away so they wouldn't hear the car door slam. Eric hopped out and then leaned in to my window to give me last-minute instructions.

"The GPS is all set up with the Erickson Ryder info, and my phone number is in Scout's phone. It has a suction cup thing so you can stick it on the dashboard if you want. I printed off some maps too, in case you have trouble with it." He shrugged. "Sometimes it goes wonky."

"Okay," I said, thinking he was making a bigger deal out of the GPS than he had to. I could have figured it out.

"Also, I installed a thing you can plug your iPod into and the music will come out of the back speakers." He pointed to the middle console.

"Great. Thanks."

He went on, impressing me with his thoroughness. "There are snacks and drinks in the cooler on the floor next to Scout's feet. The license plates are expired, so I smeared some mud on them. Oh, and the car isn't insured, so be really careful."

"What if something happens with it?" I asked. "Like if it breaks down in the middle of nowhere?"

He tapped the roof of the car. "This baby is an Eric Walker production, so you're not going to have any mechanical problems. If you need to worry about something, worry about something else."

We said our good-byes and drove away, leaving him standing by the side of the road. If his parents caught him sneaking back into the house, there would be hell to pay. If that happened, I wanted to have a lot of miles between us.

We'd driven a good while before either of us said a word. I fiddled a little bit with the controls on the dashboard, glad to see there was air-conditioning and that it appeared to work. Finally Lucas said, "You change the air so it's more comfortable for your body."

Just like that, no question, just a statement. Even though he didn't seem to need a reply, I answered, "Yes." Glancing over, I saw his profile by the light of the dashboard, and wished Lucas were here instead of this stranger. Lucas made everything fun. Something as boring as stopping for gas even, because he'd clean the windshield and draw a heart with our initials on the damp glass so I could see it from inside the car. Being alone with him was heaven; having his arms wrapped around me felt like we'd created our own world, with the two of us as the only occupants. We could talk for hours about all kinds of things—debating better endings for movies, making plans for the future. This particular future was never in the plans, though.

This new alien Lucas said, "That seems inefficient." Each word clearly enunciated.

"What seems inefficient?" I glanced at the GPS. I wouldn't have to turn for five miles.

"Why not adjust the body to the air? Wouldn't that be better?"

"Because . . ." I stopped, trying to think of how to explain. "It's not possible. Our bodies don't work that way. I mean, we can adjust somewhat, by sweating or shivering or by changing what we're wearing." I was rambling now. "But that only takes us so far. After that we have to find a source of heat or air-conditioning or a fan or something like that."

"Oh."

"Why do you ask?"

"It is just different on my planet."

"Different how?"

"Better. More efficient."

I thought I detected a slight tone of condescension. "Are you thinking your people are superior to us?"

He hesitated, maybe picking up on my prickly tone. "We have had more time to improve things." His face was turned to me now, the expression like a small child hoping he wasn't in trouble.

"Can I call you Scout?" I asked. "It feels weird to call you Lucas when you're nothing like Lucas."

He nodded. "I can be named Scout."

"We're going to be spending a lot of time together today, so we might as well get along. If you have any questions for me, just ask."

"And if you have any questions for me, you can ask," he said.

"Okay," I said, my eyes on the dark country highway ahead. I could only see as far as the shine of my headlights. "First question: Do you understand everything people say to you?"

"Almost everything. I have learned many of your words and the ones I don't know I get from where they are in the middle of other words."

"From the context?" I guessed.

Scout nodded. "Saying the words is harder for me. I understand meanings, but combining all the words in the right way is proving difficult. I am trying, though. Your language is inconsistent in its rules. I try not to speak too much so I do not make mistakes."

"You're doing really well."

"Thank you."

"You said you have a different way of communicating on your planet. How? How do you do it?"

"We sense meanings. It is easier that way. No words to be misunderstood. And when you feel people's intent, there is not as much conflict. It is like when you say you walk in someone else's shoes."

We were on a narrow two-lane highway, and I could see other cars' headlights speeding toward us, so I kept my eyes on the road. Still, I wanted to know more. "So you communicate telepathically? You can send thoughts to each other's minds?"

"No," he said, his voice flat. "It's like sending all of who we are, our feelings and ideas and images, like a movie, but with nothing hidden. We can sense feelings and project ideas and thoughts to each other."

"I don't get it," I said.

"Do not worry. It's too hard for you to understand." His tone was reassuring. "It would be like explaining mathematics to Mack."

"So I would be the dog in this scenario?"

"Yes."

He had no idea how insulting this was. "So the difference between you and me is like the difference between me and Mack?"

"In some ways, Mack is more advanced than humans."

This was going from bad to worse. I said, "How do you figure?"

He cleared his throat, an uncomfortable sound. "You are mad."

"Well, yeah, because you're being insulting. First you say I'm equivalent to a dog, then you say, no, actually a dog is more advanced than me. You don't see Mack driving you to northern Wisconsin to fix your problem, do you?"

He laughed then, a chortling sound that I'd never heard from Lucas. A nerd laugh, but sweet in a way.

"I'm glad you find that amusing."

"That is what amusing means?" he said, sounding pleased. "I did not understand the word before. Thank you, Emma."

"Glad I could help you out," I grumped. "Okay, let's change the subject. What's it like on your planet? Your bodies adjust to any temperature; you always understand where other people are coming from. Sounds perfect to me." I shot a glance his way.

"It is not perfect, but we do not have many conflicts," he said, leaning his head back against the padded headrest and looking dreamily ahead. "My planet is very different. The sky is not the color it is here, but the stars look very much the same. We have a sun, but it is different."

"Different how?"

He shrugged. "The beams are more diffused. They provide us with energy for transportation and everything else."

"Solar power. We have that too."

"Not the same way."

I was getting a clear message here. Scout's planet was a lot like Earth, only prettier, better, and more advanced.

He said, "We have animals, but we understand them and do not eat them. They help us and we help them."

"How do you help them?"

"We provide sanctuary for them, and help them with their food supply and they help us to spread plant growth. We also use their waste products to replenish our soil for our crops."

"We do that too. Kind of."

"No. Here you waste everything. On my home planet, we find a use for everything. We do not spoil where we live."

"Oh, well la-di-da."

"What does la-di-da mean?"

"It means you're being a pain." Ahead I saw the sign for the interstate. I couldn't miss the turnoff, so I didn't elaborate on my definition.

"I am sorry," he said.

"Yeah, I know. I'm sorry too."

# CHAPTER NINETEEN

Once I'd made the turnoff onto the expressway, I felt kind of bad for calling him a pain. I decided to steer the conversation in a better direction. "So what color is your sky?" I asked.

"Different, depending on the time of day. Most of the time, it looks a little like your purple, but darker. The sky . . . it *glows*, I think is the word? It is very beautiful."

I nodded, imagining how wonderful it would be to have a glowing indigo sky. But we were here, and on this planet, at this time, our sun was starting to rise—just a glint of light through the rear window in a sky that would be, if previous days were any indication, a beautiful blue. Soon enough, Mr. and Mrs. Walker would be up. How long before they noticed Lucas was gone and read the note Eric had expertly forged and left on the bed? Eric had promised to tell his parents that Lucas had wanted to sleep in and that they shouldn't disturb him. That would buy us an extra hour or two. At my house, sleeping in meant noon, but on a farm it meant seven-thirty at the latest.

"What else is different than here on Earth?" I asked. I might never meet someone from another planet again and if this trip was successful, my opportunity would be over soon. If I had any questions, the time to ask was now.

"You have so many languages here. It is very inefficient and confusing."

"You only have one language?"

He nodded. "Yes. It's not a language like yours. It's the way of communication I mentioned before. Even our animals communicate like that, at their own level. That is why we are so compassionate. You cannot hate or fear what you understand."

"But doesn't your head get cluttered with everyone's thoughts and feelings all the time?" I imagined standing in line at the grocery store and having to hear all the boring details of everyone's life: the cashier with the tired feet, the harried mother with the screaming toddler, the old lady ahead of me wanting to write a check but not able to find a pen in her great big purse. God only knew what would spill out of the old lady's head. What a nightmare. There was already too much noise in my life. I'd have a breakdown if I had to take on more. "And what if you don't want people to know something? Can you keep it private?"

"Yes, if you must. I have many things I keep to myself. And there are many things I choose not to listen to."

"It sounds like a good system," I admitted. "If we could do that here, everyone would probably get along better. Of course, we couldn't do it that way because we're not highly evolved enough." I glanced over to see if he'd nod, but Scout wasn't taking the bait. Apparently, diplomacy was part of their advanced state. "So do you have a family, like we do here? Parents, brothers and sisters?"

Out of the corner of my eye, I saw his head bob. "Each person comes from two older beings much like your parents. The two older ones, like your mother and father, contribute genetic material to make offspring. It is not dissimilar. I have twenty-two siblings, but I don't know them all very well. As soon as we are independent, we leave to contribute and work for the good of everyone."

"Twenty-two, wow." I put on my turn signal and got into the left lane to go around a semi. Even though I'd been driving for the last year, it was mostly on the roads near my house—and in a very different car. I didn't go on the expressway all that much and, right now, the speed combined with the big trucks made me clench my teeth. I breathed a sigh of relief when I made it all the way around the truck and switched back into the right lane. I couldn't believe I had signed up for ten hours of this.

Scout interrupted my thoughts. "I have an Emma too."

"What?"

"On my planet. I have an Emma."

"A girlfriend?" I glanced over to see his lips draw up in a slight smile.

"Yes, if you want to use that word."

"Really?" For some reason, the idea of Scout having a girlfriend surprised and delighted me. "What's her name?"

"I cannot say it in your language, but I have decided that her earth name is Regina."

"You decided that, huh?" I felt a smirk coming on. "Why Regina? Why that particular name?"

"There is a Regina George in one of Eric's movies that is very much like her," he said. "She has a very strong personality."

"Strong personality, huh? What else can you tell me about her?"

His fist went to his mouth, thinking. After a moment, he said, "You know the way you feel about Lucas?"

"Yes."

"I feel the same things about her. She is everything to me."

Was I imagining it, or had his voice gotten softer? I turned to look at him. "You must miss her very much."

"Very much," he repeated and I heard sadness in his voice.

So we had something in common: both of us were without the love of our life. This sucked. A dark storm cloud seemed to form above our moving car, like in cartoons. To lighten the mood,

I decided to put on some music, something upbeat and easy to sing to.

"Okay, listen up, this is what Lucas and I always used to do in the car," I said. "Whenever a good song would come on, we'd sing and do hand movements together. Car dancing, Lucas called it. It's really fun."

"I don't know," he said, his voice telling me he really didn't want to do this. "I don't know dancing."

"What's the matter? You don't have music on your planet?"

"Oh yes," Scout said, very enthusiastically. "We have music that can touch your soul. It can motivate those who hear it to try harder or think more deeply. We don't just hear it; it goes throughout our entire being, penetrating every cell."

"Yes, I get it. Our music doesn't compare well." I sighed. "Sorry. It doesn't penetrate every cell. We just listen with our ears."

"No, I . . ." He exhaled and it came out in a huff. "I don't know how to do this car dancing you speak of."

"Not to worry. I'm a most excellent teacher. Can you get my backpack? It's on the floor behind you." Scout reached back and got the backpack, which he then set on his lap. I gave him directions and he unzipped the front pocket and found the iPod right where I'd left it. He handed it to me and, even though I was driving seventy miles per hour, I was able to plug it into the dash and find the perfect song with ease. "Okay," I said before the song even began. "This is what you need to remember: 'Hate to leave you, Emily.' Can you say it?"

He repeated. "Hate to leave you, Emily." His brow furrowed, confused. "I don't know what that means."

"It doesn't matter. It's just for fun. Lucas and I would always pick the oldest, cheesiest songs on purpose." I sung the sentence for him. "Can you make your voice sound like that?" Lucas had a decent singing voice. I was curious to see what Scout would do with the same instrument.

He opened his mouth and sang, "Hate to leave you, Emily." It wasn't Lucas quality, but it wasn't terrible either.

"Okay," I said. "Now we begin."

I tapped out the first few notes on the steering wheel. "I'll sing the beginning and when I point to you, you sing your part. Okay?"

Scout looked a little nervous, but he nodded. Honestly, he was taking this way too seriously. I knew this song backward and forward. It was an old 80s tune that my mom always turned up when it came on the radio in the car. When I was little, I thought the "Emily" referred to me, Emma Leigh Garson. It wasn't until I was older that I realized the name in the song was actually "Emily," not "Emma Leigh." A little disappointing at the time. Now I belted out the lyrics, not caring that Scout was looking at me with open-mouthed wonder, and when his part came, I bounced in my seat and pointed, no small thing considering a semi zoomed past us at the same time. He sang, "Hate to leave you, Emily," and looked pretty pleased when his words matched the recording.

We got all the way through the song, him singing the one line and me doing the rest. When it finished, I took it back to the beginning.

"We're going to do it again and add some moves," I told him. Lucas and I had perfected synchronizing our hand movements, pointing out the front window during a climactic moment, pumping our fists in the air, or doing the hand jive in rhythm with the chorus. I knew we looked incredibly stupid, especially when we pulled up to a stoplight and other people could see, but we didn't care. If anyone frowned at us from another car, I figured they were jealous that we were young and happy and in love. When Lucas was sick, I missed these times, the times when we didn't have to think about treatments and pain and death. When we could just be in the here and now, living life together, being carefree.

I knew Scout was just standing in for Lucas, but for a few minutes, it was like old times. I restarted the song and we ran through it again. He loosened up after the first time, enthusiastically belting out his line and trying to copy my moves. I was a little proud, like I'd volunteered for the Big Brothers/Big Sisters organization and introduced my kid to something he wouldn't have experienced otherwise.

"Sing it, Scout," I called out, right before his part.

By the time we finished, both of us were giddy, something I hadn't experienced for a long time. "That was fun," I said, catching my breath.

"That's what fun is?" he asked.

"Pretty much. Fun is doing something just because it makes you happy."

"You and Lucas had fun?"

"All the time. How about you and your Emma?"

He shook his head. "There is nothing compared to fun where I come from. We are happy and we are content. We celebrate big occasions, but we don't do fun for no reason."

"I'm sorry," I said. Finally, I'd found one thing we did better.

# CHAPTER TWENTY

Scout sometimes had trouble processing the intensity of the emotions on this planet. The inhabitants had so many feelings, and they swung back and forth so quickly. Anything—bad news, the weather, music—could affect their moods. A rain shower made one human happy and another sad. A certain song could move one human to tears while another barely noticed it. And none of it was predictable, as far as he could tell.

It was only midday and already Emma had been worried, excited, compassionate, and now, with the car dancing, happy. More than happy. He puzzled over her feelings and decided she was "jubilant." Overflowing with joy. And he wasn't sure why. He had tried to figure out the point of the car dancing and decided there was no point. It was, as she said, just for fun. How odd it was that these people did things that didn't contribute to something else. Not for the greater good, anyway. The people just did things to make themselves feel good. So primitive, and yet, he liked it.

He tried to think of how he could explain this concept to Regina, but he knew she'd have trouble understanding. She took charge and was a doer, always setting goals and accomplishing them in short order. Regina would probably make the point that the selfishness of the individuals on Earth was the reason the planet was so backward. Still, he wanted to try sharing this idea with her, to show her how each inhabitant could find happiness from within and share it with others. It was too good a feeling not to want to recreate on his home planet.

Yes, if he ever made it home, that is what he would do.

# CHAPTER TWENTY-ONE

Many songs later, daylight broke and I didn't need headlights to see the road anymore. Around the same time the sun made its full entrance, my stomach started to growl. The cup of coffee and granola bar I'd had right before heading out the door didn't have the lasting power I'd hoped for. When I noticed a sign for a pancake house at an upcoming exit, I asked Scout, "Are you hungry? I'm thinking we should stop for breakfast."

"I could eat something," he said. I recognized the words and intonation. That was exactly how Eric always answered that very same question. No wonder Mrs. Walker didn't see anything wrong with her older son. Scout had borrowed expressions from close to home. Even though his speech was awkward, the words were familiar.

Two exits later, I got off the expressway and spotted the restaurant from the end of the ramp. In a few minutes, we were sitting in a booth, looking at a glossy menu. Our waitress took our drink order as she escorted us to our table. Apparently, it was a very efficient pancake house. Scout scanned the menu and something else occurred to me. "Can you read?" I asked.

He nodded. "Yes. It was easy to match the sounds to the symbols."

Impressive that he taught himself. Maybe he had a right to feel superior after all. "Okay, well, if you need any help, let me know."

"I do not think that will be necessary," Scout said, tapping a finger on a photo.

I looked around the restaurant, glad to see it was about half full. We weren't doing anything wrong, but I couldn't shake the feeling that we were desperadoes, the equivalent of bank robbers on the run. I didn't want to stand out too much. Our waitress came with our drinks: orange juice for Scout, coffee for me. She looked to be in her early thirties, with cropped brown hair tucked behind her ears. Earlier that morning, I'd looked in the mirror and thought I'd looked tired, but compared to this woman (Amy, according to her name tag) I had nothing to worry about. Her eyes were etched with exhaustion and she seemed preoccupied, darting a look back at the counter even as she set down our drinks. I followed her gaze to see a little girl about six years old, coloring on a paper place-mat. She was by herself, and had a scarf wrapped around her head. Almost as if she felt me looking at her, the girl turned her head and smiled, and my heart instantly melted right before breaking into a million pieces. I knew this girl. Well, I didn't know *her* exactly, but I'd seen her before in the faces of all the kids in the pediatric oncology unit when I was visiting Lucas. And then I realized she wasn't smiling at me, but at the waitress, Amy. The girl held up her picture and called out, "Look, Mommy, I made this for you."

Amy turned and said, "That's beautiful, baby. I'll be right there after I take this order." She pulled a pad and pen out of her pocket and addressed her next words to us: "The babysitter was sick." She shrugged like, *what are you gonna do?* "Are you ready to order?"

I wanted to cry, but instead I ordered a number six with a side of hash browns. Scout said, "I will have the same thing."

After the waitress gathered up the menus and walked away, I leaned across the table and whispered, "I think her daughter has cancer like Lucas had. So sad."

Scout took a sip of his orange juice. Lucas was never real big on fruits and vegetables, but I'd noticed that Scout gravitated toward them. He said, "The cancer is in her blood and the middle of her bones."

I asked, "How do you know that?"

"We went past her when we walked in." He said it nonchalantly as if this explained everything.

"Wait a minute," I said, lowering my voice again. "You can tell what kind of cancer she has just by being near her?"

"Well, yes," he said, a puzzled look on his face. "Is that unusual?"

"Hell, yeah." It had taken the doctors a million tests to narrow down exactly what Lucas had. "How can you do that?"

Scout said, "Cell empathy."

"What's that?" I glanced over at the little girl, her legs dangling off the edge of the stool. At this age, she shouldn't have a care in the world and here she had cancer. So unfair.

"I can tell the health of her cells."

"How?"

He shrugged. "How can you see colors or taste food? You just can. You have that ability because it's how you are made."

"But you're inside Lucas's body," I pointed out. "And Lucas could never do that."

"My essence is what is driving the body. And so I have retained many of my own abilities." He spoke the words slowly, reminding me once again that English wasn't his first language.

"Like, what else? What other abilities?"

"Just other abilities." He took the wrapper off his straw and stuck it in the juice, then stirred the pulp around.

His answer seemed cagey to me. Why wouldn't he say? "Wait a minute. Can you read people's minds? Do you know what I'm thinking?"

"Not exactly." He had that look on his face again, the guilty look, like he knew he was in trouble. "The little girl's name is Chloe," he said brightly.

"How do you know that?"

"I heard her mother say her name."

It did not escape me that he hadn't answered my question about mind reading. How disturbing would it be if he'd known everything I'd been thinking this whole time? His head was down now, his attention back to stirring his juice. If he thought I was going to let this go, he had another thing coming. In my mind, I yelled, *Scout, look at me. Right now! Lift your head and look at me!* Startled, he let go of the straw and met my eyes. A chill rose up my spine. He'd reacted as if I'd shouted at him. He'd heard what I was thinking.

"You *can* read my mind," I said, frowning. "That is incredibly creepy."

"I cannot do it all the time," he said. "And it is easier with some people than for others. You are the easiest one of all."

"So this whole time, you've known everything I was thinking?"

He nodded. "And feeling." He sipped at the juice again. When he was done, he looked up and said, "That is how I know I could tell you and Eric the truth, and you would try to help me and not tell the federal agents."

And that's when my eyes began to tear up. Between Chloe having cancer and Scout putting his trust in me and Eric, and me missing Lucas more than ever, my emotions got the best of me. I dabbed at my eyes with the cheap paper napkin and tried to hold back the flood. "I'm sorry," I said. "I'm just feeling a little overwhelmed."

"I know," Scout said.

My phone pinged and I pulled it out and took a look. I grimaced when I saw the text. I said, "It's from your brother. I mean, it's Eric."

"His parents found the note and are not happy."

"You picked up on that from there?" I said, astounded.

He shook his head. "That is what Eric predicted would happen."

"Well, he was right." I read off the screen, "Mom and Dad furious. Blaming you. Want to call cops." As I read, a second text came in. "I'm doing damage control." I set the phone in the middle of the table and said, "Thank God we're so far away."

The words were no sooner out of my mouth when Scout's phone rang. He picked it up and answered before I could stop him. "Hello?" he said, his face showing signs of intense concentration. "Mom, you don't need to worry. Yes, I'm with Emma and we are fine. I am safe." Even though it was up to his ear, I could hear the torrent of anger coming from his mother. I wasn't her favorite person before and she was really going to despise me now. "Mom, Mom, Mom!" he said, cutting in, and for a second, he sounded just like Lucas. "Don't blame Emma. This was my idea. She didn't want to do it, but I talked her into it. We're driving up to where we used to camp—remember, when Eric and I were little? I wanted to show Emma the lake and all the places you used to take us." He listened for a bit and I could hear her tone changing just slightly. "I've had a tough year, and I just needed a day away. Just one day. I'm eighteen and soon I'll be back in school trying to get caught up, so I thought I should do it now before I got too busy."

The waitress came with our food and silently placed the plates in front of us. "Thank you," I said.

"Mom, I have to go now," Scout said. "I love you. I'll see you tonight, okay?" And then she said something I couldn't catch before he said good-bye and hung up.

"Wow, you handled that really well," I said, picking up my fork. Really well. I hadn't heard him speak that much ever.

"Eric and I practiced many times," he said. "The mother said she will call every hour to check on us."

That figured. "Great," I said, rolling my eyes. I poured syrup over my short stack, then handed the pitcher to Scout, who followed my example. We ate in silence, me trying not to think anything weird or personal, which of course led to me only being able to think of weird and personal things. Like wondering if he could somehow see through my clothes, which would have seemed impossible earlier in the day, but now seemed within the realm of feasibility. After the waitress checked to see if we were enjoying the food, Scout watched her walk away and whispered, "Amy just got bad news about her daughter's cancer. She'd like to go home, but the boss won't let her."

"What kind of bad news?"

"I don't know. A phone call about some test results."

Amy paused to cup Chloe's chin on her way back to the kitchen and then she leaned over and touched noses with her daughter. When she pulled away, her mouth stretched into a smile, but behind the smile, I glimpsed sadness. It was the way everyone had been around Lucas—all of us pretending to be upbeat and cheerful when inside we were dying a little bit more each day, his cancer threatening to consume us all.

I felt a sudden need for reassurance. I reached across the table and grasped Scout's hand as he was sticking his fork into a piece of pancake. He looked up, startled. I said, "I have something I need to ask you, but you have to promise to answer truthfully."

"I will answer truthfully," he said, nodding.

"Is Lucas really still in there, deep inside?"

"Of course."

I let go and he lifted the fork to his mouth. "So," I said, "he's not dead? Once you go out of his body, he'll be the same as always?"

He nodded. "Yes, of course." Right behind him, two ladies were talking loudly about scrapbooking, oblivious to the alien presence one booth over.

"How do you know for sure?"

He shrugged. "I was inside Mack for a time and he survived the experience and is now fine."

Strangely enough, that did make me feel better. "Will Lucas remember what happened while you occupied his body? Will he remember today, for instance?"

"I don't think so. It is like he is sleeping," Scout said. "Or like he is in a coma. I have taken over. Lucas is not driving anymore."

Lucas wasn't driving anymore. An interesting way to put it, especially since I was now forced to be the driver on this trip. When we finished eating, I paid the check, leaving a tip equal to the amount of the bill. It wouldn't make Amy's day any better, but it might help it to suck a little less. We scooted out of the booth and headed for the door, me in the lead. After the outside door slammed behind me and I was almost to the car, I realized that Scout wasn't right behind me as I'd thought. I sighed in exasperation. It was like traveling with a little kid, constantly having to watch him and explain everything. I looked at the door for half a minute, thinking he was just walking slowly and would catch up, but when he didn't show up, I went back in, and found him standing at the counter, talking to the little girl, Chloe. When I got closer, I heard her excitedly say, "Really? Can I feel it?" Scout said yes, and leaned over to let her rub his head. I made it to his side at the same time as her mother came out of the kitchen to witness the same scene. Amy froze for a second before rushing over in alarm.

"Chloe! What's going on here?" Amy's mouth turned down in disapproval and a look of fear came over her face, something I understood completely. All I could think was of all the times kids were told about stranger danger, especially with men, and here her daughter was touching Scout in public and he was encouraging it.

"He's harmless, really," I said. The next words out of my mouth were going to explain that he was mentally challenged, a lie that would hopefully help the situation, but Chloe interrupted before I got that far.

"Mommy!" she said excitedly. "He had stage four cancer too, and they didn't think he would live and he did. He did! He's all better now and his hair grew in and everything."

"Oh." Amy seemed taken aback, but she pulled it together very quickly. "Well, I'm very happy for you, sir, but I don't usually let my daughter talk to strangers, especially about our family business."

"We were just going," I said, grabbing hold of his T-shirt. "Have a good day."

"Good-bye, Scout," Chloe said, with a small wave.

"Good-bye, Chloe," he said, letting me guide him out of the restaurant.

The sun had climbed higher in the sky while we were inside eating, and heat radiated off the asphalt parking lot. We walked to the car, me pulling his arm. "You can't talk to children," I said. "And you especially can't touch them or let them touch you." I shook my head. "You could have gotten us in a lot of trouble back there. In the future, just stick by me, okay?"

"I do not understand," he said. "Why was I wrong?"

"I know you didn't mean anything by it." We'd gotten to the car now and I unlocked the door. "But there are people who hurt kids and Chloe's mom doesn't know you. She was probably worried that you were one of those people. That's why she came running out like that. She didn't like her daughter touching your head. We're lucky she didn't call the police."

His face scrunched in confusion. "But why would someone hurt kids?"

I stopped, the key ring dangling off one finger, and tried to think about the best way to respond even as I knew there really wasn't a good answer. Why would someone hurt a kid? It defied explanation. It was a crazy, screwed-up world when adult people preyed on innocent children, and yet that was the way it was. It happened every single day. "I don't know why," I finally admitted.

"It just happens. People are mentally ill or sometimes they're just evil. It happens."

His face still had that befuddled look. "So I should not have talked to Chloe?"

"Talking to her was probably okay," I said. "But it all depends on the situation and what you're talking about. Since you don't know the difference, it's probably best just to avoid kids altogether."

I gestured for him to get into the car. I would feel better when I put some space between us and the pancake house. I had the car in reverse and was starting to back up when he turned my way and said, "Was it wrong then that I fixed Chloe's cancer?"

I threw the car into park, jolting us to a sudden stop. "*What* did you say?"

His expression, so earnest and wanting to please, changed to one of worry. "I said was it wrong for me to fix Chloe's cancer?"

"You *fixed* her cancer? You mean you cured it?" I tried to keep my voice steady, but still the volume increased. Had he actually cured that little girl's cancer?

The frown lines were back. "Did I make trouble? When Chloe's mother finds out, will she call the police?" He shot a nervous glance out the window as if expecting to see a squad car coming down the road.

"No," I said. "If her daughter's cancer is cured, she'll be very happy. Is that what you did? You actually made the cancer go away?"

He nodded. "It is not gone yet, but it will go away. The other cells will overpower the cancer cells."

"How did you . . . Oh, never mind. You did a good thing," I said, giving his arm a squeeze. "A really good thing. But you can't do it anymore. It will attract attention and we're trying not to get noticed, okay?"

"Okay. I will not cure cancer anymore," he said, returning his gaze to the front windshield. "I did not mean to attract attention."

# CHAPTER TWENTY-TWO

We were pulling out of the parking lot onto the road when my phone unexpectedly rang. I couldn't even imagine who would be calling me. A friend would be more likely to text, and my mom, if she called at all, wouldn't do it until later in the day. Right now, she was at work and would have other things on her mind. I almost ignored the ringing, but when Scout picked the phone up out of the cup holder and held it out, I saw it was Mrs. Kokesh, so I put it on speaker phone. "Hello?" I answered, while simultaneously driving around to park in back of the pancake house.

"Oh, Emma, honey, good, I'm glad you answered," she said. "We need to talk." It was Mrs. Kokesh's voice, but not her usual grouchy persona. Instead, it sounded like Mrs. Kokesh had taken Glinda-the-good-witch pills.

"Hey, Mrs. Kokesh, I've been thinking about you," I said. "I'm sorry I didn't call to give you an update, but it's been crazy—"

"Say no more. I understand," she said abruptly, sounding more like herself. "Emma, there are some federal agents here at my house asking about you and Lucas. They seem to think you know something important and they'd like you to come here right now so they can talk to you."

My throat threatened to close. "They're at your house now?"

"Yes. They'd like you to return immediately. Now, they know it will take you two hours to drive back . . ."

I heard a scuffle as the phone was handed off. A woman's voice came on the line. "Emma? This is agent Mariah Wilson. We met at the Walkers'?"

"Of course. I remember," I said, trying to sound calm.

"I need you to turn around and come back right now. It's super important to our investigation." Her voice was as smooth as the maple syrup that had covered our pancakes, but she still managed to convey that she meant every word.

I gave Scout a wide-eyed look, but even though he'd heard everything I had, he didn't appear the least bit rattled. "I'm not sure how I can help your investigation," I said. "I don't really know anything."

"We think you do."

The thumping of my heart made it hard to think straight. "Could we talk tomorrow?" I said. "We're a long way from home and Lucas wanted to show me the lake where his family used to go camping when he was a kid. We're kind of on a day trip."

"This can't wait until tomorrow," she said harshly. "You and Lucas Walker are to drive back immediately and report to us at Mrs. Kokesh's house. Please bring anything you have that is pertinent to the investigation. Not complying will be considered obstruction of justice and you will be charged and jailed. If you think I'm bluffing and that this won't apply to you because you're a minor, I promise you that's not the case. You will be charged as an adult, believe me."

In the background, Mrs. Kokesh yelled, "Emma, they can trace you!" Her voice trailed away at the end, as if someone had pulled her into the next room.

"Is Mrs. Kokesh okay?" I asked.

"She's fine. She just had to step out for a moment," the agent said. "You'll be able to see that she's safe and sound when you get here in a *timely* manner." It was a threat, barely implied. *Come back right away or the old lady gets it.* But that only happened in movies. Right? I'd always thought so, but now I didn't honestly know.

The next three seconds of silence were so thick that the words I spoke next seemed to slice right through it. "I understand," I said. "We'll come back immediately."

"Good girl," Mariah Wilson said patronizingly. One of my pet peeves: being patronized. She continued. "We'll be waiting. Don't deviate on the way back or there will be trouble. As soon as you hang up the phone, I want you to drive here as quickly as possible."

"We will," I promised. "We'll head back right away."

"Two hours," she said. "If you're not here by then, the authorities will be coming to apprehend you and we will notify your parents of your involvement in a federal crime."

After I said good-bye and ended the call, I sat in shocked silence until Scout said, "Do not worry, they will not contact the parents. She did not mean it."

"You're sure of that?"

"Oh yes," he said. "I could tell. They do not want people to know. They went to Mrs. Kokesh because they do not think people find her to be a reliable source." We were now parked alongside two dumpsters. A half-dozen cars were lined up farther away from the building, but we were the only ones out here.

"Okay." One small consolation. My poor mother would have had a breakdown if the feds had come to our place. I sighed, weighing all our options.

Finally, Scout said, his voice tentative, "So we are going back?"

"Like hell we are," I said, making a decision.

"Like hell?"

"It means no. We're definitely not going back. We have a plan and we're sticking to it." I tapped my fingers on the steering wheel, trying to evaluate the situation. Somehow, the agents had discovered that I knew more than I had told them. Had they talked to

Eric? And if so, would he have cracked? I doubted it. Eric knew what was at stake. Besides, Scout seemed to think they hadn't contacted our families. Mrs. Kokesh could have told them about Scout's pod, but how did they even know Lucas and I were connected to her in the first place?

That's when it hit me. My phone. That had to be it. They'd tracked my phone history and knew about every incoming and outgoing call, including the one I'd gotten from Mrs. Kokesh. Maybe they'd even listened to some of my calls. But I'd been careful. I didn't think I'd said anything that could come back to bite me. Had I even called Eric? I didn't think so. But they knew about Mrs. Kokesh and probably figured out that I'd visited her before and after Scout's landing.

Mrs. Kokesh had said they could trace us, and since they knew we were two hours away it was a safe bet they'd been tracking us through the GPS on at least one of the phones, and maybe both. Could they still follow our route if the phones were turned off? I wasn't sure. I turned to Scout. "Do you know anything about the tracking devices in our phones?" I asked. His blank look said it all. "I guess not, huh?"

He said, "Your equipment is basic, but I would have to examine the inside parts to know the capabilities."

"I see." I tapped my chin, thinking.

"I can look if you'd like," Scout said.

"Yeah, we don't have time for that." I held out a hand. "Give me your phone." After he gave it to me, I stepped out of the car, both phones in hand. "Don't go anywhere. I'll be right back." I glanced around the parking lot, wondering how to dispose of them. The dumpster was the most obvious choice, but being encased in metal might disrupt the signal and make the agents suspicious. I could toss them into the weeds bordering the back of the parking lot, but that would make it look like we'd stayed at the pancake house.

While I deliberated, a young guy about my age came barreling out of the employee door. He wore a black T-shirt, jeans, and a baseball cap and had coloring like mine—jet black hair and skin the color of a latte. He was cute. Very cute. Not that I was in the market, but I couldn't help but notice. He smiled at me as he came by and I caught a flash of dimples. My eyes followed as he crossed the lot to climb into an old four-door Ford. He didn't go far, though, because he then drove around the lot and pulled up right next to where I was standing. I thought he was going to say something to me, but instead he got out and headed back into the restaurant, leaving his car engine running and the windows down. "Forget something?" I called after him.

"My sunglasses," he shot back over his shoulder.

And that's when I came up with a brilliant idea. Like tossing horseshoes, I threw the phones through the guy's open car window so they landed on the floor of his back seat. Then I got back into my car. "Buckle up," I said to Scout. "This is getting serious."

We peeled out of the parking lot and onto the highway leading to the interstate. What I'd said to Scout wasn't completely right. This trip had been serious all along, but now it had a sense of urgency, a feeling that we had to hurry to stay ahead of the agents. I was glad that Eric's barn car was too old to have GPS built in and I was pretty sure that the expired plates meant he hadn't bothered to register it. It wasn't in the system, so it might as well be a ghost car. There was nothing to link it to me either. That made me feel somewhat better. I felt bad about leaving Mrs. Kokesh on her own, but if anyone could handle the situation, she could. I imagined her slipping some kind of potion into the agents' lemonade or lighting a candle that would make them woozy. Yes, she had a lot of tricks up her very baggy sleeves. I thought she would be okay. Or at least, I hoped so.

The short stretch of highway took us right to the ramp to get back onto the interstate. Once we'd merged, I breathed a sigh of relief. Scout had been quiet this whole time. He was so hard to read, unlike Lucas, whose every thought and mood played out on his beautiful face. I knew Lucas like I knew myself. I saw the struggle he had when his mother made snarky comments about me or Eric. Sometimes I could predict the words that would come out of his mouth. He always had to tread carefully when it came to his mom. Sometimes he opted to stick up for us; other times, he decided to let it go because the conflict it would create wasn't worth it. Most of the time, it didn't make a difference either way. Mrs. Walker saw the world in black and white, while Lucas and I saw every shade. She would always be color-blind, and arguing with her didn't help. Still, Lucas rose to my defense whenever she suggested he date other girls or see me less often. Both Lucas and I knew that wasn't going to happen. If anything, we wished we could be together more often. One time he had told her, "You might as well tell me to breathe less air."

"What did she say?" I'd asked, a delighted smile crossing my face.

He laughed. "Oh, the usual. That I'm young and have no idea. That everyone feels this way about their first serious relationship. That I'll meet lots of new people in college and my world will change in ways I can't even envision." Poor Mrs. Walker. She didn't know that we'd already envisioned every possible future, and Lucas and I were together in every single scenario. That was the one thing that would never change. Of course, first I had to get Scout home so I could get Lucas back.

Once the car got up to speed and we were traveling smoothly, I said to Scout, "You're probably wondering why I got rid of our phones and threw them in the back of that car."

His eyebrows arched. "I believe it was so that the agents will follow the wrong trail. They are the bounty hunters and we are like the outlaws. We need to stay ahead of them."

"Yes, that's exactly right," I said, impressed by the analogy. Amazing how Eric had figured him out. Scout had been absorbing everything about our world through movies and video clips and TV and overheard conversations. "We're going to have to drive faster," I said, glancing at the GPS. "No stopping either, except for bathroom breaks. Okay? Do you understand?"

"I understand," he said.

I fiddled with the music a little bit, switching from song to song, but my mood had shifted and nothing sounded right. I felt like a rope had coiled around my intestines, squeezing my stomach. Talking to Agent Wilson had affected me physically and emotionally. And no wonder—she'd threatened to have me charged with a crime and thrown in jail. That wasn't something that could be brushed off. I had that sick feeling like when you get called to the principal's office: the sensation of shame and impending doom even without knowing exactly what you did wrong, if anything. But I wasn't going to turn back and let them muck up our plan. It occurred to me that maybe I was making a mistake. Perhaps they might be willing and able to help. That wasn't the feeling I got, but it was possible. It would be ironic if I was fleeing from the very people who could help Scout get home and return Lucas to me. If only there was a way to find out what their agenda was.

I sat up straight, realizing suddenly that I was sitting next to someone with that very ability. "Scout," I asked. "Do you remember when the agents came to the house? You were still in the hospital bed in the dining room. It was a man and a woman. They said they were from the National Transportation Something Board investigating a plane crash." I tried to think back. "That was right after Eric and I got you on your feet and you looked out the window."

"Yes, I remember." His gaze was still on the road ahead.

"Did you pick up any of their thoughts?"

"Yes."

"So you know what it was they were after?"

"Yes, I know what they were after." And now he turned to look at me, his eyes sad. "They were after me."

"Really?"

"They want to cage me and examine me like an animal in a research laboratory." Sorrow dripped off the words.

"Don't worry. I won't let that happen," I said.

He said, "They have two faces. They will say they want to learn about the citizens from other planets, but it's not true. They just want to collect the bounty." Another reference to *The Outlaw from San Antonio*, I figured. I really had to see that movie.

"You got all that from that short time they were in the room?"

He nodded. "It was very strong. The woman, she was like Mack when he is following a scent."

"Determined? Relentless?" I guessed.

"Like a hunter." Scout said. "On a trail. She thinks she will get elevated in her job if she succeeds."

"Elevated in her job. Like get promoted?"

"Yes."

"Oh." This conversation was bringing both of us down. Ahead of us, the road stretched endlessly with not much to see on either side. Rows of trees and farmers' fields. That's what we'd be looking at for the next few hours. I couldn't change the feeling of a disaster lurking around the corner, and I couldn't change the scenery, so I decided to change the subject. "Tell me more about your planet. What if I traveled there? What would I see when I arrived?"

He smiled, thin lips stretched widely. "We have cities made of the same material as my pod. The buildings absorb energy from the sun and use the energy for our . . ." He squinted, trying to think of the word. "Technology?"

"Technology? Like computers?" I asked.

"Like computers, but we don't need to operate them. They work as they need to."

"Intuitively?"

"I think that is the right word." Even as fluent as he was, his speech was clipped, each word having its own space.

"What about plants? Do you have trees and flowers?"

"Oh yes!" he said with enthusiasm. "And they are so beautiful!"

"Beautiful how?"

And from there, he regaled me with stories of trees that swayed like they were dancing, and flowers as big as pie plates with petals as soft as Mack's fur. The trees instinctively leaned and fanned out to provide shade exactly where it was needed. "Just like the way your sunflowers turn to face the sun," he said. The foliage covering the ground was as thick as carpeting and nutritious too. The inhabitants of his planet didn't harvest crops like we did. Instead, they tapped into the essence of the plant, absorbing only what they needed, and leaving enough for the plant to repopulate. As long as Scout's people treated the planet with respect, he said, the planet gave back to them. "So different from here," he said, looking out the window.

I knew the tenor of his voice, the sadness behind the words. I'd heard it before, when Lucas's family had taken a trip to Kansas for his grandfather's funeral. Lucas had called me after the service and told me how heartbreaking it was to see his grandpa laid out in the coffin, and how his father, the usually tough-as-nails Steve Walker, had broken down and cried, shocking both his sons. Lucas had said, "Everything is wrong here, Emma. I feel like I can't breathe. It would be so much better if you were here." I could hear the yearning and sorrow rolled into his words. And that's what I heard now in Scout's voice.

"You're homesick," I said, reaching over to rub his arm.

His head dropped. Without looking my way, he said, "I want to go home."

Oh man, now he was breaking my heart. I said, "I know. You miss Regina."

"She thinks I am dead."

"No, she doesn't," I said firmly. "If she's like me, she wouldn't give up on you. Everyone else thought Lucas was doomed, but I never gave up hope. If she loves you like I love Lucas, she's waiting for you. Even if everyone else tells her it's over and that you're dead, she won't believe them. Your bond is too strong."

He cleared his throat. "Thank you, Emma. That is a nice thing for you to say."

"I'm not just saying it. I believe it. Love trumps logic every time."

And then he laughed his odd little chuckle, so different from Lucas. "Love trumps logic every time," he repeated slowly. "You are very funny, Emma."

"I wasn't trying to be funny," I said. "I believe it to be true."

After that, we didn't talk much, except to break out the snacks. When I asked, Scout rummaged through the cooler at his feet, coming up with string cheese, bottles of water, and small, red boxes of raisins, the kind my mom used to pack in my lunches in grade school. On the bottom, he found two packages of dried apple slices and a note from Eric, which he read aloud: *Sorry about all the nutritious stuff. My mom is on a crusade to abolish junk food and this is all we had in the house.* Scout didn't find it as funny as I did. I guess you had to know Mrs. Walker to realize that the word "crusade" perfectly fit her way of doing things.

I watched the GPS to see how much longer before we reached Erickson Ryder Incorporated. I imagined it as a huge office building with all kinds of security measures in place. Would we get past the front desk? "Scout," I said. "When you were getting the signals from the place in northern Wisconsin, did they tell you anything about where they came from? Do you know any names or anything at all?"

He shook his head. "They did not tell us scouts very much. I already told you what I know."

"But I thought you could hear everyone's thoughts and feelings, so I'd think there would be no secrets." I frowned.

"We can hear everyone's thoughts," he said, with the emphasis on the word *can*. "But you do not understand. We can still hold back from others. They have levels. If you are not on a high level, you will not be able to access some things."

"Like you're on a different frequency?" I asked.

"Yes," he said, bobbing his head enthusiastically. "Exactly. Very good, Emma." He sounded proud, like I was a kindergartner who'd comprehended an advanced concept. "I was not supposed to know about the friendly messages. Only someone with advanced clearance can access that kind of information. And I did not have clearance."

"So how did you find out? Did you overhear someone else talking about it or something?"

"No, I . . ." He turned his head to look out the window on his side. "I did a bad thing. I looked where I was not supposed to and found out about it."

"Oh," I said. "Well, don't feel too bad about it. I've done that kind of thing before. A person gets curious. Sometimes you can't help yourself."

His head whipped around, his mouth open in amazement. "You have done this kind of thing? Really? Oh, thank you, Emma, for saying this."

"No need to thank me. It's all true, my friend." I popped a dried apple slice in my mouth and pondered this for a moment. Scout really hadn't given us much information to go on, and what he knew came from an unverified source. From there, Eric had jumped to some pretty major conclusions. I might be on an idiot's mission, getting in trouble with the law to talk to some people who had absolutely nothing to do with the messages Scout's people had been getting. Thank God the agents couldn't get a lead on our location anymore. We would be totally screwed if they could.

When we turned off the interstate onto a county highway, I breathed a sigh of relief. Hours had passed since the pancake house with no sign of the police or highway patrol. We were that much closer to our destination and less likely to be spotted on the highway. Initially, Eric's GPS had directed us toward Ashland, Wisconsin, but Erickson Ryder was actually about thirty miles away from Ashland. Now that we were on a two-lane highway, we were less than an hour from our destination.

I didn't realize how much I looked at my phone until I didn't have it with me anymore. Even when driving, I usually listened for incoming texts or glanced to see what was new with friends. I never texted and drove, and I was proud of that because, believe me, even though I'd been tempted to do it many, many times, I always held back. When I first got my license, a kid from my high school, Derek Taylor, rolled over his car while texting, and he wound up being in the hospital for a month. The school held two different assemblies on the horrors of texting while driving and showed us disturbing video clips with wrecked cars covered with blood, and other clips featuring funerals and crying parents. One of them had a paralyzed teenager sitting in a wheelchair, sobbing that she'd only looked away from the road for a second. Just one second. Every single student in my school, even the ones who were too young to have a license, signed a contract promising never to text when driving. Not everyone stuck to it, but I did.

Now I had both hands on the wheel, eyes on the road, going just over the speed limit with no other vehicles in sight when a flash of brown leapt through the trees directly into our path. My heart seized up and my brain registered everything at once: the fact that it was a good-sized doe, along with the knowledge we were traveling way too fast to stop in time. It all happened so quickly that my reflexes took over. The deer jumped in front of us, and I braked and turned wildly to miss her, skidding and sliding into the ditch next to the road.

I felt the yank of the seat belt across my shoulder as we slammed into the ditch. It wasn't until it registered that we'd come to a full stop that my heart started up again, pounding at how close we'd come to total calamity. The ditch was deep and wide and the front end of the car tipped downward, so I felt like we were falling forward. I cursed loudly and slammed my hand against the steering wheel. "You okay?" I asked Scout, who didn't look at all upset. He nodded to let me know he was fine.

I knew we weren't going to be able to drive forward so I threw it into reverse and stepped on the gas. "I can't believe I was so stupid," I said.

The tires spun, making a horrible, mocking noise that told me we were going nowhere without a tow truck. Still, I tried rocking it back and forth, getting more frustrated each time, but not giving up. I was like a maniac, determined to make the unworkable work. Throughout all of this, Scout said nothing. His silence made me wish for Lucas, who would have known what to do. Honestly, this accident wouldn't have happened if Lucas were around, because with him driving, we wouldn't have wound up in a ditch.

Finally, I gave up. I turned off the engine and put my forehead against the steering wheel, letting the tears come. I didn't hold back, didn't worry about how I looked, which was probably ridiculous and pathetic. My chest heaved as I sobbed. I knew that carrying on like this accomplished nothing, but it was the culmination of months of stress and sorrow and worry and I couldn't help it.

I was still crying when I felt a hand on my back. It was Scout, awkwardly patting the space between my shoulder blades. "Don't be sad, Emma," he said. "You have done a wonderful thing."

"Oh yeah?" I looked up and wiped my eyes with the back of my hand. Thank God for waterproof mascara. "What wonderful thing have I done?"

"You saved her from pain and death," he said, pointing in the direction the deer had disappeared. "She was afraid when we came close, and when the car did not hit her, she felt relieved. Her baby was alone. If you had killed her, the baby would have died. You are a hero, Emma." His eyes glistened with admiration.

"You got all that in the one second she was in front of us?"

"Fear is one of the strongest emotions," he said solemnly. "And fear for a loved one is stronger yet."

He was so sweet. Too sweet, really. There was no way he'd have survived if he'd been an earthling. The kids at my school would have seen that sweetness as weakness and pulverized him. I took a deep breath. "That's very nice, Scout. I'm glad the deer can go to her baby. But do you realize that we're stuck? Because of me we're totally screwed. We are this close to Erickson Ryder." I held my thumb and pointer finger a few inches apart. "This close! And now we can't get there."

"We will work something out," he said, with way more confidence than I was feeling.

His attempts to cheer me up had *not* cheered me up, but at least I didn't feel like sobbing anymore. Scout and I got out of the car, and I showed him how to push on the front, then I got back inside to drive. We tried every combination, forward and back, the engine whining from exertion, but nothing worked. If anything, the spinning wheels grooved us in even deeper. When I got a whiff of something burning, I decided to officially give up.

I yelled out the car window, "Okay, that's enough. You don't have to push anymore." I rolled up the windows, gathered up the water bottles to put in my backpack, grabbed my car keys and both pairs of sunglasses, and got out of the car. I handed Scout his sunglasses and he put them on without question.

I slung the backpack over one shoulder. "Let's go," I said, gesturing to the road ahead.

"Where are we going?" he asked.

"We're walking. Looking for help."

I recognized the look on his face. He was puzzled. "Who will help?"

"We don't know that yet," I said. "But we've been here for twenty minutes and no other cars have passed us, so it doesn't make sense to wait here. There has to be a farmhouse or something ahead, and maybe those people can help us push the car out of the ditch."

I watched as he processed what I was saying and then he nodded, as if my idea suddenly made sense. "Okay, Emma. I understand."

"Okay, let's go." I was ten steps down the road before I noticed he wasn't with me. Looking back I said, "Scout? Teleporting isn't an option. We're going to have to walk."

He stared at the back end of the car, then glanced my way and back again. "I cannot leave without it." He lifted his arm and pointed toward the trunk.

I sighed and backtracked. "What are you talking about?"

"Inside. It belongs to me."

I got out the car keys and unlocked the trunk. The lid popped open. "What is it you're . . ." He reached in quickly and snatched up a cloth bag. From the general size and shape, I instantly knew what it was. "Your pod," I said. "You didn't tell me it was in the trunk."

"I told Eric it had to come with me," he said.

Of course. When I wanted it to show Mrs. Walker proof that I wasn't lying, no one would let me have it. But now, magically, here it was. "You want to put it in my backpack?"

"No. I will carry it."

"Have it your way." I shrugged. "Anything else before we leave?"

"No. That is all."

As we walked down the highway, I felt like the refugees in other countries you see on CNN. The ones who are uprooted from their homes and have to relocate with nothing but the clothing on their backs and a few possessions. I may have been a little dramatic in my thinking, but that's how it felt anyway, walking in the heat with my backpack over my shoulder alongside Scout, whose cloth shopping bag held his pod, his only connection to his home planet.

I kept waiting for a car to come by so I could jump into the middle of the road and stop it like they do in movies. When you're desperate, normally risky behaviors start to sound reasonable. I never got a chance to try my stuntwoman moves though, because we walked for half an hour without encountering any signs of human life. We heard birds chirping in the woods on either side of the road, and the humming of an insect, the kind that sounds like a live electrical wire. I started to wonder if we'd just keep walking until we hit Lake Superior and then we'd die of starvation, when off in the distance, I heard what sounded like music.

"Do you hear that?" I asked. Not waiting for a reply, I quickened my pace. Music meant people. People meant air-conditioning and a place to sit. And help. Maybe we were approaching a town that had a gas station with a tow truck. If that was the case, they might be able to get us out of the ditch right away. I was tired of walking and I had a good feeling about this. I was ready for our luck to change.

# CHAPTER TWENTY-THREE

Scout knew that his curiosity had been the problem. He didn't have high enough clearance to know about the radio messages from Earth, but Regina did. That kind of classified information was part of her job. Of the two of them, she was smarter and more assertive, and more likely to become a leader. Already, she was a master communication specialist, a perfect fit for her intellect. Frequently, when they spent time together away from their jobs, she would allude to a new development in the broadest of terms, just as a topic of interest, but she never betrayed a confidence. Regina would never do anything that would prevent her from ascending the ranks.

He was the one who blundered, the one who broke the rules by delving into Regina's archived work records when she wasn't around. Scout knew the information was off-limits and that his behavior was appalling, but curiosity overpowered him and he couldn't help himself. Very few people on his planet would have done such a terrible thing, but when he'd confessed this horrible deed to Emma, she had acted like it was not a big deal. She said she had done that kind of thing herself. It made him both look down on the people of Earth and feel a kinship with them, all at the same time.

The radio messages came from a coordinate close to Lucas's house. Close by spaceship standards. The messages were simple in nature, a rhythmic tapping that substituted numbers for meanings. An easy code to crack. Eventually, the source transmitted what he now knew to be video clips. The document he read said that the code experts believed the communication to be friendly and that there was a possibility that this planet might be ready for contact. They were going to proceed cautiously. When he got his orders and knew Earth was the destination for his next job, he knew this was not going to be a standard mission. Of course, he had no way of knowing he would become stranded on Earth indefinitely.

# CHAPTER TWENTY-FOUR

Scout had to break into a jog to catch up to me. Even though his legs were longer, I'd gone into fifth gear, my legs moving so fast they were a blur. He didn't complain, though. I could say that for him. He wasn't a whiner.

As we got closer, I could tell the music was some kind of upbeat country music. Not the new country music, but the old timey stuff. The kind with the fiddles. As we approached a bend in the road, the music came through more clearly. Over the sound of the music, I heard a man's voice calling out some words I couldn't quite make out. "We're close now," I told Scout. "Once we get around the curve, we'll be able to see where it's coming from."

We rounded the bend and sure enough, a building that looked like a converted barn came into sight. The letters painted on the side were as tall as a person. They spelled out "Bar None." Vehicles weren't parked in front of the building as much as they were scattered. It was as if the drivers had just pulled up anywhere on the gravel lot. There were a few motorcycles and some pickup trucks along with some older cars. A lot of words crossed my mind, none of them good. Hicks, bikers, hayseed, rednecks. To me, this looked like the place where the unsophisticated and maybe even somewhat scary people hung out. My excited, good feeling was dampened by a shroud of caution. "Bar None," I read aloud. "That's what the place is called."

"Why?" he asked.

"It's a play on words," I explained. "A bar is a place that serves alcohol, but the expression 'bar none' means no one is excluded." I'd never walked into a bar before, much less an up-north country bar. I didn't like the thought of going in, but we'd walked for so long and it was so hot outside . . .

"Emma?" Scout said. "Do you want to go inside for help?"

His voice broke me out of my trance, making me aware that I'd stopped in my tracks. "Yes, we still need help," I said. "But I'm not sure these are the kinds of people who will help us. They might be scary. Here's the plan: we'll go in and ask about a tow truck, but if I want to leave right away, just follow me, okay?"

I didn't wait for a response, just walked over to the entrance. There was a regular-sized screen door and I pushed through, aware of Scout coming in behind me, right on my heels. As my eyes adjusted to the light, I did a double take when I saw that we'd walked right into a square dance. A platform on the far end of the building held an announcer bellowing into a microphone. Behind him played a live band of old guys. Fossils with instruments. The dancers were all senior citizens, the women in the poufy skirts you see sometimes on the dolls you win as carnival prizes. For the most part, the ladies were a bit thick in the middle and had tightly permed hair. The men looked somewhat better in shiny black shoes, dress pants, western-style shirts, and bolo ties.

"Whoa," I said.

"What is it?" Scout stood next to me.

I leaned in and whispered in his ear. "This is called square dancing."

The announcer was totally getting into it. "Circle left and promenade!" he called out, a big, cheesy smile on his face. The dancers swung around and around, all of them looking deliriously happy like there was nothing they'd like better than to circle left and promenade.

"Square dancing is fun?" Scout said.

"They think so," I muttered. I looked around and got the lay of the room. A wooden bar stretched along one side of the room; a bored bartender was pouring soda from a two-liter bottle into a row of plastic cups. Clustered in front of the bar were a number of tables and chairs haphazardly pushed to one side to make room for the dancers.

I dragged Scout across the room, maneuvering around the empty tables to talk to the bartender. "Is there a ladies' room?" I asked, raising my voice and leaning forward. When he pointed to a hallway in back, I led Scout to an empty table and told him to sit down. He took the seat, the cloth bag with his pod clutched to his front. "I'll be back in two minutes," I said, then leaned down to whisper in his ear. "Don't do anything until I get back. I don't know about these people." I shook my head. They looked harmless, but you never knew.

In the bathroom, I made full use of the stall before checking my appearance in the mirror as I was washing my hands. Not as bad as I feared. I had been perspiring, but the waterproof mascara had done its job and my hair had held up well. My naturally tan skin was advantageous for these types of conditions. Even after crying, my skin wasn't usually blotchy. I heard the music stop and the announcer say something about taking a break.

I smoothed the front of my button-down shirt and dress pants. I'd been so careful to dress nicely so that I'd look respectable for Erickson Ryder, but now I was a hot, rumpled mess. A pair of shorts and a T-shirt were in my backpack, but I wasn't going to change at this point. I splashed some water on my face, patted it dry, then picked up my backpack and headed out of the bathroom. A few older women were heading in as I swung the door open, and I had to step aside to let them in.

In the dancing area, the older people had shifted over to the bar side of the room, some talking in clusters while others were rearranging the tables. On the bar top, soft drinks in plastic cups were lined up for the taking.

When I reached him, Scout was still at the table, right where I'd left him, but he wasn't alone anymore. An older couple sat on either side of him. The sight alarmed me even though a casual observer might think he was just a young guy with his doting grandparents. Scout had a cold drink in front of him, something clear and fizzy, and he was taking a sip as I walked closer. "What's going on here?" I asked, taking the empty seat.

"This drink is called Sprite," Scout said. "These people got it for me. It is very good. You should have some Sprite, Emma." Now that the music was off, his normal speaking voice seemed abnormally loud. Several people looked our way. So much for trying not to attract attention.

The old guy sitting to Scout's right stuck out his hand. "I'm Roy Atkins and this is Beverly, my wife." He had a full head of white hair, cut short, military-style, while she had a short haircut, a bob that ended at her chin. Both he and his wife looked to be retirement age plus ten years.

I reluctantly shook his calloused hand. "I'm Emma."

Beverly gave me a finger wave. "Would you like a soda?" she asked. "Roy will go up and get you one."

I shook my head. "Our car is stuck in a ditch," I said. "And we really need to figure out how to get it towed out."

"Oh, that's too bad." She clucked with grandmotherly concern. "Didja take a turn too fast?"

"No, I . . ."

I didn't get the rest of the sentence out because Scout felt compelled to speak up right at that moment. "Emma saved a deer's life," he said proudly. "She did not hit her."

Absolute silence while they digested this bit of embarrassing information about my terrible driving. I couldn't believe it. The guy who almost never talked chose this moment to take a stand and make a public announcement about my stupidity. "The deer ran right in front of the car and I didn't have time to stop," I explained. "I swerved to avoid it and wound up driving into a ditch."

"Good for you, Emma!" Roy said. "A collision with a deer can do a lot of damage to a car."

"But now we're stuck," I said. "Is there a garage around here? We really need a tow truck."

"Nothing like that around here," Roy said. "Are you kids alone?"

"I am not alone," Scout said. "I am with Emma." *Oh boy.*

"We can pull them out, can't we, Roy?" Beverly said, tipping her head to one side. Then she spoke right to me. "Our truck's parked around the side and we have a hitch and a strap. It won't take but a minute."

I gave them a long look, trying to decide. They seemed trustworthy. I looked to Scout, hoping he'd say something either way, but he had turned his attention back to his Sprite.

Roy must have noticed my hesitancy, because he said, "Beverly and I've got grown kids and grandkids. All the folks here have known us our whole life." He pushed his chair back and stood up. "You all know me. Anyone here willing to tell these kids I'm a nice old guy who wouldn't hurt a fly?"

Voices came from around the room.

"Yeah, we know you, Roy, but we wish we didn't!"

"He looks trustworthy, but he still owes me money."

"I could vouch for him, but I won't!"

There was a lot of laughter. I nudged Scout with my elbow. "What do you say, Scout. Is Roy Atkins someone we can trust?"

"Oh yes," he said, taking a pull on his straw. "He is a very nice man. He will help us."

After Scout was done with his Sprite, I reminded him to use the bathroom and walked him to the door. When I got back to the table, I said to Roy and Beverly, "This is really nice of you. I don't know what we'd have done otherwise."

"Not a problem," he said, brushing off my thanks. "We were just about to head out soon anyway and we're glad to help."

Beverly placed a hand over mine and leaned in to whisper. "One of our grandsons is a little slow like your friend. It's a really good thing you're doing, taking him along with you."

"He's not as slow as he seems," I said, not sure what else to say. "Just very innocent."

"Oh, honey, that speaks well for him. If you ask me, the innocents are better than the rest of us," Beverly said, not quite catching my meaning. "I always say that some people are on this earth to teach lessons and the rest of us are here to learn. I think your friend is here to teach us." I looked at her blankly, and she continued. "Things like compassion and caring and to trust in each other. To be more childlike. We've all lost that childlike wonder."

"I guess," I said. If only she knew.

When Scout came back and the three of us got up to leave, the people in the bar shouted good-byes as we headed out the door. "A friendly group," I observed.

"The best," Roy said enthusiastically. "I've known some of these guys since grade school. We're like brothers, only better."

"I have a brother," Scout said, and I practically palmed my forehead in frustration. Again, with the talking. "His name is Eric."

"That's great," Roy said, leading us around the side of the building to where his truck was parked. "Are you close to your brother?"

Scout nodded, his head bobbing up and down in an exaggerated way. "Yes. He is a good brother."

Roy's pickup truck had a faded, red paint job, dented hubcaps, and an open cab in back. I saw the problem as soon as we approached—there wasn't enough room in the front for all four of us. Or even three of us. Beverly saw me stop, and said, reassuringly, "You and your friend can ride in the back. It's perfectly safe. Our boys used to do it all the time." I still hesitated and she added, "I'd sit back there myself, but I really can't in this skirt." She had a definite point.

Roy flipped down the tailgate and gave me a hand up. Scout was able to scramble in by himself. Right away, I noticed we'd be sharing the space with a large pile of something covered with a tarp. I peeked underneath to see a mound of damp wood chips; the smell almost knocked me over.

"We'll be there in no time," Roy said, seeing my nose wrinkle up at the smell. "And then I'll pull your car out lickety-split. I promise you'll be back on the road before you know it."

He and Beverly climbed in front. When the engine started up, the vibration in the back was terrible, so I told Scout to grab onto the side. The back window had sliding glass and it was open, so I could give them directions to our car. I had to duck my head down a little bit to talk. Not ideal, but I couldn't complain. We were being driven and the distance passed quickly. As it turned out, we'd walked a long way.

"We're getting closer," I said, pointing. "It's up ahead beyond the curve."

As we got closer, I spotted the white Grand Prix off in the distance. It was still in the ditch, but it wasn't alone anymore. Three other cars had stopped nearby, one in the road alongside our car, and two in front of it. Several men dressed in dark-colored slacks and short-sleeved, button-down shirts stood around the car. A few stared into the windows, while two others had some kind of device they waved over the outside of the vehicle. Everything about the scene screamed federal agents. They'd found our car, but they weren't looking in our direction just yet.

"Please just drive past," I begged through the window opening. "Just keep going. It's a matter of life and death." I turned to Scout.

"Get down," I hissed. "Don't let them see us!" He looked puzzled, but he ducked down like I did. I grabbed the edge of the canvas tarp and yanked it over our heads.

All this time, Roy didn't say anything, but I felt the truck come to a stop and heard a voice call out to him. "Sir? Do you live in the area?"

Under the tarp, my legs were tucked under me in an uncomfortable position, the smell of the mulch making it hard to breath. Scout had folded his body into mine, our foreheads touching, his arm slung protectively around my waist, like he sensed danger. Or maybe he just sensed my fear; my anguished thoughts and the pounding of my tell-tale heart. Luckily, Roy was as cool as a secret agent himself. His calm folksy voice didn't give anything away.

"Beverly and I live just down the road," he said. "Can I give you fellas a hand?"

"No, sir. We're conducting an investigation. Is this the first time you've seen this car? We're looking for the occupants, a young woman and young man, both teenagers. They might still be in the area." A slight pinging noise, the sound of some kind of meter, accompanied his voice. What were they checking for?

Roy said, "Nope, never saw that car before now. My wife and I just came from square dance practice over at the Bar None. We've been there all morning. Our group is called the Senior Squares on account of we're all senior citizens and we're square dancers." He chuckled. "Did the kids in the car rob a bank or something? Should I be putting out the word in the community? I'd be glad to warn people if you want."

"No, sir, they're just wanted for questioning in another matter."

Roy laughed. "Too bad. We could use some excitement around here."

Even though I knew he was playing it cool, part of me was thinking, *just go, just go, just go!* How long before one of them glanced into the back of the truck and discovered us? I had to force myself to breathe through my terror. Scout hugged me tighter as the agent's voice called out, "You may proceed, sir. We don't want to hold up traffic, do we now?"

"Righty-o. Have a good day, gents."

The truck lurched forward and I breathed a sigh of relief. Scout and I had lost a car, but at least we'd escaped being detected and arrested, so I was taking it as a win. When fifteen minutes or so had passed, I felt the truck slow and heard the sound of an automatic garage door opening. When we came to a halt, I heard Beverly's voice call out, "It's okay, kids. It's safe to come out."

I lifted my head from the tarp to see we were inside a large garage. Parked right next to us was an ancient station wagon. I knelt and brushed wood chips off the front of my clothes. So much for looking dressed-up and presentable.

Roy and Beverly got out of the truck and gave us a long look. Roy said, "Let's go in the house and you kids can tell us what in the heck is goin' on."

# CHAPTER TWENTY-FIVE

The inside of Roy and Beverly's house looked a lot like them—comfortable and worn. The entrance from the garage went right into a homey kitchen, complete with scuffed linoleum and gold-flecked laminate countertops. The kitchen table was covered with a red-checkered vinyl tablecloth. Roy gestured for us to have a seat and I reluctantly sunk into a chair. They'd saved us from the agents, I'd give them that, but there was no way I could tell them the truth. Even worse than that, I had no idea what we were going to do from here.

Once we were all at the table, Roy said, "Do you want to tell me what kind of trouble you kids are in?"

"I just want to go home," Scout said miserably.

I shushed him, trying to think up a story that would work for this situation. "We haven't done anything wrong," I said. "I swear we haven't broken any laws or done anything that would hurt anyone."

"Do your parents know where you are?"

"We're both legal adults," I said, which technically wasn't true, but whatever. "But yes, they do know. They don't know that someone is after us, though. We didn't want to worry them."

"I see," Roy said, his brow furrowing in concern. "Who were those people and what do they want with you?"

"I'm not sure," I said.

"Emma, we can tell him," Scout said, his hand squeezing my upper arm. His movements were so awkward, but it was starting to get endearing, like when toddlers are figuring out how to hug, but don't quite do it right. "It is okay. He will help us."

I sighed, putting a hand to my forehead. I was starting to get a headache. "Okay, it's some agents from the federal government. They think we know something about an aircraft collision. They threatened to have me arrested if I didn't go back today and tell them what I know." I gave him a pleading look. "But we can't go back today, because Scout needs to get home. It's very complicated."

"Wait a minute," Roy said. "They threatened to arrest you? On what charges?"

"Oh, um. I don't know." I tried to think back to my phone conversation with agent Mariah Wilson. "I think it was withholding evidence or something. But I already told them everything I know."

"So you've already spoken to them?"

"Yes, they questioned me and I told them everything. Then they started tracing my cell phone and bothering a woman we know. A friend of ours." Was I saying too much? My brain seemed to shut down, while my mouth went into overdrive. "All we want is to be left alone."

"Well, that's just a load of bull crap," Roy said, looking to his wife, who nodded in agreement. "Tracing your calls? Harassing your friend? Unbelievable."

"It's been a nightmare," I said.

Now Roy was revved up. "That's the problem with our government today. They're all up in everyone's business. It's almost like they've forgotten we have rights." His anger on our behalf was making me feel better.

"We really haven't done anything wrong," I said. "I swear to you." This was easier than I'd thought. Their outrage was keeping them from asking too many questions.

Beverly said, "We've had some problems with the government ourselves. It's ridiculous."

Roy shook his head. "This makes me sick. I never thought I'd live to see the day the United States of America, my country, would go so low as to hunt down a nice young lady such as yourself who is taking care of a special boy like your friend."

"He *is* special," I said, shooting a glance at Scout. Special, but not Lucas. Somewhere though, on another planet, far, far away, there was a girl waiting for him. She was going to be overjoyed when he came back. If he came back.

Roy clucked. "It's a sad day, let me tell you. It makes me ashamed to be a citizen."

"So what are you kids going to do now?" Beverly asked, concerned.

"We'll figure out something," I said, pulling on the strap of my backpack just to reassure myself it was still there. I still had the handgun Mrs. Kokesh had given me. She said it was my ace in the hole, something to use as a last resort. I hoped I didn't have to use it ever, but I felt better knowing it was there.

Both Beverly and Roy were looking at me now, which made me nervous. I said, "Would you mind if I visited your bathroom? I'm feeling sweaty and I'd like to change my clothes."

"Not a problem," Roy said, gesturing to a hallway. "First door on your left."

"Oh no, not that one! It's a mess," Beverly said. "Use the upstairs bathroom. Top of the stairs on your right."

As I made my way up the stairs, I heard Beverly offer to get Scout something to drink and his answer: "Yes, please." In the bathroom, I turned on the fan, shimmied out of my pants and unbuttoned my shirt. Standing there in my underwear, I felt vulnerable and defeated, but a little bit cooler too. I grabbed a wad of tissue and got it wet, then dabbed my face and the back of my neck. I was a hot mess, and I could still smell the damp wood chips from the back of the truck. The odor had permeated my skin and now surrounded me. I pulled on my shorts and a T-shirt and stuffed my dirty clothes into one of the compartments of my backpack. Just having fresh clothes made me feel much better.

I got out my money and counted through the bills. Enough to rent a car, if there had been a car rental place around here, which I was pretty sure there wasn't. Not to mention that I'd need a credit card and wasn't old enough, so that idea was out. How frustrating. We were so close to our final destination. Thirty or forty miles, I thought. In a car, that would be nothing. I had a sudden thought— maybe if I paid Roy, he'd be willing to drive us there. That seemed like a good possibility given their reaction to our dilemma. But if he refused, we'd have to hitchhike. Whatever we did, we'd have to do it soon. If we didn't get there by the end of the afternoon, it would be too late and the building would be closed. It would be ironic to travel so far and arrive after everyone had gone home for the day.

I headed back to the kitchen, following the sound of Scout's voice saying, "And so we need to go to the place called Erickson Ryder to see if we can communicate with the people on my planet."

Inwardly, I groaned. I walked into the room to see Roy and Beverly leaning forward, intently listening to everything Scout said. Hopefully, they'd think Scout's story was just him being special. "I'm back," I said brightly, hoping to change the subject.

"So now we need a different car because we need to get there soon," Scout said, still talking to Roy and Beverly.

"He gets confused sometimes," I said. "Really, he doesn't know what he's saying . . ."

But no one was paying attention to me. Roy and Beverly had their heads together and were whispering between themselves, while Scout sat back with folded arms, a self-satisfied expression on his face. The couple talked for a really long time, maybe five minutes or so, which made me nervous. Scout thought these two were okay, but we really didn't know them. What if they called the police or tried to keep us trapped here? We didn't have phones to call 911 and even if we did, I didn't know where we were. Roy and Beverly whispered back and forth, looking from Scout to me and back again. I gestured to Scout to get up. "I think we have to get going," I said.

Roy held up a hand to signal we should wait. A second later, Beverly nodded and he said, "I think we can help you out."

"How?" I asked.

"Bev and I have a vehicle you can borrow," he said.

# CHAPTER TWENTY-SIX

Less than half an hour later, we were back on the road, me at the wheel of what looked like a brand-new cargo van, Scout in the passenger seat. I still couldn't believe complete strangers would just lend us a vehicle without even wanting to look at our IDs. It was a matter of trust, Beverly said, and the right thing to do. The van was white, with two windows in back, and it came, Roy said, with a full tank of gas. And that wasn't all it came with.

"This here vehicle is something pretty special," Roy said with a grin, clearly proud. We'd walked around to the back of the house where it was parked, hidden from the road under a carport. "My son and I have been making modifications to it since day one, and believe you me, there isn't another one like it in all the world."

It looked like a regular van to me, the kind that made deliveries. "Like what kind of modifications?" I wondered aloud.

"I'm very glad you asked," he said.

"Just wait until you see," Beverly said, rubbing her hands excitedly.

"This compartment on the top. It just looks decorative, right?" he said.

"I guess."

"But there's something in it that comes down," Scout said.

"Righty-o young man!" Roy beamed. He flipped up the lid of the compartment and pulled a flexible sheet down all the way until it completely covered the side of the van. It stuck on by itself, like it was suctioned. "Magnetic," he said, by way of explanation. The sheet was smooth and dark in color. It had the words "Henderson Family Locksmith Company" above the image of a family gathering, the people all in silhouette. Below the family image was a picture of a lock and a key next to a phone number and the words, "One call and your troubles are over."

"Wow," I walked up and smoothed my hand over the surface. Even up close, it looked like it was part of the van.

"There's one on the other side too," Roy said. "Besides that one, we have other magnetic signs for all kinds of businesses in the back of the van. There are different license plates too. You just slide 'em right into the slot. You can make this van look completely different in just a few minutes' time."

"The locksmith one is the only one that completely covers the van," Beverly said. "But some of the others do the trick almost as well. One of them is an exterminator and there's a big bug in back that you can clip onto the top of the van. That one's my favorite."

"There are also brochures and business cards in back for all the businesses, just in case," Roy said. "And fake ID badges." He opened the back of the van and gestured to Scout to come over so he could show him. From where I stood, I could see a large plastic bug the size of a dachshund lying with its legs in the air. Everything else, the brochures and business cards he'd mentioned, was tucked into plastic boxes. Between the boxes were several large flashlights the size of small fire extinguishers. Scout crawled into the back of the van behind Roy, and he and Roy continued the discussion.

"But why?" I asked Beverly. "Why would you need to make the van look different?"

"To throw off the feds, of course. You get spotted, then you pull off the road, change your license plate and the way the van looks, and when you get back on the road, you're unlikely to get stopped because they're looking for something else. They aren't as smart as you'd think."

I stared at her in bewilderment.

She gently took my arm and pulled me off to the side. "Your friend told us about your troubles and we understand what you're going through."

"He's not quite right. He gets confused sometimes," I said, ready to launch into my story about his compromised mental status, but Beverly would hear none of it.

"Don't say that," she said, waving a finger at me. "There's nothing wrong with that young man. He just has his own version of events. Roy and I figured it out right away because our grandson does that too."

"Does what?"

"Makes a story out of things he doesn't understand, so it makes sense to the way his mind works," Beverly said. "I can tell you're very protective of Scout, so I won't ask you to tell me your secret, but if I guess it, will you let me know if I'm right?"

"Sure. I guess." This was getting weird and time was passing us by. Roy and Scout were crawling out of the back of the van now and Roy was still talking about custom features and emergency switches. They walked around to the front and Roy said, "Climb on in, son, and I'll show you everything on the dashboard."

Beverly leaned in so close her mouth was nearly up to my ear. She whispered loudly, "Scout told us about being an alien and needing to go home to his planet. And that you told him he couldn't cure cancer here." She smiled, the lines around her eyes crinkling. "When you say it like that, it doesn't make much sense, does it?"

I shook my head. "No, it doesn't."

"So Roy and I came up with a theory of our own." She put a grandmotherly hand on my shoulder. "We think your friend is an illegal alien who needs to get to Canada for medical care, and that if you get stopped by the authorities, you'll get in trouble because he's been here illegally."

I sucked in a breath, stunned at what they'd come up with. "That's exactly right," I said.

"I knew it. I knew it!" She practically crowed with satisfaction. "Roy figured out he was an illegal alien, but I was the one who figured out the cancer. Something about him just looks a little off, you know. I notice things." She smiled. "I mean, he's a good looking kid, but there's something that's different."

"I know."

"That cancer is a vicious thing." Beverly tilted her head to one side and gave me a long look. "You really love him, don't you?"

Her question caught me off guard. The answer was complicated. First and foremost, Lucas was the one I loved. As for Scout, well, originally all I wanted was for him to get out of my boyfriend's body and be gone for good. I wouldn't have cared if that meant an end to Scout's life. And even knowing he had cured Lucas's cancer, I'd considered him a trespasser. How dare he take over someone else's body? What gave him the right?

But in the last few hours and days, my attitude had softened. This was a crazy, mixed-up galaxy and Scout was a lost soul just trying to get home. And I was the only one who could help him.

And it was more than that. When I looked at him now, I saw more than a stranger who'd taken over Lucas's body. I knew Scout now. He was curious and sweet and thoughtful. Beverly was still waiting for my answer. "Yes, I really do love him," I said.

She nodded. "I told you I notice things. You know, they're curing cancer so much more now than they were even a few years ago. New treatments, new drugs. Your friend will probably be just fine."

"I hope you're right," I said.

When Roy came back around to where we stood, he ceremoniously handed me the keys. "Scout says you'll be the driver. Take good care of my baby."

I took them and said, "When do we have to have it back?"

"Don't matter," Roy said, wiping his palm across his forehead. "A few hours, a few days, a few weeks. Whenever you're done getting this boy home." Next to him, Scout stood smiling, the happiest I'd ever seen him.

"Thank you," I said. "I have some money. It's not much, but I could—"

"No, no, no," Beverly said. Next to her, Roy shook his head. "You keep your money. We want to do this."

We climbed into the front and Roy spoke to me through the open window. He explained how to take an alternate route, a back road where we were unlikely to run into the agents. "You'll loop around for a while, but eventually, it will take you back to the highway."

"Will do." I patted the dashboard. "Thank you again for helping us out," I said. "I don't know how I can ever repay you."

"My pleasure," he said. "You just take good care of this guy and it will be payment enough."

I rummaged in my backpack and got out the keys for the Grand Prix. "If you want to go pick up our car after the agents leave, you can," I said. "I don't think they can trace it back to anyone. It was my friend's barn car to begin with and I'm pretty sure he never registered it."

Roy nodded and took the keys. "If I get it, I'll hold onto it for you." He grimaced. "But judging from personal experience, they're likely to haul it away as evidence."

I nodded. "Sounds about right. Well, thank you again." I started up the engine and it came to life with a powerful roar. As we drove down the driveway, Scout turned to look behind us. When I glanced back, I saw the couple standing together in front of the house, Beverly blowing kisses and her husband waving. As we turned onto the road, Roy cupped his hands around his mouth and yelled, "Don't forget to go the way I told you."

I wasn't about to forget. We drove down a narrow country road paved in crumbling asphalt. There were no street signs and even the van's GPS didn't have a name for the route we were traveling on. It seemed fairly safe, but still I kept glancing in the rearview mirror, just in case.

We drove up behind a guy on a tractor and I veered around him, pretty sure federal agents wouldn't be driving mud-splattered farm equipment. The tractor driver, an old guy in overalls, gave a friendly wave as we went past and Scout responded, his hand moving enthusiastically across the width of the open window. I sighed. So much for not drawing attention to ourselves.

When we reached the highway, I breathed a sigh of relief and the GPS voice seemed happier too. She cheerfully announced the turn as if pleased to know the name of the main road, although her tone of voice might have been my imagination. "Twenty-seven miles until we get to the Erickson Ryder place," I said. "When we get there, let me do the talking, okay?"

"Okay," he said, his gaze straight ahead. "Emma? Do you think the communications to my people came from Erickson Ryder Incorporated?"

"I don't know for sure," I answered. "But it's a strong possibility. I mean, look around." I gestured. "It's not like there's much else around here."

"Emma?"

"Yes?"

"Can I ask you a question?"

"I think you just did."

It was an old joke, but not one Scout had ever heard before, because a look of wonderment came over his face and he laughed.

"Sorry about that," I said. "Go ahead and ask."

He composed himself and said, "Why did you think the people at the Bar None would be scary?"

"Because I saw the motorcycles and old trucks parked outside and I thought maybe it was a biker bar full of scary rednecks."

"Rednecks?"

"That's a word that means . . . forget it. It's not a nice word. I shouldn't have said it."

"Why did you think these people would be scary?"

"Biker bars usually have a rough crowd and sometimes things get ugly. Fist fights break out. People get drunk and start pushing people around. That kind of thing."

"So you know of these fights? Have you seen the pushing?"

"Well no, not personally."

"Is this something that is reported all the time? On the television?"

"No, I . . ." I stopped to think, but couldn't recall where I'd gotten the idea that biker bars were bad news. It was just a general sense I'd always gotten. From movies, maybe? "I can't tell you, Scout," I finally said. "It's just a thing people know."

"But it was not true. All of the people there were good people."

"You're right, it wasn't true at that bar."

"So maybe it isn't true at all?"

"Maybe."

He shook his head. "This is a very confusing planet. People believe things that aren't true about other people just because of how they look and what kind of vehicle they drive. Why can you not wait and see who they are inside before you make a decision?"

"Because we're afraid," I said. "If I had trusted them and they turned out to be bad people, they might have robbed us or attacked us. It's better to be cautious."

"That is a sad thing," he said. "Always thinking the worst of other people."

"Sad, but that's the way it is. We have to judge them on how they act and what they wear and how they look. We don't have any other way of knowing about them except what we can see on the outside. It takes a long time to really get to know someone, and even then, they can fool you."

"But I knew they were nice," he said.

"Well, I wish I had your ability, but I don't." I tightened my grip on the wheel. Just as Roy had predicted, the road looped around and the terrain was getting hillier too. "People can be a mystery. Like Roy and Beverly Atkins. You told me they were nice and they were nice. I mean, they lent us this van, which is unbelievable, but I'm still confused. Why do they have it rigged to change its appearance? Beverly said it was to shake the feds, but why would an old couple who live in the middle of nowhere need to hide from the law? They're definitely doing something illegal."

"It is the drink," Scout said. "The drink that they make. They need the van to transport it."

"What drink?" I glanced over to see him looking ahead, a dreamy expression on his face.

"I can't tell you what it was called. It was an odd word, like two words together." His forehead scrunched and when he couldn't remember, he waved the problem away. "They make the drink and drive it places in this van and people buy it."

"Did Roy tell you that?"

"Oh no, but I knew. He was thinking about the drink. He thinks about it *a lot*. They make it on their land, in these big metal . . . kettles? It looks a little like Eric's mother's tea kettle, but much bigger and the kettle is connected to other metal containers," he continued. "You add different things and it makes the drink. And when you drink it, it gives you a kick."

Realization dawned on me. "They make moonshine?"

Scout grinned. "Yes! That is the word. They have made it in Roy's family for a long time. His father and his father's father and all the way back. And now he makes it with his son. It is a . . ."

"Tradition?"

"No, that's not it."

"Pride. That is the name of it. They will say, 'I'm going to brew me up some Pride.'" Scout's voice deepened like Roy's when he did the quote, reminding me of Lucas when he used to do impressions. He'd mimic scenes from movies, doing all the parts, even the women. Sometimes he made me laugh so hard I'd be doubled over, praying I wouldn't pee. "Roy tells the customers, 'This here Pride is the real deal—one hundred and twenty proof and pure. White lightning. Not the kind that would make you blind, so don't you worry about that.'"

"I didn't know people still did that," I marveled. "I can't believe I met an actual moonshiner and now I'm driving his van. Unbelievable."

"Oh no, it is believable," Scout said. "I can tell you that it is real and it happened, so you can believe it."

"Okay," I said and didn't even bother to explain.

# CHAPTER TWENTY-SEVEN

Scout was quiet for the next half hour, and I didn't talk either. I couldn't speak for him, but my silence had to do with the nervousness of driving toward our final destination. What were the chances two teenagers would get anyone at a research facility to take them seriously? *Not likely*, I thought. I was starting to question this whole outing, but I'd already defied federal agents, had Scout lie to Mrs. Walker, and borrowed a van from moonshiners. I didn't have a better plan, so I had to see this one through.

Trees lined the sides of the road and, at one point, we passed what had to be a Christmas tree farm. When the GPS directed us toward Ryder Drive, it turned out to be just one more country lane. The road went on for at least another mile and I was starting to doubt we were on the right track when the building came into view and the GPS announced we'd arrived.

Nothing about the outside of the place looked top secret. As office buildings go, it was on the large size, taking up about two city blocks. It was three stories tall and flat on top. The square windows were spaced evenly apart, like in a child's drawing, and the glass was tinted to keep out glare. The lines on the parking lot were bright white, as if they'd recently been painted onto the asphalt. I managed to get a space a few rows back, not too far from the front entrance. It took some maneuvering to pull in backward, but

I thought it was worth it so we could leave quickly if we had to. The front of the van faced the building. We sat for a second, looking straight ahead. "This is it," I said, not knowing if the obvious was obvious to someone from another planet.

"Erickson Ryder Incorporated," he said, his voice flat.

"Yes." I reached over and touched his arm. "If we're lucky, they'll agree to send out a signal right away. Do you have any idea how long it would take for a message to reach your planet?"

"I don't know. Not very long."

It just now hit me that I didn't know exactly what I expected to happen from here. First, we had to get through the door, and then we had to get someone to listen to us. If all went well and the Erickson Ryder people admitted that they'd been the ones sending the friendly signals, it was just one more step to get them to agree to send a communication about Scout. And what would Scout's people do? Send a ship for him? That's how it worked in *E.T.*, but of course, that was just a movie. "Once they find out you're here, how long will it take for them to come get you?"

He turned to look at me and I saw terror in his eyes. "I don't know if they will come for me. I did not follow the proper procedure."

"You mean because you ejected? You think they might leave you behind just because you didn't follow the rules?"

His head drooped and he didn't answer. My heart ached for him. "Come on," I said firmly, opening the door on my side. "Let's get you home."

We both got out of the van, me still hanging onto my backpack and him carrying the cloth bag containing his pod. A small sign next to the front walkway said "Erickson Ryder Incorporated," but there was nothing indicating what kind of business was conducted inside. I held the door open and Scout walked through slowly, like a man heading to the gallows.

"It's going to be okay," I said. "I'm not going to leave you." And then he did something that startled me. With his gaze still ahead, his fingers found his way to mine and he grasped my hand. He did it just like Lucas used to, and if my heart was starting to break before, this finished the job. We were two broken people trying to find comfort from the other. Neither of us had signed up for this madness, and yet, here we were together, trying to make the best of it.

Inside the glass doors, a wide reception desk dominated the space. I'd never seen so much white and chrome in one spot before. Off to one side, a white leather couch was pushed up against a wall behind a chrome coffee table. Both pieces were stark and new-looking, like they were part of a furniture display. A young woman, not much older than me, sat behind the reception desk. When we walked in, she had her feet up on the desk and was leafing through a magazine. As we approached, she closed the magazine and sat up. "Welcome to Erickson Ryder Incorporated," she said primly. "What is your business here?"

I was relieved to see we were off to a good start; the first person we came across wasn't at all intimidating. Besides looking so young, the woman had fair skin and freckles, with brown hair chopped unevenly like she'd cut it herself. She glanced over to a closed door to the right of her desk that had a sign saying, "No one admitted beyond this point." On the left side of her desk was another door, this one with the universal silhouettes indicating it was a unisex bathroom.

"We'd like to see one of the scientists," I said. The air-conditioning was on so high that I felt a sudden chill. The pants and dress shirt I'd had on originally would have been a better choice. Too bad they were crumpled and sweat-stained.

"One of the scientists?" Her forehead furrowed, like she had no idea what I was talking about.

"Yes."

"Your names please?"

I spoke for both of us. "Emma Garson and Lucas Walker."

She didn't write anything down, but her mouth twitched from side to side like she was considering what to do next. "What is your business here?"

This was the second time she'd asked that question. Apparently, she worked off a script. I said, "We'd like to talk to one of the scientists. It's regarding some signals sent to outer space from this building."

"Signals sent to outer space?" She repeated the words slowly.

"Yes."

I matched her stare until she blinked. I leaned over to Scout and, out of the corner of my mouth, I whispered, "Is she okay?" He nodded an affirmative.

After a long, uncomfortable silence, she said, "So, I'm sort of new here and so far I've only had to sign for deliveries. No one told me what to do about visitors. If you take a seat, I'll call someone."

We sat down on the couch, side by side. Scout squeezed my hand and I edged closer to him and whispered, "The second something feels wrong, let me know."

"What should I say?"

"Say, 'It's time to go, Emma.'"

"What will we do then?" he asked.

"We'll leave. Fast."

The girl behind the desk spoke animatedly into the phone, her eyes flickering across the reception area to where we sat. For once, I wished I could read lips. I was willing to bet she was giving someone a description of us and repeating what I'd said. When she finally set the phone down and addressed us, her smile gave me hope.

"Dr. Kessler can be with you in a few minutes." She smiled. "He said you'll have to wait because you didn't have an appointment and he's finishing up a meeting, but he'll be happy to talk to you."

"Okay," I said. My heart pounded with a mixture of fear and anticipation. Maybe I shouldn't have used our real names. It was, I realized, entirely possible that Erickson Ryder had been contacted by the agents and would try to detain us. So stupid of me. She didn't ask for IDs, so I could have told her anything at all, but I didn't. I glanced sideways at Scout who still held my hand and was now playing with my fingers, gently running his thumb over each knuckle, one at a time, while watching as my fingers flexed back and forth like it was the most fascinating thing he'd ever seen. I whispered, "It's going to be okay," and he lifted his head to meet my gaze. His eyes were all Lucas's—hazel green with gold flecks and blond lashes longer than any guy should be allowed to have—but the expression was all Scout, weary and lost. He nodded, but I'm not sure he believed me.

A few minutes later, when the receptionist answered the phone and announced, "Dr. Kessler says you can go on back," I was ready to get this thing over with. I hoisted my backpack over my shoulder and Scout carried the cloth bag in front of him. The girl buzzed us through the door saying, "Down the hall, second door on the left." Scout took my hand and led the way.

We walked down a hallway so wide we could have driven the van through it. The floor was a conventional beige tile, but the walls were made of ridged metal like a corrugated roof. I quietly asked Scout if he was picking up anyone's thoughts and he shook his head. He reached out and tapped the wall as we walked past and it resounded with a dull thud. "This is like a barrier."

We went a long way before we reached the first door on the left, which was closed. The second door, our destination, was wide open. I expected a lab or a manufacturing area, but this was just a small office. A young guy wearing a short-sleeved shirt and dress pants stood there waiting for us, and greeted us as soon as we walked in.

"You're Lucas and Emma?" His skinny, white spaghetti arms surged forward to shake our hands and he got so close I could smell his coffee breath. "I'm Trent, Dr. Kessler's assistant. He'll be here in a minute. Please." He gestured to two vinyl-padded chairs up next to the open doorway. "Just take a seat and he'll be right with you."

The room was small and furnished like an office in an 80s sitcom: tall plant in the corner, desk with a nameplate that said "Trent McCord," fluorescent lights, and a large framed picture of autumn trees. A door on the far wall presumably went into Dr. Kessler's office. I was starting to get a not-great feeling about all this waiting, but Scout hadn't sounded the alarm, and really, what did I know? Maybe this was how it went when you showed up at a secret research facility without an appointment. We took our seats and Trent sat back behind his desk, facing us like he was the principal and we were students who'd violated the rules.

"It's nice to see some new faces around here," he said. "Are you from the area, or just visiting?"

I wasn't feeling up to small talk. I leaned forward in my seat and asked, "So what exactly does Erickson Ryder do?"

"What do we do?" His face had a blank look like I'd asked a very complicated question.

"Yes. This is a research facility, right? So what is it you're working on?"

"Oh." His face relaxed. "Communications. We specialize in satellite communications, but we also—" His phone rang right at that moment and he held up an index finger while he answered. "Trent McCord answering for Dr. Kessler." His eyes widened while listening to an angry squabble on the other end. "I'm sorry, I don't understand what you're asking."

Scout nudged me and indicated the artwork on the wall. He whispered, "There are people watching us from behind the glass." I studied the picture of an autumn landscape, a matted and framed watercolor fronted by glass. The image did have a slight pixilated look to it. We were being watched through the picture? Like suspects in an interrogation room?

Trent continued his phone conversation. "Christy Carversen? No, Christy doesn't work here anymore—"

Just as he said that, an older man burst into the room and grabbed the phone out of his hand. Right away, I noticed his surly expression and the way his face reddened around his thinning hairline.

"Who is this?" the man barked, as he pulled on his tie. A moment later, he said, "Dr. Carversen no longer works here. Furthermore, we don't comment on our employees and we will not tolerate nuisance calls. If this persists, we will take legal action."

The anger in his voice made me involuntarily rise to my feet and Scout, seeing me, did the same. Even Trent appeared startled at this turn of events, cringing like a cornered animal. The man slammed down the phone, smoothed his hair back and seemed to collect himself. He turned to us.

"I'm sorry you had to witness that bit of ugliness. We've been getting harassing phone calls." He held out a hand, palm up. "You must be Lucas Walker and Emma Garson. I'm Dr. Kessler. It's nice to meet you."

I was shaking Dr. Kessler's hand when I heard Scout say, very, very softly, "It's time to go, Emma."

I pulled back and looked straight at Scout. "Run," I said, not even trying to keep my voice down. I grabbed his arm and we took off through the open doorway, going as fast as we could down the long hallway. I think at some point I stopped breathing and was running on pure adrenaline. Behind us, I heard men's voices shouting.

"Stop!"

"Come back!"

"Make sure that door is secure!"

I wasn't sure who was yelling. It could have been any number of people, but in the rush, all the voices sounded the same to me. It really didn't make a difference. All that mattered was getting out of there. We tore down the hall, and I heard footsteps behind us, but I didn't turn to look. By the time I reached the door, I was one step ahead of Scout. I tugged on the handle and my heart sank. Locked. Like an idiot, I pulled on it again, like it would work the second time, which it didn't. The voices behind us were getting closer, and I made a quick decision.

"Stand clear," I said to Scout as I rummaged around the bottom of my backpack, and he obeyed, stepping to one side of me. When I found Mrs. Kokesh's handgun, I pulled it out, released the safety catch and aimed at the door. Boom!

I'd seen guns being used in movies and TV, but never even held one until Mrs. Kokesh gave me this one. I wasn't prepared for the kickback and the smell that rose off it like something burning.

"They've got a gun!" one of the men yelled.

"Watch out, she's got a gun!"

Time shifted and went in slow motion as several things happened at once. Out of the corner of my eye, I saw Scout jump behind me, raising his bag as he went, and at the same time, the door buzzed, signaling the lock was being released. I grabbed the handle and pushed it open, turning back to see a beam of light shooting toward me. Pencil-thin, it was as translucent and shimmery as the heat waves coming off a road on a hot summer day. Scout held the bag like a shield and it blocked the ray.

"Come on," I yelled, going through the open door and reaching back to yank on Scout's shirt. He followed, but paused to pull the door shut. "Just leave it!"

The girl in the lobby jumped up and frantically cried out, "What's going on?" but we raced past her to the glass doors leading out to the parking lot and didn't stop until we got to the van.

As we jumped into the van, I put the safety on the gun and tossed it and my backpack on the floor near Scout's feet. Within seconds, I had the vehicle in drive and we had pulled out of our space.

My heart felt like it was in my mouth. *Ba thumpa thumpa thump.* "Are they following us? Look, quick. Are they back there?" Our tires squealed as we tore around the side of the lot toward the road.

Scout turned to look into his side mirror. "A few are standing and watching us go. Two of them are running after us."

"How many of them in all?"

"Seven."

I gulped and tried to breathe normally, but I felt like I couldn't get enough air. "I can't believe what just happened."

"You can believe it," Scout said. "It did happen."

I kept an eye on the rearview mirror as we raced down the road, relieved to see that none of them were following us. I couldn't believe how fast I got the van up to eighty miles an hour. Pretty impressive for a cargo van. One of Roy's modifications had to be for speed. When we reached the Christmas tree farm, I pulled off the road onto a narrow dirt drive and, from there, drove between two rows of trees. We wouldn't be visible from the road, but if they had helicopters or spy satellites, we were screwed. I shut off the engine and closed my eyes, talking myself through the crisis. *Breathe, Emma. Just breathe.* I could hear myself taking ragged breaths, trying not to cry. Finally, I felt like my lungs were back on track and my heart rate was steady.

Still, I sat like that until I felt a gentle hand on my shoulder. "Emma?" Scout said.

"What the hell was that thing?" I asked. "The laser thing they shot at us? What was that all about?"

"It was a stream of energy designed to short-circuit the human body," he said. "I knew it was coming and used my pod to stop it."

He held up the bag to show me a clean, circular hole in the fabric. Presumably, that's what it would have done to one of us.

"But didn't some of it hit you?" I asked.

"No. The pod is meant to absorb energy. That is what it does best."

"Would it have killed us?"

"No, it would have just stopped us. For a long time."

"Oh." Like a Taser. I had another thought. "Why did that girl open the door for us?"

"One of the men called her to tell her *not* to open the door, but she couldn't hear what they were saying because the gun was shooting. She got confused and opened it," he explained.

"You picked that up from what she was thinking?"

"Yes. Fear is a very strong emotion, and she was very afraid."

*Poor thing*, I thought. Up until now, all she'd done was sign for packages. I said, "Lucky for us, I guess, that you can read minds."

"So, Emma," he said, "now what do we do?"

"Now we change the way the van looks and wait until the coast is clear."

We got out and set to work. The locksmith covering did more to change the look of the vehicle than the other options, so now we were locksmiths and members of the Henderson family. Together, we managed to pull the sheeting down on both sides and secure the pieces in place. Rummaging around inside the van, I found some laminated nametags with various Henderson personas. I tossed one to Scout. "Hang onto this," I said. "If we get stopped, put it on. If anyone asks, you're John Henderson."

"Okay," he said, examining it front and back.

"And I'm Janette Henderson," I said.

"So I should call you Janette Henderson?" His forehead wrinkled as he puzzled out this new development.

"No, you can still call me Emma. We're only the Hendersons when other people are around. And don't say Henderson, just call me Janette."

"This is a very odd planet," he said.

"Yeah, I know."

I found an assortment of license plates and grabbed one to slot into the back. I took out the old one and replaced it, glad that Roy had planned for quick-changes.

The doors to the back of the van were open and Scout watched as I worked. "Look around and see if there's more Henderson Locksmith stuff back there," I said. I'd never had a take-charge personality, but here I was again, plotting and planning. I'd never thought of myself as a strong person, but now I knew it was only because I'd never been in a situation where I had to be strong. This was proof that I could bring it if I had to.

Scout rifled through a stack of stuff and held up two square signs displaying the Henderson logo and phone number. "What about these?"

"Good," I said, taking them out of his hands and positioning one below each of the back windows. I stood back and admired our work. In a very short time, we'd transformed the look of the van right down to the license plates. Still, any van spotted on these quiet country roads was bound to raise suspicion.

"Emma?" Scout said, interrupting my thoughts. "Do we need any of this?" He held up two metal boxes. One was labeled "Universal Kit," and the other said "Locksmith Certifications."

"I don't think so, but let me see." I climbed into the van and examined the first box, opening it to see various metal rings holding bulky, odd-looking keys, along with directions for faking being a locksmith. The other box contained a stack of certificates that looked like diplomas. I was glad to see that Janette Henderson was included in the stack, and that she had completed the training and classes necessary to be considered a master locksmith. I felt oddly proud of my alter ego. "Let's just leave this here for now," I said, shutting both boxes.

I rifled through another stack of boxes, noting that we were also equipped to impersonate dog groomers and a catering service, neither of which came with a fun prop like the plastic bug belonging to the exterminator business.

"What about this?" Scout asked, holding up a large glass jug with a screw-on top.

I took a look. It was about the size of a gallon of milk, but shaped like a wine jug. The kind that usually held cheap wine, judging from the beverages served at my Uncle Kevin's family get-togethers. The liquid inside this particular jug was clear. I was pretty sure I knew what it was, but I unscrewed the lid and took a sniff. It was so strong, it burned my nostrils.

"This, my friend, is what you call moonshine. Where did you find it?"

He gestured to a milk crate sitting off to one side. I peered inside to see red plastic cups stacked in the corner of the container. Scout said, "There was a cloth covering it up."

"I bet there was. They didn't want anyone to see it." I grabbed two cups and poured us each a small amount. "This might be our only chance to try moonshine ever." I handed a cup to him and said, "Cheers."

Scout put it up to his mouth and stopped, his nose wrinkled in distaste. "I must drink this?"

"You don't have to drink it," I said. "But *I'm* going to try it." I took a small sip and, immediately, the overpowering taste made me want to spit it out, but I didn't. Man, it was strong, and not in a good way. The roof of my mouth burned and my eyes went bigger than they ever had before. "Whoa," I said. "It would take a lot to get used to drinking that."

Scout put the cup up to his mouth and his expression changed to horror as he took a sip and coughed slightly, putting his fist up to his mouth. "Why would you want to get used to drinking it?"

"People like the feeling they get from the alcohol," I said. "When you drink enough of it, you get drunk, and it makes the world seem like a better place." I added. "Most of the time."

"Why don't the people just make the world a better place and then they wouldn't need to get drunk?"

He had a point. "I don't know," I admitted.

"Emma? Don't you think we should be doing something?" He looked out of the open van doors. A slight breeze brought the scent of fir trees. "They could find us here. They want to catch us. And they were thinking terrible things. They want to kill you."

"What?"

"They want to kill you." Seeing my shocked expression, he clarified. "To make you dead."

I sucked in a sharp breath. "I understood what you said, I just don't get it. Why would they want me dead?" But even as I said the words, it came to me. Scout was the alien, the one they wanted to capture and study. I was the witness, the one who could tell the world what had happened. They wanted me dead because dead girls can't talk. I held up a hand and said, "Wait. You don't need to answer that. Just tell me, what exactly were they thinking about killing me?"

"That it would have to look like an accident," he said miserably. "A car accident that created a fire explosion. They can do that. And then, they would tell Lucas's parents that he died too, and they would keep me."

"But they'd have to give his parents a body . . ."

He shook his head. "Not this body. One that is burned so you cannot tell who it is."

"But how did they know who we were to begin with?"

"The agents called Dr. Kessler today and he has been waiting for us," he said.

A shiver of fear went up my spine. "Oh."

I scrambled out of the van as a sudden wave of nausea hit me. I was four steps away when the contents of my stomach heaved out and onto the ground. I hadn't thrown up since middle school and I'd forgotten how nasty it was: the bile in the back of my throat, the burning in my nose. I wiped my mouth with the back of my hand, thinking I was done, but then another surge hit. This time it wasn't so bad and when it was done, it felt more final. I felt a little better.

I wiped my lips and turned around, smacking right into Scout, who wrapped his arms around me, holding me in a gentle hug. I leaned against him, burying my face in his chest. He patted my head and made the kind of reassuring, shushing noise Lucas would have made, but it didn't help. Every second counted, and we should be on the move, but I was paralyzed with fear. I knew that our best bet was to get as far away as possible, but they'd be looking for us on the road and I wasn't convinced that changing the van's appearance was enough. If we were stopped, that would be it. No escaping. It would be certain death for me and imprisonment for Scout. But staying here wasn't the answer either.

We couldn't stay, but we couldn't go. I understood now why animals caught in steel traps sometimes chewed off their own legs.

# CHAPTER TWENTY-EIGHT

"I'm sorry," I said, pulling away from Scout. "I must smell awful." I smoothed back my hair and leaned over to spit on the ground.

"It is a bad smell," he said agreeably. "But I do not mind." He tilted his head to one side and gave me an intense look. "You were thinking we must leave here, but you are afraid to go?"

"That's exactly right," I said, walking to the front of the van to get my bottle of water out of the front seat. I handed it to Scout, who took a sip and handed it back. I took a swig, gargled, and spit it out. It was a beautiful, sunny summer day in northern Wisconsin, the kind we wait for all winter long. Most of the residents in the state were enjoying the sunshine while I was thinking I was as good as dead.

Scout had followed me and was watching. "So we should hide." Like that was an obvious conclusion.

I took another sip of water, swallowing this time. My stomach gratefully received it. I put the cap on the bottle and shook my head. "There's nowhere to hide. I think our best bet is to wait here until dark and try to leave on the back roads. With the van disguised, there's a chance we might get away."

He shook his head. "They will have the expressway roads blocked. They will not let us get away this time."

"Well then, I've got nothing."

"We should not go back. They will find me at the Walkers' house and they will go to your house too."

"Yes, but we'll be safer with other people around," I argued, even as I wasn't entirely sure that was true. "My mom wouldn't let them take me." Not if she could help it. That much I knew.

"But if we leave, we will never know how to get the signals to my planet." His voice was tinged with desperation and I could see the agony in his eyes.

"But staying here isn't going to help us get signals to your planet either. Obviously, Erickson Ryder isn't going to help us." I heard the anguish in his voice and understood. He was a lost boy trying to get home and I should have been comforting him, but all I could think was that getting signals to his planet was now the least of my worries. "I give up then," I admitted, throwing up my hands. "I don't have a plan or a phone."

"It is better to be moving than be found sitting," he said. "We are going now, Emma. Give me the keys. I will drive." He held out his hand, palm up.

"You seriously think I'm going to give you the keys? You've never driven before."

"I have watched. It does not appear difficult," he said, his voice completely confident.

"You don't have a license," I said.

He raised one eyebrow, something I'd never seen Lucas do. "The keys, please."

"Okay, have it your way." I fished the keys out of my pocket and dropped them into his hand. This was going to be interesting. "Do you have any idea where you're going?"

"I have an idea," he said, slamming the back doors.

Once inside the van, I watched as Scout expertly adjusted the mirrors before putting on his seat belt. As it turned out, he had been paying attention. I clicked on my own seat belt and watched as he started up the engine and put the van into reverse, slowly backing out between the rows of fir trees to the wide driveway before going forward. When he approached the road, he looked both ways before turning the wheel hand over hand to the right. "Pretty good, huh?" he said, sneaking a glance in my direction.

"Not bad," I admitted. "So where are we going?"

"There is a big lake north of here. Some of the houses on the lake will be empty right now. We will go there and hide until we have a better plan."

"How do you know about the houses on the lake?"

"Eric and I discovered this on the computer. It seems silly, but some people here have two houses and only go to the house on the lake for the weekend."

I nodded. "Oh yeah. Lake cottages. Sometimes they rent them out too."

"You know about this?" he asked, surprised. We were the only vehicle on this country highway and he whipped the van around a turn with amazing precision.

*Too wild and too fast*, I thought. "Hey, take it easy," I said. But before I could tell him to slow down, a minivan pulled out of a driveway ahead of us and stopped in the middle of the road, blocking our path. "Stop!" I yelled, but Scout had other ideas. He veered wildly into the left lane, almost going into the ditch, before careening back onto the road, accelerating as we went. My heart leapt into my throat and I was glad there was nothing left in my stomach or I probably would have thrown up again. "What do you think you're doing?"

He didn't answer, but gripped the steering wheel harder, his eyes darting to the rearview mirror and then back to the road. When I turned, I saw what he'd seen—the minivan was following close behind us, two men in the front seat, one of them holding a gun aimed straight at us. Frantically, I said, "Faster. They're gaining on us."

Scout pressed the accelerator down and the engine roared. The trees on either side of the road were a soft blur now and still we weren't going fast enough. They were getting closer by the second and I found myself slouching down to make myself less of a target. Scout, however, didn't seem to know enough to duck down. His posture was perfect. I glanced back to see the man on the passenger side had opened his window and had a gun aimed right at us. "He's got a gun!" I screamed.

"We have one too," Scout said, shrugging.

I leaned down and found the handgun on the floor. I held it on my lap with a shaking hand. When I'd used it back at Erickson Ryder, it was only because I was trying to break through a locked door. I didn't want to die today, but I also didn't know if I could kill a person.

A man's voice blared through a loudspeaker from behind us. "Pull over. No one will be hurt. Just stop the vehicle. We need to talk to you."

"What do you think?" I asked.

Scout slowed. "It is a lie," he said. "They will hurt you if they have a chance."

"Stop the van and put down any weapons," the voice blasted over the loudspeaker. "No one will be harmed. We just need to talk to you."

"That is not true," Scout said, easing his foot off the gas and braking gently.

"Then why are we stopping?" I asked as the van slowed to a halt. We were at a standstill now, stopped in the middle of the road. I craned my neck to look back, only to see the two men getting out of the minivan, both with guns drawn. From the back of the vehicle, more men poured out, all of them dressed in office attire as if they were going to a convention. I opened my mouth to yell, but Scout had already stepped on the gas and was speeding down the road. Behind us came the loud crack of gunfire. The vehicle lurched like it'd been hit and Scout spun the wheel, zigzagging back and forth. I flinched, expecting the worst.

"Do not worry, Emma," Scout said. "Roy said the windows have bulletproof glass."

We barreled down the highway, but I knew they'd catch up and be on our butt in no time at all. I looked back a few seconds later and sure enough, they'd gotten back into the van and were now in hot pursuit behind us. Scout's trick had gained us some distance, but there was no way this could end well, I thought. The windows might be bulletproof, but it was a safe bet the tires weren't.

"I have a really bad feeling about this," I said. "Maybe we should turn ourselves in to the police and take our chances."

"No," he said, shaking his head and continuing to drive like a maniac.

Scout ignored the stop sign at an intersection ahead, narrowly missing a silver SUV crossing from the other direction. The van behind us was forced to slow down for the other car, but only for a moment and then they were back on our tail. As we hurtled down the road, I didn't know where to look, so I wound up craning my head back and forth from the road ahead to the van in back. They had given up on the loudspeaker, but the metallic rain of bullets grazing the van showed they meant business. "If they hit the tires, we're screwed," I said.

"They are not aiming for the tires," he said. "They do not want an accident where I might be killed. They only want you dead."

"Oh." My stomach squeezed tight with the realization that today was the day I was going to die. I wished I had left my mom a note explaining everything that had happened and telling her I loved her. But I hadn't even thought to because I had assumed everything would work out fine. Why had I been so stupid? "Do you think they're federal agents?"

He shook his head. "They are just from Erickson Ryder. They do not want the federal agents to know what they've done."

"And what have they done?"

"They want to be the first ones to make contact with other planets, so they have broken the rules. If the federal agents find out what they've done, they will be shut down and sent to jail." A grim expression came over Scout's face as he drove erratically around a bend and past a picture-perfect farmhouse accompanied by a red barn and fields that stretched on forever.

"What's your plan?" I asked. "You have a plan, right? You know where you're going?"

"Yes," he said.

I glanced back again, alarmed at what I saw. "There's another one!" A second car, a white sedan, was in the left lane, and the two vehicles were driving side by side right behind us. He slowed, which was not the reaction I was going for. "Go faster, they're gaining on us."

"Do not worry, Emma," he said. "I will take care of this." We rounded a slight curve and, when the road straightened, he reached down to the bottom of the dashboard and pushed a knob I hadn't noticed before. I heard a gush of liquid pouring out behind us and looked in my side-view mirror to see a trail of something dark spilling out of the back of the van. "It is a kind of oil," Scout said, answering my question. "Roy said it was only for emergencies."

The two cars behind us skidded on the oil, the minivan sliding almost gracefully to one side, the sedan careening into it and bouncing off into the ditch. Scout turned another knob on the dashboard and pushed hard. "What's that?" I asked, my head swiveling to see. Behind us, a wall of thick, black smoke filled the air, making it impossible to see the vehicles. *Oh no, what did he do?*

I waited for the boom I knew must follow oil and smoke. There had to be a fire somewhere in there, and when it reached the vehicles, they'd explode. I tensed, ready for it, but it never came.

"They will not blow up. It is only smoke to provide a screen," Scout said, reading my mind again.

"But they'll still find us," I said. "They won't give up."

"Maybe," he said. "But we won't give up either."

"You seem different," I said, studying his face. "Just now. What happened?"

"I had to change," he said with a sigh. "I did not want to be like your people. I did not think I could be. But I want you to live."

"Oh," I said, touched by the confession that Scout had gone against his very nature to keep me safe. I knew he wasn't Lucas, but the love I felt at that moment was every bit as strong. Was it possible to love two guys at once, but in completely different ways?

"You know," he said. "The outlaw in the movie said that when things get bad and it looks like you're reaching the end of your rope, then you have to get mean. Really mean. Mean as a rabid dog." He repositioned his hands on the steering wheel. "I did not think I could get that mean, but it is not as hard as I had thought."

# CHAPTER TWENTY-NINE

He had not lied to Emma when he told her Lucas was present deep down underneath, the equivalent of sleeping, but that wasn't entirely true either, because recently Scout had felt a change. Lucas was stirring, making his wishes known. It happened in bits and pieces. When Emma was paralyzed with fear, Lucas pushed for Scout to console her. It was Lucas who'd had the idea to stop in the road and then take off when the men got out of the minivan. The idea to release the oil? That was Lucas too. He'd apparently heard all of Roy's instructions, even the ones that had gone over Scout's head.

Scout was glad to get the help, but he knew the truth. Lucas wasn't just trying to be helpful. He wanted his life back.

# CHAPTER THIRTY

We kept to the back roads and didn't encounter anything out of the ordinary for the next ten minutes, but every time we passed a house or another car, I was sure that something bad was going to happen. Scout stayed on a northward course, reasoning that we were bound to hit the lake sooner or later. I looked at Scout, driving as confidently as if he'd been doing it for years. Only a few hours before, he'd been waving like a child to other drivers. My baby boy had grown up before my eyes.

"Try not to worry," he said gently, glancing over at my hands, clenched tight into fists. "We will be there soon."

"I can't help worrying," I said, flexing my fingers. We'd reached a country road that had houses every half mile or so. I read the names on the mailboxes as we drove by, trying to get my mind on something else. The Dembiec mailbox was decorated with sunflowers. The Hunt's was planted in a concrete cylinder to keep country thugs from playing mailbox baseball. The one that said C. Carversen was—

"Stop, Scout! Turn around," I yelled. He slowed slightly and gave me a puzzled look. "We need to go back," I said.

I'd recognized the name on the mailbox and the realization hit me like a bolt of lightning. C. Carversen. I knew that name. Christy Carversen was the former employee at Erickson Ryder. I didn't know what had happened to her, but the mention of her name had made Dr. Kessler furious, so it had to be something important.

Scout pulled to the side of the road and spun the wheel around, pointing the van back the way we came. "You are thinking that this C. Carversen is the same one from Erickson Ryder?"

This mind-reading thing was getting to be pretty handy. "Yeah, that's exactly what I'm thinking. It has to be her. What are the chances there would be two people with that name living in this area?"

He shrugged and pulled into the gravel driveway, following the slight curve up to the garage. The house was typical of what we'd seen up and down this road: one story, white clapboard siding, asphalt-shingled roof. Not much to look at, really. Black shutters on either side of the two front windows were the only decorative element. Otherwise, the house was a rectangular box with a concrete stoop in front of a red door. A large tree in front loomed over the house, casting shadows over the entryway. The garage door was down and the curtains were drawn, making the house look lonely.

Scout frowned. "I do not think anyone is home."

"Do you know that for sure?" I asked. He shook his head and I said, "Wait here, I'll check." I hopped out of the van and slammed the door shut, then went up to the front door. As I pressed the doorbell, I noticed a fuchsia-colored bike on the ground next to the stoop. I heard a ding-dong as the doorbell echoed inside the house. I rang again and heard approaching footsteps.

"Just a minute." A woman's voice called from the other side of the door. I heard a chain lock disengage before the door gave way.

But when the door opened, it wasn't a woman at all, but a girl my age. She wore a halter top that showed off significant tan lines and a tattoo of a Celtic cross that covered most of her right shoulder. The frown on her face showed she wasn't all that excited to see me standing there. "Yes?" she said, jutting her chin close to the screen.

"I'm looking for Christy Carversen?" As soon as the words slipped out, I heard my mistake. There was too much question in my voice when what I really needed was confidence.

"She can't come to the door right now." The girl folded her arms in front of her. "Can I help you?"

"I can wait. When will she be available?" I tried to sound a little more assertive this time, but knew I was failing miserably.

"Who wants to know?"

Before I could answer, Scout bounded up onto the porch next to me, nearly knocking me over. "Hi," he said, a huge smile crossing his face. I recognized the look. It might have been Scout behind it, but the smile was all Lucas, pearly whites gleaming, along with an expression designed to lure anyone caught in his spotlight. "Lacey, right?"

"Yeah, that's me. I'm Lacey." She dropped her arms, and her annoyance was replaced with puzzlement. "Have we met?"

"No, but Aunt Christy told me if I got here early that you might be looking after Boo," he said, giving her a smile that could melt an iceberg. "I'm Lucas. Did she forget to tell you I was coming?"

*Boo?* I held my breath, listening to him outright lie to this girl. Was she going to buy it?

"Oh, right. Lucas." She took a step back and opened the screen door. "I'm pretty sure she's talked about you before, but she didn't say you'd be coming by. I would have remembered."

Unbelievable. With only a smile and a name, she let us into the house. A house that belonged to someone else, no less.

I followed Scout inside, but now that he'd charmed his way in, I was forgotten. There were three of us standing in the front hall, but as far as Lacey was concerned, it was just the two of them. She chattered away about how she'd been getting the mail and taking care of the cat all week and how Christy would be gone for at least another night, which sucked because Lacey had a chance to go camping with some friends for a few days up at Badger Lake. They were leaving that evening.

"I already told them yes, because this is our last year before my friend Mandy goes off to college, and you know how that goes," she said. "Next year, my whole group is going to be split up after graduation and it will never be the same."

Scout had one hand on the wall and was leaning toward her, giving her all his attention. He nodded as if he understood exactly what she was going through. "I hear you," he said, sounding exactly like Lucas.

"So, I'm thinking it's no big deal if I go," Lacey said. "My mom or dad can just swing by and take care of the cat and get the mail and check on things, but then my mom says," here she let out a huge dramatic sigh, "that since I was the one Christy made the arrangements with, I need to live up to my obligation and stay. I'm like, really?" She threw up her hands. "So I'm not supposed to go camping just because I have to stop over here for fifteen minutes a day? That's ridiculous and so unfair. Usually I can get my dad on board, so I begged him to help me out, but this time he agreed with her. He said my friends should change their plans and go a day later to wait for me. Like, how ridiculous is that? God!"

"So ridiculous," Scout echoed, then added, "good thing we're here now. We'll take care of things so you can go camping with your friends."

"Would you?" She practically shrieked. "Oh, that would be so awesome. I'll show you where the cat food and the litter box are."

"Is the litter box still in the second bedroom in the closet?" Scout said.

"Yes." The next sentence, she and Scout spoke together: "And the cat food is in the cabinet with the canned goods."

"Jinx!" Lacey grinned. "If you know where she keeps the cat stuff, I guess Christy really *is* your aunt."

"She really is my aunt," Scout said. "Don't worry, we've totally got this. I'll stay until Aunt Christy gets back. You don't have to worry about anything."

"Who is she?" Lacey said, her head swiveling sharply, her attention suddenly on me.

"She's no one," Scout said before I could answer. "A neighbor. I brought her along as a favor to her parents." He leaned in again. "She doesn't get out much."

"Thanks," I said, but the word was lost in Lacey's laughter. I suddenly felt a familiar pang of exclusion, the kind I'd last felt in fifth grade when my two best friends suddenly and inexplicably ditched me midway through the year. I knew Scout was acting, reading Lacey's thoughts and telling her what she wanted to hear, but still, it hurt. Until recently, he'd seemed so innocent that this new version of him caught me off guard.

"I'll walk you out," Scout said to Lacey and the two of them went out the front door without another word to me.

I watched through the screen as Lacey picked up her bike and walked with Scout toward the road. They paused under the tree and Lacey began talking to him in earnest, one hand resting on his forearm. If I hadn't known better, I would've thought they were boyfriend and girlfriend. As I watched, I felt something soft and furry brush up against my calf.

"You must be Boo," I said, reaching down to pet a chubby black cat. The cat flopped over on her side, asking for more attention, and I complied, running my fingers through her fur. When I straightened up a minute or two later, Lacey and Scout were standing closer together and the skank had her hand on his face, stroking his cheek. An objection froze in my throat and I watched, horrified, as she stood on her tiptoes to kiss his lips, then laughed and hopped on her bike to ride away.

When he came back inside, I said, "What was that all about?"

"I got her to go," he said happily. "Now we have a place to hide."

"No, I mean the kiss. Why did she kiss you?"

He shrugged. "She wanted to, I guess. She asked if she could kiss me and I said yes."

"Just like that. Some girl you never saw before in your life asked to kiss you and you were okay with it?" My mind was at war with my emotions. I knew that it was Scout doing the kissing, but he was doing it with Lucas's lips, and I was having trouble differentiating between the two. "Just like that." I heard my voice get ugly as I did a derpy impression of Lacey. "I want to kiss you." And then I mimicked his response, equally derpy. "Okay."

His face froze and he tilted his head to one side, like he was picking up radio signals only he could hear. "She needed it," he finally said. "It made her feel good about leaving. She thought it was fate that she was here when I arrived and that we had a connection."

"And did you?"

He shrugged. "I did not feel a connection with her. My only emotional connection with a human on this planet is with you."

A smile crept over my face. "Good. Try not to forget that."

"How could I forget it?" he asked, puzzled. "It is a fact."

"Okay," I said, sighing. "Should we go through the house and look for evidence that Christy Carversen was involved with the radio signals sent to outer space?"

"Yes." He nodded vigorously. "But first I would like to put the van in the garage so it is out of sight."

# CHAPTER THIRTY-ONE

Once, when I was twelve, I stole gum from the grocery store. I knew it was a terrible idea, but I still did it, spurred on by peer pressure and stupidity. Afterward, it bothered me so much that I didn't even enjoy the gum; it felt like dirt in my mouth. That night, knowing the rest of the pack was in my dresser, I couldn't sleep at all because of the guilt. In retrospect, the gum heist wasn't even much of a crime. But this? Entering someone's home without their permission? This was a thousand times worse than shoplifting gum. But Scout seemed so sure that everything was going to be fine and he somehow *knew* things, things no one else would know. I wanted this journey to have a happy ending, and I wanted to believe him.

Scout drove the van into the garage, which was fairly empty except for a motorcycle parked on one side. Once in, we lowered the door and locked it. From the road, no one would be able to tell that anyone was in the house. With the van taken care of, we locked all the doors and went through the place, room by room, looking for anything that might help us.

The house was nothing special. The air-conditioning was on, which was one positive, but everything else looked dated and worn. If I had to guess, I'd say the owner of the house was about sixty-five. In the kitchen, a white refrigerator wheezed in the corner. Grocery store coupons covered the front, held in place by daisy magnets. The plain pine cabinets and white countertops were exactly like the kind my mom and I had in our trailer. The whole place could have been the "before" photo for a home-remodeling website.

It was not a large house, and we went through it very quickly. A basic eat-in kitchen, a living room, one bathroom, and three bedrooms. One of the bedrooms was obviously where Christy Carversen slept. The second was empty except for a bag of litter and few cardboard boxes in one corner, and a litter box on the floor in the closet. I combed through the boxes hoping to find something significant, but all I found were some photo albums and books. The third bedroom was set up as an office with a bookcase and a desk, the old wooden kind. The desk was massive with multiple drawers, all of them full of things like yellow legal pads, markers, and pens.

There wasn't a sign of anything modern anywhere in the house. Not even a computer or a tablet. Maybe whoever lived here wasn't the former Erickson Ryder employee? But no, Lacey had confirmed that the homeowner's name was Christy Carversen and the mail sitting on the kitchen table was addressed to that same name. And it didn't seem like there could be two Christy Carversens in one small area. Maybe she was a lower-level employee? Someone from the loading docks who'd been caught stealing or something. Wouldn't that just cap off the day? We'd been chased and shot at by the very people we'd thought might help us, and now we'd illegally taken refuge in the house of someone who had nothing to do with our problem. Of course, getting caught trespassing was the least of our worries right now.

"Ready to check the basement?" I asked and Scout, nodding, followed me down the rickety wooden stairs. The light at the bottom had a metal pull chain that switched on one bare bulb.

Three of the walls were concrete block. The fourth wall was shiny wood paneling, bare except for an empty bookcase right in the middle. The paneling wasn't much of an improvement over the concrete. On the opposite side of the room, a washer and dryer sat underneath a narrow window. A wooden table next to the appliances held laundry detergent and a box of dryer sheets. With the basement's lack of head room and musty smell, it wasn't anywhere I'd want to spend much time. I squinted into the dim recesses of the basement. Empty. There weren't even boxes.

"Nothing here." I surveyed the space, hoping to spot something, anything, but nope, it was just your basic basement with a washer and dryer. "I hate to say it, but I don't think Christy Carversen has anything to do with your radio signals," I said, ready to turn around and go back upstairs.

But Scout's outstretched arm stopped me. "What's behind that wall?" he asked, pointing to the paneling.

"Nothing?" I said.

"No." He strode across the room and pulled another light chain, making it easier to examine the empty bookcase. He sized it up from each side before grabbing one side and pulling it away from the wall. It swung forward like a door, and behind it was an actual door, solid metal from the looks of it. "Something is hiding back here."

Scout turned the knob but it didn't give, not even a fraction of an inch. He yanked on it, pulling back with all his weight, but nothing. Instead of getting impatient, like Lucas would have, Scout took a step back and ruminated on the situation, his fist to his chin. I recognized it as his thinking look. Finally, he ran his hand along the doorframe, looking for a way in, but it was solid metal, bolted to concrete.

"Did you see any keys upstairs?" he asked.

"No," I said. "But Lacey had the key to get into the house. She left it on the kitchen table."

Scout shook his head. "Lacey did not have this key. The opening is the wrong size."

I remembered our getaway at Erickson Ryder. "Maybe I could shoot the lock mechanism to get it to open like I did before?"

He turned and gave me the kind of look you give little kids when they offer their allowance so the family can go to Disneyland. It was a sweet idea, but not practical. "Your gun did not open the door at Erickson Ryder," he explained patiently. "The noise of the gun confused the girl and she opened the door with her buzzer."

"I know," I said. "But I didn't aim well. It might have worked if I'd done it right." What he'd said was true. Still, it always worked in movies and we didn't have any other options.

"Shooting a gun in a small space might be dangerous," he said, slowly. "But if you want to try it, we can do it."

I nodded and held up a finger indicating he should wait, then bounded up the stairs to get the gun out of my backpack. When I came back down, he was right where I'd left him, standing directly in front of the door. When he saw me approach, he held his hand out. I gave him the gun, glad not to be the one doing the shooting.

"Put your fingers in your ears," he said.

I did as instructed, and then took a few steps back, watching as he carefully turned the gun sideways before pulling the trigger. Even with my ears covered, the crack from the gunfire was deafening. The smell made me cough. I waved a hand in front of my mouth as Scout unsuccessfully tugged on the door again and again. Finally, I put my hand on his shoulder.

"Enough. It's not going to open. I'm hungry. Let's get something to eat and we can think about it and maybe come up with something else."

I led the way upstairs, talking as we went. I tried to cheer him up, saying it was just as well. Once Christy came home, we'd find out more. "Why did you turn the gun sideways before you pulled the trigger?" I asked.

"Oh!" His face brightened. "I learned that from a movie. That is known as the kill shot."

"I don't think it's any more accurate that way," I said.

"I know, but it looks cooler."

Scout was one stair below me and I stopped, forcing him to halt in his tracks. I gazed down at his earnest face and grinned. "Did you say it looks cooler?"

"Yes. Everyone thinks so."

I reached down to muss his hair and he did nothing to stop me. "You have no idea how adorable you are right now. I wish I had my phone so I could record you saying that." I brushed his hair back into place and continued up the stairs.

"I do not understand. What is adorable about me?"

"Everything," I said without turning around.

In the kitchen I found a packaged pizza in the freezer and some bottles of soda in the fridge, and figured that would have to do for dinner. While I was rummaging around looking for a pizza cutter, Scout was double checking all the drawers for keys. He started in the kitchen and worked his way through all the other rooms. I could even hear him pulling things out of the bathroom drawers and cabinets, like a key would be hidden in Christy Carversen's box of tampons. When he came back fifteen minutes later, his defeated look and empty hands told me he hadn't had any luck. By this point, I'd already preheated the oven and popped the pizza onto the rack.

"If you want to be useful," I said, "you could open up the blinds facing the back of the house. It's really dark in here."

A second later, he called out from the living room, "Emma, you are brilliant!"

"What? Did you find something?"

"Yes, I did. Come and see. You will not believe it."

# CHAPTER THIRTY-TWO

I joined him at the big window and let out a low whistle. Outside, there was a satellite dish mounted on a concrete patio slab, but it wasn't like any satellite dish I'd ever seen. This one was enormous, at least twenty feet across. The space above it was open to the sky, but the yard was surrounded by a wooden fence too high for anyone to peek over. No one could see this thing except from inside the house. And from overhead too, of course. Maybe we'd found the right Christy Carversen after all.

"Whoa. That's one big dish. I'd say she gets all the channels."

Scout's nose wrinkled in confusion. "I don't think this is for the television, Emma," he said. "I believe it sends out signals to space."

I hugged Scout, who just stood there, calm as can be. "This is good news, Scout! This proves we're in the right place. All we have to do is wait for Christy Carversen to help us send a message and you can go home." *And I can get Lucas back,* I thought. "Pretty soon this will all be over and both of you will be where you belong."

He frowned. "But what if she will not help us?"

"She has to!" I bounced around, doing my happy dance. "She *will*. How can she not? Look at this face!" I patted his cheek. "How could she resist?" Besides, she was on the outs with Erickson Ryder and so were we. What was the saying? The enemy of my enemy is my friend?

Scout cleared his throat. "But if she does not help us, can I stay?"

"Stay?" My happy bubble burst as I realized what he was asking. "Stay inside Lucas, you mean?"

He nodded. "If we can get safely back to the Walker house, could you be happy with me? If I was here forever? I would need your help to get through school and to know what the Walker parents expect from me."

"Oh, Scout . . ." I said. "It's not going to come to that. We'll get you back to your home planet, and if that doesn't work, we can always find another body for you to go into. Someone who is dying, who wouldn't have used it anyway." Said like that, it sounded really creepy. It was a solution, not a very good one, but at least it was something.

"I don't want to go into someone else," he said sadly. "It would not be the same."

"I know, but you can't stay inside Lucas. I need him back."

"So are you saying you don't care about me? Me, Scout, not Lucas. Because I can feel that you do." He tapped his chest with the flat of his hand. "I told you the truth that I was inside Lucas, but if I didn't, you would never have known. You would have thought I was Lucas and you would have loved me then."

"But I knew something was different. You weren't like Lucas. I saw the change. I knew. I could tell."

"You would have gotten used to me," he said. "And I would have learned more of how to be Lucas and would have been better at it. After some time it would have been the same to you."

"Oh, Scout," I said. "It never would have been the same. I do love you, but just as a friend. My heart belongs to Lucas."

"You could *learn* to love me." Scout put his hands gently on my shoulders and leaned in so close our noses touched. He whispered,

"I know everything about you. If you would think carefully about the times you had with Lucas, I would know the memories too."

I took a step back, shaking him off. "No. It wouldn't be the same. Yes, I care about you, Scout, but you could be in his body for a hundred years and I'd never feel the same way about you as I do about Lucas." I blurted out the words, but when I saw his hurt expression, I almost wished I could take it back. What made it worse was that the pain I saw was Scout's, but it was written on Lucas's face. It was true that the line between the two of them was beginning to blur for me, but I couldn't deny that Lucas was my true love, my one and only. And I knew that Scout understood that, deep down. I gave his shoulder a gentle squeeze. "I don't know why we're even talking about this. You're going to go home soon and it's all going to work out fine. Imagine how excited Regina is going to be when she finds out you're still alive."

"Yes," he said with no emotion in his voice. "Regina will be surprised."

In the kitchen, the timer on the stove dinged.

"Come on," I said, pulling on his arm. "Let's eat the pizza. You'll feel better once you have something in your stomach."

# CHAPTER THIRTY-THREE

My biggest concern that night—besides getting shot by Erickson Ryder or caught by federal agents—was worrying about my mom back home. She wasn't the kind of parent who invented things to stress about, but even the most laid-back mother couldn't ignore her teenage daughter not calling or coming home by nightfall. I could only think she was imagining the worst. And I had no way to tell her otherwise. There wasn't a landline in Christy Carversen's place, which was a good thing because I knew I'd be tempted to call her, which might lead the agents straight to us.

I rationalized that this was the tradeoff: in exchange for a few frantic days, all of us—Eric, his parents, my mom, and me—would get Lucas back. I hated to put them all through grief, but there wasn't any other way around it. In the meantime, at least Scout and I were safe enough for now. The only loose end I could think of was Lacey, the ditsy cat sitter. Hopefully, she was already camping with her friends.

Both Scout and I were exhausted, so after we cleaned up our plates and fed the cat, I suggested getting some sleep. "I know it's early, but we're both tired," I said, like I was speaking to a child. Scout nodded wearily, then followed me into Christy's bedroom.

"This side of the bed is mine, okay? There's plenty of room for you on your side," I said, positioning the pillows. Maybe tomorrow

I'd see if Christy Carversen had any clothes that would fit me while I washed my own, but for tonight, I was sleeping in what I had on.

I left the light on in the hallway and left the door open a crack. We hadn't seen much of Boo the cat since we arrived, but I wasn't going to worry about her. Cats pretty much took care of themselves.

I thought Scout understood what it meant to stay on his own side, but as I was drifting off to sleep, I felt him nestle up to my backside, spooning against me. "Don't get any ideas," I grumbled. I was so tired, it took everything I had to get the words out.

He didn't answer, but now his arm was looped over me, pulling me into a warm hug. "Emma?" he whispered.

"Uh-huh?"

"What if Christy Carversen won't help us?" he said. Here we went again.

"Then I will *make* her help us," I said. "I've got a gun, remember?" I opened one eye halfway and could see the dark outline of the gun on the nightstand table. I yawned. "Now stop worrying and go to sleep."

There was a long pause and then he said, "Emma?"

"What?"

"I don't think Regina wants me back."

The worry in his voice pulled me out of my drowsiness. "Why would you say that?"

"On my planet, we do not choose our match. It is chosen for us."

"Yeah?"

"It's just . . ." His voice faltered. "Regina hates me."

I sat up. "She hates you?" I couldn't believe my ears. He was the sweetest soul ever. Hating Scout would be like hating Dory from *Finding Nemo.* "She said that?"

"No, but I can tell what she feels about me and it's not the same as what you feel for Lucas."

"Well, everyone's different," I said, "but if she doesn't love you, then she doesn't deserve you." I turned around to face him. "And who knows, maybe her feelings will change in time and she'll grow to love you."

"Regina likes doing things the right way and I did not follow orders. I left my ship." The anguish in his voice pierced through the darkness.

I reached out and stroked his head. "The orders were stupid. If you'd listened to them, you'd be dead like the others. Instead, you thought for yourself and were the only one who survived. That has to count for something."

"Maybe."

"Now go to sleep." I settled back down, my head on the pillow.

"Okay." He exhaled heavily. "But can I ask you just one more thing?"

A person would have to be pretty mean not to listen to just one more thing. "Sure, go ahead."

"Why do you say you are less than three?"

"What?"

"Why do you say you are less than three?" he repeated.

"I've never said that, Scout."

"Yes, you did." His tone was adamant. "In your emails to Lucas, you would put less than three next to your name."

"You read my emails?" I asked, irritated. Even given the circumstances, it seemed a violation of privacy.

"Yes, and they did not make sense. Why would you tell Lucas about the things you did together? If he was there, he would already know these things, wouldn't he?" His voice was tentative.

I sighed. "Yes, he already knew about most of it, but that wasn't the point. I wrote those emails so there would be a record for all time. So that our children and all the future generations to come would know about our love and what things were like for us when we were young." Tears filled my eyes. "Just forget about it. It was stupid."

"Why was it stupid?"

"Because there aren't going to be any future generations." I spoke quickly, wanting to get this over with. "The cancer treatment made Lucas sterile. He can't have children." I hoped this would end the conversation. "Good-night, Scout."

There was a long silence and then, as if he just couldn't help himself, Scout floated another question. "But why would you say you were less than three? It does not make sense. Your age is seventeen, and it is not the number of your house, or your phone number. I have been thinking very hard about it and I do not understand what it means."

I sighed. "It means 'love,' okay? That's just the way I signed everything I wrote to Lucas. Don't think of it as a number. It stands for love." I closed my eyes. It seemed like a week had passed since I'd left my house that morning. If I didn't get some sleep soon, I was going to lapse into a coma of my own.

Still, his voice, uncertain and soft, came drifting toward me. "But how does 'less than three' mean love?"

How to explain this? I thought for a moment and then said, "When you put the symbol for 'less than' next to the number 'three,' it looks like a heart on its side. And love comes from the heart." Outside, I could hear crickets chirping. If anyone pulled into the driveway, we'd hear it since the bedroom window faced the front.

"But you know, love doesn't really come from the heart," he said, eager to educate me. "The heart is a pump for your blood, which carries—"

"Go to sleep!"

"Okay, good-night, Emma."

"Good-night, Scout."

# CHAPTER THIRTY-FOUR

Scout couldn't sleep. He had an underlying awareness that the solution to the problem of the locked basement door was within his reach, but he couldn't quite figure out what that would be. When he finally remembered, he sat up suddenly.

"Emma?" he whispered, leaning over her. But she was sound asleep, one hand curled over her eyes like she was trying to block out the world. She looked so peaceful that he hated to disturb her.

Emma had been through a lot today, and all of it was because of him. His fault. He could feel her stress and worry, and knew it was a heavy load. He decided to let her sleep. He could take care of this problem himself.

When one of the universal keys he'd retrieved from the back of the van actually worked, and he saw the equipment set up in the secret room, he felt a shiver of anticipation, something he'd never felt on his own planet where so much was placid and predictable. The setup was primitive, but logical, and once he got it up and running, he knew how it all worked. The communications device was already sending out signals, a repeating pattern that he overrode with one of his own—a simple numeric language that everyone on his planet learned during their early educational years. Archaic, really, a throwback to earlier times. Communication for infants. He'd balked at having to learn it at the time, never imagining how useful it would prove to be when he was fully grown and stranded in another galaxy.

He tapped in his message over and over again, and paused between, waiting for a response. When one finally arrived, a smile stretched across his face. And when he discovered exactly who was on the other end, his fist involuntarily pumped upward in a burst of glee. The reaction felt perfect, but was so unlike him. Yes, this planet had definitely affected him.

# CHAPTER THIRTY-FIVE

The overhead light flicked on, making the bedroom as bright as day. I blinked and sat up in shock, finding myself staring down the barrel of a gun. My gun, the one Mrs. Kokesh gave me. A woman standing over me had it pointed right at my face.

"What are you doing in my house?" she said through gritted teeth.

I went from sound asleep into adrenaline overdrive in two-and-a-half seconds. "Don't shoot, don't shoot!" I raised my hands. "I can explain."

"You can explain to the police," she said.

"No, no," I said, protesting. "Don't call them." My mind reeled. "Or did you call them already?"

She hesitated and I saw from the look on her face that she *hadn't* called them. Yet. My hands still up, I said, "You're Christy Carversen, right?" My eyes were working well enough now that I could see that the gun's safety catch was still on. "I'm Emma Garson. We came here—" I glanced behind me and that's when I realized Scout was gone. "I'm here with a friend. We know about the radio signals you're sending out to space and we need your help. We were just waiting for you to get home."

Her face softened; I'd caught her off guard and she was unsure what to do next. The hand holding the gun was shaking and there was a healthy measure of fear in her eyes. "What makes you think I'm sending radio signals to space?"

"Well, you are, aren't you?"

Instead of answering, she lobbed a question back at me. "How did you get into my house?" Her avoidance of my question about the radio signals confirmed it for me: the big monstrosity in the backyard was for sending messages to other planets.

"Lacey let us in." I dropped my hands. "Could you put the gun down so we can talk? I promise I'm harmless."

"Lacey let you in," she repeated in disbelief, shaking her head. "Great. Just great."

I was willing to bet Lacey's cat-sitting days were over. "Lacey said you wouldn't be back for another day."

"I came back early to get . . . never mind, I just came back." Christy lowered the gun but didn't put it down. Still, I saw it as progress. "How many other people are with you?" Without the gun pointing at me, there was nothing scary about her. Just a skinny woman in her forties with severe features, a ratty T-shirt, and pants that were too short.

"Just one. My boyfriend," I said. "Well, he was my boyfriend. Now he's someone else." I stopped myself before I could go nervously rambling off topic. I took a deep breath. "Listen, I know how this looks, but could you just let us explain before you do anything?"

Her eyes darted to one side, like she was considering what to do, so I jumped in full speed before she could decide something I wasn't going to like. "My friend desperately needs to send a radio signal to another planet and we need your help."

Her eyebrows furrowed. "Who sent you here?"

"We came on our own." I got up off the bed and faced her, trying not to seem too menacing, which wasn't hard because she was at least six inches taller than me. "Once you talk to Scout, you'll understand why we need your help. It's a matter of life and death."

I gestured to the door. "He probably just got up to go to the bathroom or something. He wouldn't have left." I pushed past her and went for the door.

"He's not in the bathroom," Christy said, her voice trailing behind me. "Don't try anything. I still have the gun."

*Yeah, yeah.* I knew all about the gun. The one with the safety still on. "Scout? Scout!" Where could he have gone? I felt a clutch of fear, wondering if one of the agents could have captured him. No, I'd been sleeping right next to him. I would have woken up if anyone had tried to take him.

"Your friend's not here," Christy said. "I've already searched the house and you're the only one I found."

*Could he have gone outside to look at the satellite dish? In the dark?* Now I was starting to worry. *Where could he be?* "Scout?"

"Your boyfriend's name is Scout?"

"Yes." I kept going. When I walked past the basement door, I noticed a sliver of light underneath. We'd turned off the lights earlier, I was sure of it. "He must be downstairs," I said, flinging open the door and bounding down the wooden stairs.

Behind me, I heard Christy say, "You better not be trying something."

"I wouldn't do that," I said over my shoulder. "Not when you have a gun."

Downstairs, I was relieved to see the bookcase swung away from the wall. The metal door was now unlocked, and slightly open. I couldn't see into the room, but I could tell that the light was on. I stopped short in the doorway, stunned to see Scout sitting in a desk chair with his back to the door, headphones on his head. His head was bobbing as if he was listening to music and he was tapping away at a keyboard like he was writing a novel. The cat, Boo, was nestled in his lap. In front of him was the kind of console and semicircle of monitors I knew from the movie famous for the classic line, "Houston, we have a problem." One of the screens showed a graph, the line rising and falling like a lie detector; the second displayed an audio line, the kind you'd see in a recording studio; and the third was filled with columns of numbers scrolling at a dizzying speed. On the dashboard were dozens of levers and dials. I had trouble reconciling the one side of the basement, the laundry side, with this hidden room. Who would have guessed that Christy Carversen had her own secret space station under her house?

I went to get Scout's attention, but before I even got close, I was yanked back by Christy Carversen. "Not so fast," she said, her voice harsh. She came up behind Scout and ripped the headphones off his head, then stuck the barrel of the gun next to his ear. "Get up. We're going upstairs *now*."

Scout turned around and, when he saw me, a smile spread across his face. "Emma," he said, "I have found a way to email Regina." His voice rang with happiness.

"Get up *now*," Christy said, waving the gun.

"Scout, this is Ms. Carversen," I said. She had a wild-eyed look that worried me. "We need to go upstairs now to talk to her."

"Hi, Ms. Carversen," he said, extending his hand.

"It's *Doctor* Carversen," she said. "How did you get in this room?" Her voice had such a sharp edge that she scared the cat, who leapt off Scout's lap and ran past us and up the stairs.

"With a universal key," Scout said. "There are many possible combinations and one of them worked with this lock."

His explanation made me want to slap my forehead. Of course! The box in the back of the van labeled "Universal Kit." The one that held the weird-looking keys. How did that slip my mind? So stupid of me. I could only guess that he couldn't sleep, remembered the contents of the box and tried the keys, and then, once he got the door open, went straight to work. I wished Scout had come and gotten me. He had either wanted to let me sleep or thought I would slow him down.

Even though she'd asked, Christy didn't seem all that interested in the answer. She said, "I want both of you to walk in front of me. Slowly. When we get upstairs, sit down at the kitchen table. You're going to be answering some questions."

After all of us had trooped upstairs and were seated at the kitchen table, Christy relaxed a bit and actually set the gun down on the table in front of her. "I'll give you five minutes," she said, "and I'd better like what I hear."

"So you're not going to call the police?" I asked.

"No. Yes. Maybe."

Scout leaned forward, both hands flat on the table. "She does not want to call the police because she's afraid they might find out about the satellite dish and the radio signals. And then the people at Erickson Ryder will know about it too. She is only talking to us because she's worried about what we know."

One glance at Christy's face and I knew he'd picked up on her thoughts. She stuttered, "Erickson Ryder? So you're with them. Did they send you here?"

"No, no, no. Not at all," I protested. "The opposite really. We've been trying to get away from them. Believe me, we're here on our own."

A slight smile crossed her face. "Okay, then. You said you needed my help. That it was a matter of life and death. So talk. And make it fast."

I took a deep breath, thinking about where to begin. A quick look at Scout showed that he wasn't going to be any help. His lips were pressed firmly together and his gaze was at Dr. Carversen's forehead. I said, "We need your help sending a radio signal to the planet Erickson Ryder was able to reach. My friend here—" A jolt of pain hit my calf as Scout kicked me under the table. I bit my lip and sucked in to keep from crying out and he took over in that split second.

"We are students of astrophysics," he said with conviction. "And we are taking part in SETI at home."

*What?* I gave him a questioning look, but he was concentrating on her and didn't see it.

"SETI at home?" she asked, sounding puzzled.

"It stands for Search for Extraterrestrial Intelligence," he said. "We have been assisting the US government in receiving radio frequencies from space and determining if there is an intelligent pattern."

My mouth dropped open. *Why was he saying this?*

"I know what it stands for." Christy sounded impatient. "But what does that have to do with you breaking into my house?"

He went on. "I've picked up data that shows you've made contact and that the alien spacecraft will be landing nearby sometime tonight. It will happen in a clearing that you gave them coordinates for." His eyes flicked from me to the gun on the table in front of Christy. A message. "We are here because we want to witness this. You will need to take us to the landing area."

"You're talking crazy," Christy said, her eyes narrowing. "I don't know where you got this so-called information. Alien spacecraft?" She leaned back and laughed theatrically. "That's rich."

"Our sources are reliable," Scout said. "The information is good."

Christy shook her head. "We've all had a good laugh, but I'm done placating you. You kids need to get your van out of my garage and toodle on home. You're lucky I don't call the authorities on you."

Scout gave me a subtle nod of his head, and I grabbed the gun, aiming it right at Christy.

# CHAPTER THIRTY-SIX

"Whoa, whoa, whoa," she said, holding up her hands and pushing her chair back. "What the hell is this?"

"Don't move," I said, not sure how to answer the question. My eyes darted to Scout, who calmly stood up.

"We need to leave right away," he said. "How far is it to the landing area?"

"Is that a real gun?" she asked, her voice quavering.

"Of course it's real," I said. "And when you release the safety catch, it even shoots." I made a show of doing just that. I turned to Scout. "What's the plan?"

"Christy Carversen walked here tonight from the landing site, so it cannot be far. She forgot something and came back to get it." His forehead furrowed as he spoke; he was listening to her thoughts. "A camera. She and her brother want to blow up this ship like they did the other one and she wants to record it. Her brother is Woodcarver on the message forum."

I said, "No kidding?"

Scout said, "No, I am not kidding." His tone was so serious I almost laughed. He continued. "She was fired from Erickson Ryder for stealing company secrets about the radio signals. Erickson Ryder wanted to be the ones to make the first contact because it would make them famous for history. But she and her brother shot the ship down."

"Where are you getting this?" Christy asked. "Who have you been talking to?" Her eyes flashed with anger.

Scout looked around. "We will need flashlights to see and we need to hurry. They arranged this meeting with the ship some days ago and it will happen tonight."

"That's it, I'm calling the police," Christy said, but I still had the gun aimed at her and she didn't move, not even an inch, so I knew it was an idle threat.

"Why do we need flashlights?" I asked. "Can't we drive there?"

Scout shook his head. "It is deep in the woods and there are no roads. Christy and her brother own all the property for miles around. They inherited it from their grandparents."

I asked, "But why would your people send another ship if the first one was blown up?" After the last fiasco, I would have thought they'd avoid our planet altogether.

"They are coming back to get me," Scout said, a thin smile stretching across his face.

I had a million questions then, but the words never got a chance to leave my mouth because at that moment, Christy rushed at me and slammed me in the face with her fist, knocking me against the wall. The back of my head hit the wall so hard I saw an entire constellation. Off balance, I slid to the floor, the gun still in my hand. It happened so fast I didn't have time to react. I was on the floor, dazed and in pain, and could only watch as she wrenched open the back door and ran outside.

"Hey!" I yelled weakly. "Get back here or I'll shoot!" My empty threat trailed her as she fled through the back door.

I staggered to my feet, intending to go after her, but Scout held out his arm to stop me. "We need to follow her," I said, waving an arm in her direction, frantic we might lose the trail.

"Not to worry, Emma. She showed me in her thoughts where it is. I know the way."

"But what if she calls the police?" I sputtered. "Or gets her brother and they come after us?"

Scout shook his head. "She knows there is no time. The ship will be here soon." He tipped his head to one side and placed a hand on my sore cheek, flinching at exactly the same time I did, feeling my pain. "Nothing is broken," he said. "I am sorry I did not stop her. I only knew she was going to do that as she did it. She is not a person who thinks things through."

I nodded and then suddenly remembered: "There are flash-lights in the van."

A few minutes later, we were out the back door, lights shining ahead of us. I'd grabbed my backpack and stuck the gun, safety on, in the front zippered compartment. Without the guts to use it, it was just a chunk of metal, but who knew? It still might come in handy. Better to have it and not need it, than need it and not have it.

Scout led the way, past the enormous satellite dish and through the open gate, which Christy had left ajar. She had a few min-utes on us, but she couldn't be too far ahead. The moonlight was blocked by the canopy of tree branches overhead, so we had to rely on the flashlights to see the way. I found myself walking carefully, not wanting to trip over any roots or branches, unable to focus on anything but the next step.

"I don't understand," I said, going right behind Scout, my fin-gers pinching the back of his shirt. "A ship is just going to appear to pick you up? How did this happen?"

"I was able to send a message to Regina. She told me they have been able to retrieve information from the ship that exploded and so they knew one of the pods had ejected to safety. She suspected it might be me. They have been looking."

"How did they retrieve the information if the ship exploded?"

"You know about an airplane's black box?"

"Yes."

"This is like that. But it's not black." He exhaled loudly. "And it's not a box either."

Deeper and deeper into the woods we went, pushing branches aside, stepping over roots and logs. I still had questions. "How are they getting here so fast?"

"Christy Carversen set it up some time ago. She told them she had something left over from the crash and arranged a meeting. They thought it would be me, but really she did not have anything. It was just a trick."

"Not much of a trick," I muttered.

"She and her brother want to blow up this ship too. They have missile launchers that sit on a person's shoulder. He was going to destroy the ship and she was going to film it."

"But why go to all that trouble? For what reason?"

"There is not a good reason. They have just decided that those from other planets are the enemy." I heard the shrug in his voice. "Like you said, some people here are mentally ill, or just evil."

Before I could ask my next question, Scout had already anticipated it. "Do not worry, Emma. My people will be prepared this time. No harm will come to them."

We continued on, deeper into the woods. In another lifetime, a dark summer night like this was made for Lucas and me. Because of his mother, we cherished our time alone and really made those minutes count: holding hands on the porch, sneaking out to the barn, kissing under the stars. But if those memories felt like a dream, this night, this walk in the dark, was my nightmare come to life. The swing of the flashlight beams turned the tree limbs into monster arms reaching for us, and the clammy night air made my T-shirt stick to my back. Around us, unidentifiable rustling noises worried me. Worse still was the knot in my stomach, the nagging feeling that we were walking into a trap. Ahead of me, Scout moved faster and faster, spurred on by the promise of Regina and home.

Scout must have sensed the dread I was feeling because he stopped and said, "It's okay, Emma. It will all be fine."

"How can you be so sure?" My hand tightened around his arm, the bicep nearly as strong now as Lucas's once was.

"Because Regina was not mad, not at all," he said, as if that explained everything. "Remember how you said if she loved me she would never give up on me? I did not believe it, but you were right, Emma. She did not give up. She was happy to hear from me. She told me that I was smart to eject and that it was resourceful of me to find a host. And Regina said if I had died she would never have taken another match. She said she would have been alone until the end of her days."

"That's real nice, Scout, but that Christy woman is a complete wacko and her brother has a missile launcher. Has it occurred to you that they might attack us? They might be here right now, hiding behind those trees, ready to jump us." I pointed to a thicket just to the right of where we stood.

He stuck the flashlight under his arm and put a hand on either side of my face. "I would feel them if they were nearby. Really, Emma, it is going to be fine. Regina said they are coming and they will take me home."

"Okay, well, how is this going to work? I mean you'll go out of Lucas, but how exactly? Will they have another pod for you or something?" I thought about his original pod, still locked up in the van.

"I will not need a pod to go home. Regina said they have it all worked out."

I wiped my forehead and sighed. "And how is it that you were able to email Regina?"

"It wasn't really email, Emma," he said, shaking his head at my foolishness. "That's just what I called it so you would have a point of reference. Our communication was done by manipulating radio waves. Primitive, but effective." He took my hand. "Come on, we'll walk together. Soon you will have Lucas back and I will be going home and everything will be fine."

There didn't seem to be a path as far as I could tell, but Scout moved as surely as if he'd grown up in these woods. He had a firm grip on my hand and I let myself be pulled along, even though I felt sure we were heading to our doom. We'd probably only been walking for fifteen or twenty minutes, but it felt much longer.

"Are we getting close?" I asked and Scout said, "Yes."

*Stupid me*, I thought, *asking the guy who came from another galaxy if a clearing in the north woods of Wisconsin is close.* Relatively speaking, to him, everything on Earth was close.

A few minutes later, we sloshed through a small creek. We heard the rush of water before we saw it. It trickled in a shallow bed so narrow a person could lay across the width of it and touch each bank. I flashed my light over the creek and nodded as Scout indicated we needed to be on the other side.

"The landing place is just ahead," Scout said, steadying me as we crossed. Our shoes became soaked, but there was no time to think about it, because after we made our way through it, Scout broke into a jog. As excited as he was to get there, I felt just the opposite. He still had my hand, but I wasn't in step with him anymore. In fact, I lagged behind, trying to be the voice of reason.

"Let's scope out the situation first," I whispered. For all his time on Earth, all the movies viewed, articles read, and thoughts and feelings he'd taken on, he still seemed innocent, like a child who knew bad things happened, but didn't seem to think they could happen to him. I knew that his intellect surpassed anything on Earth, but sometimes, frankly, he just seemed dumb.

I pulled him back to explain my plan—that we could hide in the woods just beyond the clearing and see if Christy and her brother were there, then wait to determine if they had weapons. I

wasn't sure what we'd do then, but knowledge is power and I figured staying hidden would give us an advantage. I had only just
started explaining this to Scout when I was interrupted by a rhythmic noise that came from above us. I tipped my head to listen as
the faint sound became louder and louder, finally becoming deafening. I'd know that sound anywhere. The chopping noise of the
blades of a helicopter. The air stirred as it passed overhead. And
then, after that, there came another helicopter, and then another.
Three enormous helicopters flying above us.

"Come on," Scout yelled, pulling on my arm. "Something is
happening."

# CHAPTER THIRTY-SEVEN

Scout released my arm and broke into a run. I hurried after him, my backpack banging against my hip, branches whipping across my face. I didn't even watch to see where I was going. I just followed the spike of his light waving ahead of us. The helicopters were loud, and as the noise got more intense, I knew they were landing somewhere just ahead of us. My current level of exhaustion made it hard to sort through all the thoughts running through my head. Were Christy and her brother expecting helicopters? Scout hadn't mentioned it, and he rarely missed anything.

"Wait," I called out, but Scout wasn't waiting for me or anyone else.

When the clearing was in sight, he stopped so quickly that I slammed into his back. A space the size of a baseball diamond had been scraped bare, the edges rimmed with the kind of solar lights you buy at a gardening store. There was no sign of Christy or her brother, but we saw the first helicopter land on the far side. The noise echoed across the field while the blades stirred up a cloud of dust. The chopper was nothing like the news helicopters I'd seen around town. This one had a body almost as long as a school bus and a shape that screamed "military." As we watched, the doors to the helicopter opened and eight people in camouflage carrying automatic weapons jumped out. While the blades wound down, a man and a woman in civilian clothes exited right behind them, the man holding his hand out for the woman, who pushed it aside and got out of the helicopter without assistance. I caught a glimpse of her face when she jumped to the ground. I would have known her anywhere. Federal Agent Mariah Wilson. Which meant the guy next to her was her crony, Agent Todd Goodman.

In short order, the second and third helicopter landed, and just like with the first, a crew of armed soldiers jumped out. The soldiers fanned out and went into the woods at precise intervals, following the orders of one man. Meanwhile, Agent Wilson spoke into a handheld radio. I heard yelling off in the distance, but I couldn't make out the words. They weren't close to us now, but if they were doing a thorough sweep they'd find us in no time. I pulled Scout farther back into the woods and put my hands on either side of his face.

"We have to leave now," I said. "If we hurry, we can get back to the van and drive somewhere while they're busy looking out here."

"No," he said firmly. "I am not leaving."

"We *have* to go." I grabbed his arm to steer him back the way we came, but he was immovable. A rock. He threw his arms around me and pulled me into a deep hug, forcing me to stand still. My face was buried in his chest, my ear so close I could hear the beating of his heart. On the other side of the field, I was aware of movement and the voices of men shouting directions. It sounded like a war movie right before the gunfire started. "They're going to find us," I said, lifting my head to look in his eyes. I pleaded, "Let's just go back."

Scout smiled and sang, "Hate to leave you, Emily," and stroked my hair. "Remember that?"

We didn't have time for a journey down memory lane. "Of course, but—"

"I will never forget it," he said, his voice calm. "I will never forget the car dancing, and what it is to have fun, and all the feelings.

So many feelings. I want to remember my earth brother who believed me, and I will remember seeing your blue sky, so pale and changing. I have learned so much on this odd planet. The people, all so different. Some are cruel, but so many are good all the way through. Everything is different here. I did not like being here at first, but now I know I will miss it. And I will miss you, Emma."

A lump formed in my throat. He thought he was leaving tonight, but I didn't see how that was going to happen. His ship certainly wouldn't land with all these people here. Even if they were willing to risk being seen, the field was full of helicopters. There was no place to land.

"Scout, if you don't go home tonight, we can always figure something else out. Now that Regina knows you're here—"

"One more thing. I have changed this body and I am leaving a gift for Lucas," he said, smiling. "He will have perfect health and he will never get cancer again."

"That's good. Thank you."

"I am leaving a gift for you too. Generations to come will read your emails."

I blinked, thinking I'd misheard. "I'm sorry," I said. "I don't understand." But a second later his meaning hit me, and I *did* understand. Generations to come. He meant our children and grandchildren and great-grandchildren. Scout was saying that Lucas wouldn't be infertile anymore. Someday, there could be a baby.

Hearing my thoughts, he nodded in affirmation, then leaned down and kissed my brow.

"Oh." I looked up at him, not knowing what to say. When the doctor told Lucas the cancer treatment would make him sterile, he'd been bitter about it, but I'd told him I didn't care. That all I cared about was that he would live. And this was basically true, but now, knowing I could have his child was like getting a gift wrapped in a miracle.

Scout said, "When I'm gone, will you remember me?"

Tears filled my eyes. "Every day of my life." I wiped my eyes with my fingertips. "Thank you."

There was a commotion out on the field. Distracted, we peered through the bushes and saw one of the soldiers walking Christy Carversen out of the woods, his gun aimed at her back. She had her hands up. A resolute look crossed Scout's face and he released me from his grasp.

"Good-bye, Emma," he said. "I need to go." And then, before I could stop him, he ran out onto the field, straight toward the soldiers, his hands raised in the air.

# CHAPTER THIRTY-EIGHT

"Scout, no! Wait!" I dropped my backpack and flashlight and followed him out onto the field, my arms raised in the air, my breathing ragged. The soldiers, grouped in clusters across the clearing, caught sight of us a moment later, and their guns snapped to attention right at us. Scout, oblivious to how this worked, kept on going. A cannon-sized light swung in our direction, blinding me for a moment.

A man's voice boomed out over the field: "Drop the weapon immediately!"

I stopped, confused. Neither of us had a weapon. Why did they think we did? "We're unarmed," I yelled. "Scout, stop!" I could barely see him through the glare as he trotted forward, not listening.

"Drop your weapon *now* and get on the ground or we'll shoot." The voice came over some kind of speaker as loud as an announcer at a sports event. I threw myself down, not wanting to die that night, or any night really, but definitely not that one. Above my head, gunfire cracked, making me shudder, and then, just like that, it was over. I raised my head to look and saw soldiers trotting across the field toward me, their boots eye level with my face. I flinched, waiting for the inevitable, but they went right past me. I craned my neck to look behind me and saw a man down on the ground, a rocket launcher lying a few feet away from his out-stretched arm. Some other men jogged by with a stretcher, and a lone man came after, toting a medical box. I watched as they lifted the man I assumed to be Christy Carversen's brother, Woodcarver. The patient shouted out a string of curse words as they attended to his injuries. So he wasn't dead, just wounded.

Suddenly, Agent Mariah Wilson was standing above me, her hand extended. I took it and she pulled me to my feet. "We meet again, Ms. Garson," she said. "You're not so good at following directions, I see."

My fear melted into despair. In a minute, we were going to be hauled off, interrogated, and maybe killed, or charged with some fake crime. All of this, the planning, the car ride, the close calls, opening the locked basement door, reaching Regina—all that, and Scout still wouldn't make it home? No, this just wasn't right. It couldn't all be for nothing.

Downfield, I saw Scout talking to Agent Goodman and point-ing to the sky.

"I don't have anything to say to you," I said, thinking that Scout was probably saying plenty already. "Why can't you just leave us alone? We're not hurting anyone. Why can't you just go and forget you ever saw us?"

She shook her head. "That's not going to happen. Come with me." I hesitated and she said, "I asked you nicely. If I have to ask again it's not going to be so nice." I looked around at all the soldiers with guns and knew I didn't have a choice.

Agent Wilson gripped my elbow so tightly I swear her fingers dug all the way in until they found bone. She pulled me along, past one helicopter and a group of soldiers who barely looked my way. When we reached Agent Goodman and Scout, she said, "Cuff 'em. I don't want to lose these two again."

Agent Todd Goodman said, "Do you think that's necessary? They're just kids." She raised both eyebrows, and he said, "Okay.

Got it." He pulled two sets of handcuffs seemingly out of nowhere and then had Scout turn around while he clicked a set onto his wrists.

When it was my turn, I blinked tears away, determined to be strong. "Are we being charged with something?" I asked, remembering what Roy Atkins, the senior citizen–square-dancing moonshiner, had said. "Because I don't think you can hold us if you aren't charging us."

"Yeah, we're charging you with disturbing the peace," Mariah Wilson said, chuckling.

"Can't we just wait here for a while? My friend is meeting someone here. They'll expect him to be here tonight." I made a good case, I thought, but she didn't even turn her head in my direction.

She ignored me, tapping on the side of the chopper and addressing Agent Goodman. "Get 'em inside."

It wasn't easy to climb in with our hands cuffed behind our backs, but Agent Goodman helped guide us to our seats, then buckled our seat belts for us.

"I'm sorry it ended up this way," I said to Scout, who sat next to the window. He was watching as they loaded Christy Carversen and her brother, strapped to a gurney, into another helicopter.

He gestured out the window with a tip of his head and spoke softly. "Christy and her brother hate people from other planets, because their grandfather was taken once by a spaceship and probed. He said they hurt him badly. It is a family story that has caused much hatred."

"Do you believe that story?" I asked. Out on the field, soldiers were getting their final orders and lining up to get back on the choppers.

"I have heard of it happening." He shrugged. "But no one from my planet would do such a thing. It is not our way."

The two federal agents sat down in seats facing us, the pilot behind them. A crew of soldiers entered the chopper from the opposite side and filed in, barely glancing our way as they moved past to take their seats. If they were curious, they didn't show it. None of them would have helped us, even if they knew the whole story. They knew their duty. The world was divided into us and them, and we weren't them.

After the doors slammed shut, Agent Goodman turned around and gave the pilot the okay to take off. The engine started up with a mighty vibration, accompanied by the roar of the whirring blades. I yelled, "Where are you taking us?"

Agent Wilson just shook her head and looked annoyed. We lifted sharply into the air, the suddenness giving my stomach a rollercoaster-ride lurch. It didn't help that the cuffs dug into my wrists. I leaned against Scout and tried to give him a reassuring smile, even though I wasn't really feeling it. He met my eyes and nodded before turning his attention back to the window.

We hovered above the tree line, and I saw the lights of the other helicopters as they rose and flanked us. Our seats rumbled as we were jostled from side to side; the noise was incredible. If my hands had been free, I would have covered my ears. Through the window, I saw the field, dotted with the solar lights, so very small from up here. I felt someone's eyes on me and I looked up to see Mariah Wilson, her arms folded and a grin on her face. I didn't need to have Scout's ability to pick up on her smug satisfaction. The chopper went up again and then, abruptly, it stopped and I saw Mariah Wilson's expression change to surprise, her facial muscles moving in slow motion. And then everything began to happen in slow motion.

The sound of the blades became muffled and the view out our window softened. We could still see the dark night sky, but it seemed to be off in the distance, like looking through a sheet of waved glass far beyond. The best I could make out was that the helicopters had been lifted up inside of something enormous that now encased us, causing our actions to slow down like moving through water.

"What's . . . going . . . on?" Agent Goodman yelled, the words stretching like someone had reduced the film speed.

Peering down, I saw that, below us, what looked like giant glass doors, larger than the landing field, were pulling shut, and now the ground below appeared as gauzy as a dream. All around us, the stars shone as if we were seeing them through a prism. My sense of reality had become distorted; I was mesmerized by the way time and space were reshaping around us, but having trouble making sense of it.

If I had to guess, I'd say we were inside a giant, transparent spaceship. The helicopters were stuck in place, and the space outside the window was hazy. I was able to make out movement within the opalescent murkiness. People? I wasn't quite sure. The shapes were generally right: a head, body, and limbs, but it was so indistinct I couldn't tell.

It took an enormous effort to turn my head to look at Scout. His smile confirmed my guess. His ship had come and, instead of landing on the ground or beaming him up like in the movies, it had swallowed all of us whole. Just as Mrs. Kokesh had predicted, we were in the belly of the whale. Scout leaned forward, his movements deft and quick compared to the rest of us, and he rested a hand on each of the agent's knees.

"Once you land, you will need to let Emma go. Do you understand?" he said, speaking firmly. "You have to release her *right away*. Nothing will be more important than letting her go." Both of them nodded compliantly. He added, "Do not bother her, or anyone she knows, ever again."

Then he sat back and turned to me, a warm smile stretching across his face. "I have to go now," he said, leaning over to kiss my cheek. "You have been everything to me, Emma. Do not forget me."

The door opened and closed, and he was gone before my lips could even part to speak a word. Where he'd been sitting, the seat belt was unfastened, and the handcuffs, now open, rested on the empty seat. He left so quickly it reminded me of a magician's stage show where they disappear in a puff of smoke. Except there'd been no smoke. One second, Scout was in the seat next to mine, and the next, he was gone in a blur and the slam of the door, taking my boyfriend's body with him. Through the window, I saw the outline of that same body walking away from the helicopter. Other forms rushed toward him as if in greeting. Happy to have him back.

The last thing I remember was calling out to him, my words coming out thick and slow. "Scout, wait—what about Lucas?" I can't honestly say if this part actually happened. Later, it all felt like a dream.

# CHAPTER THIRTY-NINE

We all came to at about the same time, gaining consciousness as if we'd been in a deep sleep and were slowly waking up. The helicopters were down on the ground now, parked on the landing field. The engines were off, so everything was dead silent and dark. I had no idea how much time had elapsed or how we'd gotten from inside an alien ship back to Earth. I blinked a few times, wanting to rub my eyes, but my hands were still cuffed. The agents, still sitting across from me, were trying to make sense of what had happened. They remembered much less than I did and I wasn't about to bring them up to speed. Scout's empty seat and instructions loomed in their minds, but they couldn't recall the specifics. Just the feelings he'd imparted, and the importance of letting me go and not bothering me or anyone I knew, ever again.

Agent Wilson got up to talk to the pilot and I heard his voice as he spoke to the other pilots via the radio. There was no record of the interruption and no one seemed to know what had occurred from the time of the first takeoff until now. "We'll proceed as originally planned?" the pilot said and I held my breath.

"Just one minute," I heard Agent Wilson say. The light came on in the cabin. She came back to her seat and spoke to Agent Goodman. "Take the cuffs off her."

He got up dutifully and released my seat belt. I leaned forward and twisted so he could reach my hands, and in a few seconds, I was free. I rubbed my wrists and shook my hands to get the cramps out. "What are you going to do?" I asked, but now they were whispering to each other, not paying any attention to me.

Mariah Wilson roughly slid open the door and pointed a finger at the opening. "Out you go," she said.

I looked at the field delineated by the dim solar lights and weighed my options. If I left now, how would I ever contact Scout and arrange to get Lucas back? Or maybe, and this was a horrible, unthinkable thought, maybe this had been Scout's plan all along. Perhaps he lied to get me to help him all the while having no intention of returning Lucas to me ever. Maybe there was no way to extract Scout from Lucas's body and have Lucas remain unharmed. I knew it was possible but I didn't want to believe it. After all, Scout had said he'd been in Mack's body, and the dog was fine after he left.

I hesitated and then said, "Is there someone who can help me send a radio signal to a planet? The one Christy Carversen contacted?"

"Get. Out. Now," she said.

I scrambled out of the helicopter and looked back to see her making a shooing gesture, like I was an annoying fly. I walked away from the helicopter, in the direction of the woods that stood between me and Christy Carversen's house. From behind, I heard the helicopters start up, engines rumbling, blades whirring. The motion stirred the night air and lifted my hair off my shoulders. I stopped to look back and saw them rise up above the tree line, then take off in formation. Two minutes later, there was no sign they were ever there. It was just me, all alone in northern Wisconsin, feeling more desperate and afraid than I'd ever felt in my life. I looked up at the stars.

"Where are you, Lucas?" I said aloud, but there was only the rustling of the wind and the chirp of insects in response.

I wandered slowly to the edge of the field and found my flashlight and backpack right where I'd dropped them. I slung the backpack over one shoulder and turned on the light. I focused on getting back to Christy Carversen's house, and tried to block out my fear and grief, but still I had nagging thoughts. How could I return home without Lucas? And more importantly, how could I live without him? I took a deep breath. *Just one step in front of the other* became my mantra. I pushed aside branches and stepped around tree roots, hoping I was heading in the right direction.

I walked for what seemed like a long time, and more than once, I wondered if I'd made a bad turn and was actually lost in the woods. I could die out here, I realized, and no one would know it. The thought scared me and brought me some odd comfort too. If going on this trip caused me to lose Lucas, what right did I have to keep on living? I was sure Mrs. Walker would agree with me.

When my flashlight shone through the last cluster of trees and reflected off something metallic, I breathed a sigh of relief. I had reached the open gate in Christy's backyard, right behind the giant satellite dish. Even knowing that no one was home, going into the house by myself in the dark seemed scarier than before, when Scout and I had gone in together. The back door was still unlocked and I let myself in, flipping on the light switch. I stood there frozen. *Now what?* I got my answer when a black cat came out from hiding and wound her way around my ankles.

"Hey, Boo," I said, leaning over to rub her ears. Poor thing couldn't help it if her owner was a sociopath.

I went to the kitchen cupboards and got out several large bowls, then filled them with water and cat food. Who knew how long Boo would be here alone? Then I went downstairs to see if I could use the computer in Christy's secret lair to contact someone on another planet.

# CHAPTER FORTY

When Scout thought back on his time on Earth, he compared it to *The Outlaw from San Antonio*. Just like in the movie, there were bad guys: the Carversens who did evil deeds to avenge their grandfather; the people from Erickson Ryder who broke the law so they could be the first to make contact; and the federal agents, especially Mariah Wilson. She had no problem with wrong-doing if it helped her get ahead in her job.

Revenge. Pride. Greed. He recognized all of these things from the movie and marveled at how they existed in real life as well. Humans were willing to kill others for such silly reasons.

But there were heroes on Earth too, just like in the movie. Eric, of course, and Beverly and Roy Atkins. But the biggest hero was Emma. She was afraid so much of the time, but it did not stop her. She risked her life for Lucas, and for Scout too. Love trumps logic every time, she'd said. He didn't understand it at first, but now he did.

# CHAPTER FORTY-ONE

More than an hour later, it was nearly morning, and I'd given up on being able to contact Scout's planet using the computer system in Christy's basement. I had no idea how Scout was able to do it. I could turn the thing on and that's where I stopped. After that, I was stuck and frustrated, randomly hitting keys and typing in fake passwords, none of which worked. I couldn't think straight and I was getting angry. How could Scout have done this to me? He knew the deal. I would help him return to his home planet and he would make sure I got Lucas back. I'd kept my end of the bargain, but he just took off, knowing there was nothing I could do about it. I felt betrayed. I slammed my fist on the keyboard. In the movies, this would have magically linked me to the right feed. Instead, the side of my hand hurt like hell and I felt like an idiot.

When I finally decided to give up, it was a relief. I plodded up the creaky wooden stairs, leaving the creepy basement behind. There was nothing for me here, and as long as I stayed, there was a chance I'd get in trouble for trespassing. I fished the keys to the van out of my backpack, gave Boo one more pat, and went out to the garage.

Once I'd backed down the driveway, the GPS set for home, my despair came to the surface. I couldn't hold it back any longer. There were too many tears for me to wipe them away; my sobs were loud and ugly. I drove down the winding road, the sun coming up over the horizon. A new day for everyone else, but the end for me. I'd foolishly believed that if I did everything right, I'd get Lucas back. How could I have been so trusting? I gripped the steering wheel wondering what I was going to say to Mr. and Mrs. Walker. How could I explain that we'd left together, but I'd returned alone? They were going to hate me, but not any more than I hated myself.

I could barely see through my tear-rimmed eyes, but it didn't matter. There was no traffic this time of day. The glint of the sun on the dewy grass made everything sparkle. The ditches were lush with wild tiger lilies, their beauty a contrast to my feelings of despair. For a split second I was distracted by the flowers, and when I returned my gaze straight forward, I was startled to see a man off in the distance. He stood stock-still in the middle of the road, his feet planted on either side of the center line, his familiar silhouette outlined by the rising sun. I slammed on the brakes and the van screeched to a halt, stopping twenty feet short.

Throwing the van into park, I jumped out of the vehicle, running and throwing myself at him. "Lucas!" I said, and that's all I could manage. The tears were coming fast and furiously, but they were now tears of joy.

He wrapped his arms around me, giving me his warmth and strength. I started shaking and clung to him. He smoothed my hair and said, "It's okay, Emma. It's okay. I'm back. Everything's going to be fine."

# CHAPTER FORTY-TWO

At some point, Scout knew he would need to take Lucas's body with him. They had been together so long that the extraction process would be complex, requiring a team effort. On the ship, the experts set to work immediately, separating his essence from Lucas with such care that the host body remained unharmed. How much easier it would have been to just pull out Scout and cast off the body he no longer needed, but that was not an option. He could not do that to Emma.

Once Scout was out, and Lucas had recovered from the trauma, the team focused on Emma's location as she traveled away from the house, calculating the distance and time, then transporting Lucas so he would be directly in her path. Scout was not able to see the resulting reunion, but he knew it would be joyous. He would have given anything to have felt that emotion along with them.

An interesting thing happened as a result of the two of them, Lucas and Scout, existing for a time as one. A small part of Scout remained in every fiber of Lucas's being; as for Scout, he now experienced life as someone who had once been Lucas.

He was forever changed.

# CHAPTER FORTY-THREE

Getting back in the van and putting on our seat belts, I couldn't help but stare at Lucas sitting in the passenger seat. He caught me looking and smiled. "Yes, it's me," he said.

But, of course, I'd known it was Lucas the moment I'd laid eyes on him.

"What do you remember?" I asked. His voice was the same and he looked like himself, although his clothing was rumpled and dirty. "Do you know what happened?"

"I remember some things," he said. "I remember being sick in the bed in the dining room and my parents talking about me dying. I didn't want to die, but I felt so terrible and I was so tired. And then. . ." His voice trailed off and he looked straight ahead at the windshield.

"And then?" I prompted, reaching over to run the back of my hand over his cheek.

Lucas turned to look at me. "And then it seemed like someone took over and my body felt so much better after that, but I was submerged sort of. I can't really explain it. I felt like I did when I was going under anesthesia right at the end where you hear the doctors talking off in the distance, but you can't get a grasp on things. I was there, but I wasn't really there . . . I know it doesn't make sense."

"Do you want me to tell you what happened?" I asked.

He ran his fingers through his hair. "That would help."

So I told him the whole story, beginning with my visit to Mrs. Kokesh to get the potion and ending with the helicopter dropping me off at the field and my failed attempt to contact Scout's planet using the equipment in Christy Carversen's basement. "And then I got in the van to drive home and I was crying my eyes out when I saw you standing in the middle of the road. After that, well, you know the rest." He took some time to let it all sink in and when a minute or two had passed, I said, "I know it's hard to believe."

"Oh no, I believe it," he said. "Now everything makes sense. I felt like I was possessed, kind of. I remember bits and pieces. There were times I even had a little bit of control. Sometimes I would try to tell him what to do."

"You did? Like what?"

"I told him to lean in because that girl wanted to kiss him."

"What girl?"

"The one watching the cat."

"Lacey?"

"Yeah."

I playfully slapped his arm. "Why would you do that?"

"She so wanted it and I knew if he kissed her, she would leave without a fuss." He took in my disapproving stare and laughed. "What? It wasn't me, it was him."

"Still. It was your lips."

He grinned. "Does anyone know about this besides you and Eric?"

"Just Mrs. Kokesh." *If she were still alive, that is*, I thought grimly.

"My parents didn't figure out that something was wrong?"

I shook my head. "Not a clue."

"That's good." He nodded. "My mother couldn't have handled it." He leaned over and I thought he was going to kiss me, so I leaned in too, but instead he brushed my hair away from my face. "Emma Leigh Garson, you are very beautiful."

"No, I'm not." I grinned. "I'm sweaty and dirty and my mouth tastes like road kill."

"And despite all that, you're still very beautiful."

I started the van and we headed toward home, fine-tuning our story along the way. The plan was to say that we'd been carjacked by two guys who also stole our phones. A nice man lent us this van. It was lame, but it was the best I could come up with.

"But wait for them to talk first," I said. "In case they heard something from the federal agents that will contradict our story." I knew the agents had been to Mrs. Kokesh's house, but I wasn't sure if they'd contacted our parents. Scout had said they wouldn't, and I was hoping he was right.

As it turned out, all of our practice wasn't necessary. When we got to the Walkers', Lucas's mom burst out of the house as soon as we pulled into the driveway. She ran with her hands fluttering like she was about to have a seizure. "Lucas, Lucas!" Tears streamed down her face. "Thank God you're home. Are you all right?"

"I'm fine, Mom." He hugged her and turned on the Lucas charm. "Emma and I just had a few adventures we weren't counting on. I'm sorry I didn't call."

"All that matters is that you're home and safe." She pulled away to inspect him. "You're really okay?"

"I told you, I'm fine."

"Well, don't ever pull anything like that again." She wagged a finger at him. "When you didn't answer your phone, I went out of my mind thinking the worst."

"That I was dead in a ditch?" Lucas said and threw his head back and laughed. Oh, how I had missed that laugh.

"I don't think that's funny at all," she said, narrowing her eyes.

"I'm just teasing you, Ma. Is there anything for breakfast? Emma and I are starved."

She glanced over and gave me a look of disdain. "I believe Emma needs to run along home. I'm sure her mother is out of her mind with worry." Mrs. Walker took Lucas's arm and steered him toward the house. The way she turned her back on me made it clear that she'd reclaimed Lucas and I was once again the outsider. Sighing, I went to open the van door, when I heard Lucas's footsteps behind me. "Emma, wait!"

And just like that, he was back, wrapping his arms around me and pressing his lips against mine, kissing me like he'd been waiting a long time to do this and didn't want to wait another minute. When he pulled away, I was breathless, my heart happily pounding. "Lucas," I said, tilting my head toward the house, "your mother can see."

"Let her see," he said. "You saved my life. I think I'm entitled to a kiss." He whispered in my ear. "I love you. Go home and get some sleep. I'll see you later."

I watched as he dashed up the steps to the house. As he went inside and through the screen door, I got a glimpse of Mack jumping and yelping as he realized his boy was home. As I backed down the driveway, Lucas was rubbing Mack's head and speaking what I was sure were words of reassurance.

In a way we'd lucked out. Mrs. Walker was so glad to have her son home alive and well that we didn't get interrogated. With time, this would all blow over.

I took one last look at the house and saw Eric watching me intently from the living room window. That kid didn't miss a thing. When he saw me looking, he saluted and I waved right back. Since I'd managed to bring his brother back, I had a feeling he'd forgive me for losing the car.

# CHAPTER FORTY-FOUR

Two weeks later, Lucas and I took another kind of road trip when we went back on the road to return the van. The logistics of this trip were staggering because in order to get permission to go we had to do damage control from our previous outing.

When I'd returned from the first trip, my mom met me at the door, upset and worried, reacting just like Mrs. Walker had (without the flappy arms). I was so happy to find out that the agents hadn't been around that I wound up telling her the truth about our car trip, with a few omissions. Like, I didn't mention aliens or federal agents or getting airlifted into a giant spaceship. I did tell her about almost hitting a deer and putting the car in a ditch, losing our phones due to a mishap at a diner, and that we had to borrow a van from a nice elderly couple. That we met up with a friend named Lacey who let us spend the night at her house because by then it was so late and we were too tired to drive.

My mother folded her arms in front of her and said, "And there were no working phones at Lacey's house? No cell phones, no landline?"

Oh, she got me good. And I'd been doing so well. I tapped my chin with my finger. "Um . . . see, what happened is—"

She sighed dramatically. "I have a feeling we're about to take a bad turn here. How about you're grounded for two weeks and we save this story for ten years from now when I'll think it's funny?"

"I'm good with that. Except—"

"Except what?"

"I need to get the van back to Mr. Atkins. And I'll have to borrow your car to do that."

Reluctantly and miraculously, after many days of campaigning on my part, she agreed to let me go, but only after I reminded her that, when *she* was my age, seventeen, she and a friend had hitchhiked across the country to go to a concert. She said, "Different times, Emma. Those were different times." But I could tell from the smile on her face that she was giving in.

When Lucas's mother dropped him off at my house the morning we were leaving to take the van back, she wasn't smiling, but she did get out and make small talk with my mother in front of our trailer. "Your daughter has my son under some kind of spell," she said, trying for a joking tone, but I wasn't buying it. "Lately, all he does is follow her around like a duckling."

My mom said, "It sounds like Lucas has very good taste." From the look on Mrs. Walker's face, that wasn't what she was hoping to hear.

We didn't stick around much longer. Lucas had borrowed Eric's phone and I had replaced my phone, so we were set that way. We said our good-byes and headed out. I drove my mom's car and Lucas followed in the van, and we traveled for hours without stopping until we got to Roy and Beverly's house. I knocked on the door, but they weren't home, which made things easier, actually. I had Lucas pull around to the back of the house and park under the carport. I stuck the keys under the sun visor and left a long thankyou note on the dashboard, along with some money. Payment for gas and the jug of moonshine I'd appropriated.

When I was done, we got back in my mom's car and headed home with me at the wheel. Driving, just the two of us, with no worries, was like old times. We laughed and talked and listened to music and ate junk food. And we did a little car dancing too. It was a lot of driving for one day, but with the right music and the right person sitting next to me, the miles melted away and I didn't even notice the time.

We were nearly home when I told Lucas, "We have to make one more stop. I want to see Mrs. Kokesh." Lucas grinned, knowing what I had in mind. I'd already told him how I'd tried to call Mrs. Kokesh numerous times since we'd returned. The first time, she'd answered and told me curtly that she didn't want to talk to me. "Those agents tore the house apart and scared my cats near to death," she said. "If they find out I'm talking to you, it'll start right up again. You just leave me alone, Emma Garson." Slam. She hung up the phone and every time I tried to call after that, it rang and rang and rang.

I saw her point, I did, but I still wanted to see her, to show her that Lucas was himself now, and to give her a thank-you gift. I turned down the country highway that led to her house. It was still light out, nearly dinnertime, and I was pretty sure she'd be home. Per usual, a cat lounged on the front porch and it didn't budge even when we stepped over it to knock on the door.

"Mrs. Kokesh?" I called through the screen. "It's me, Emma. I know you're home."

I waited a minute and knocked again. "I've got Lucas with me. He's back and everything is great."

Lucas stepped closer to the door, his mouth nearly on the screen. "Hello, Mrs. Kokesh? It's me, Lucas Walker."

"Please?" I pleaded. "We just want to talk to you for a minute."

"Okay, okay," she yelled from the top of the stairs. "Hold your horses!" The steps creaked as she made her way down. At the door, she said, "Emma Garson, knowing you has only brought me grief.

You got nothing I want or need." Today, she had a paisley scarf wrapped around her head, held in place with a brooch like she was a fortune-teller.

I held up a glass jug. "I brought you a gift. It's moonshine."

"Moonshine, huh?" A thoughtful look came over her face. "That I could use." She pushed open the door. "Come on in, but just for a minute." We followed her into the kitchen. "Put it on the table," she instructed. "What kind of moonshine is that? It's not going to make me blind, is it?"

"It's not going to make you blind," I promised. "It's from northern Wisconsin." I tried to remember how Scout had quoted Roy. "This here is called Pride and it's one hundred and twenty proof and as pure as it comes."

"Pride, huh? I've heard of that, I think." Mrs. Kokesh unscrewed the cap and gave it a sniff. "Okay. I'll keep it." Like she was doing us a favor. She screwed the cap back on. "So, what else is new?" She cackled then, like she'd told one whopper of a joke. "You want to tell me what those agents wanted?"

"Oh, that," I said, waving a hand to show it was nothing. "That's over now."

"What?" she said sharply. "They come and terrorize me looking for you and you don't want to tell me what it was about?"

Lucas stepped forward. "If you really want to know, they were looking for an alien from another planet. He crash-landed here and took over my body until Emma was able to drive him to a place where he could reconnect with his people. That's where she was when the agents were here tearing up your house."

"Huh." She gave Lucas a nod of approval. "But everything is okay now?"

"Never better."

I reached into my purse. "One more thing." I pulled out her gun, safely in its case, and put it on the table. "I want to return this. Thank you. You were right. It was good to have."

"I had a feeling it might be," she said, putting it back in the kitchen drawer.

# CHAPTER FORTY-FIVE

That night, Lucas and I took a walk behind the barn to look at the stars. It was a good night for doing just that—the night sky seemed to stretch endlessly overhead, the stars shining brilliantly, all of them competing to be the most beautiful. I swear I even saw a few of them twinkle.

I thought about how we'd look from above. Two tiny people out of billions living on planet Earth. One planet, in one solar system, in one galaxy. Insignificant in number, and yet out of all the people on this particular planet, we were the ones Scout had wound up coming to for help and friendship. Us. It had to be fate.

I said, "I always knew it was possible that there were other planets like ours, with intelligent life, but it didn't seem real, you know?"

"I know," he said, putting his arm around my shoulders. "But it is real. They're out there." I still had Scout's pod in my closet at home, and occasionally Lucas and I took it out and marveled over it. Proof that the whole thing had actually happened.

More proof that it happened? The night before Lucas and I had watched a movie on TV, and we didn't shut it off when the news came on, the way we normally would have. When the anchorwoman announced an upcoming story, I sat up and held my breath. The banner across the bottom of the screen repeated her words: a little girl in northern Wisconsin miraculously cured of cancer. When Chloe and her mother, Amy, appeared on the screen, I grabbed Lucas's arm. "I know them," I said, excitedly. "That's the girl I told you about."

We watched in silence as Amy spoke, her eyes filling with tears. "They told us that the cancer was throughout Chloe's entire body and that they couldn't do any more for her. I prayed and prayed and prayed." She put her hands together to illustrate. "But instead of getting worse, she seemed to get better. She had so much energy and she gained some weight. When her hair started growing back, I asked them to run some more tests. When they said it was gone, no cancer anywhere, I knew it was a miracle."

Chloe bounced in her seat next to her mom, a big grin on her face. The headscarf was gone and her hair was short and fine as dandelion fluff, but she looked more like a little girl with a cute, short haircut than a cancer patient. When the anchorwoman asked how she was feeling, Chloe proclaimed, "I feel great!" I thought of Scout leaning over to let her rub his head. He'd done a good thing. The world was a better place because he'd been here. And now he was home, and both he and Lucas were where they belonged.

As we stared at the night sky, a question came to me and I turned to Lucas. "Did you go to Scout's planet, do you think? Do you remember?"

He shook his head. "It's pretty hazy, but I think everything happened on the ship while it was hovering above Earth."

"Tell me again what it is you remember exactly from when they took Scout out of your body."

Lucas looked up at the sky, thinking about that night. "It almost felt like going into surgery on Earth. I was lying flat on a table, and I had that groggy feeling. I couldn't see anything, but I knew they were all around me, working on me. I could tell when Scout was lifted out. There was sort of a rushing feeling, like a wind going through my body, and then I was myself again."

"And then they brought you down and I found you on the road." My own personal happy ending.

"You know, I just remembered something else," Lucas said, pulling me closer. "At least, I think I remember it." He shook his head, like trying to shake it off. "So weird that I forgot about this until just now."

"What is it?"

"Right before they brought me back, Scout communicated with me. He must have done it telepathically, because I heard it in my head. It was a message for you, but it doesn't make sense, so maybe I'm not remembering it right."

"A message for me?" I straightened up in surprise. "What was it?"

"Let me think how it went." He put his hand up to his forehead. "I think it was, 'tell Emma that I am sending her less than three.'"

I couldn't hold back my smile, a smile so bright it radiated beams out into the night sky and off to the rest of the universe. "That guy is unbelievable," I said, grinning.

"So you understand it?"

"Yeah."

"But what does it mean?"

I gazed at the velvet sky, scattered with bursts of light, and imagined Scout on his planet looking at his glowing indigo sky with Regina at his side. I'd wanted him gone in the worst way, but I missed him now. If Scout was indicative of what people on other planets were like, we were missing out by keeping to ourselves. He had a good heart and was true to his word. He'd kept his promise to return Lucas to me and he'd left us a gift for the future as well.

"It means . . ." I said, trying to think of how to break the news to him, ". . . that he loves us. And there's something else too." Lucas regarded me curiously and I felt a wellspring of joy rising up from within. "Wait until I tell you," I said. "You're going to be so happy."

# ACKNOWLEDGEMENTS

A heartfelt thank-you to everyone at Skyscape and Amazon Publishing for helping this book find its way into the world. It's an honor to be associated with such a dedicated, talented group of people. For this book and others, I've benefitted from the expertise of Courtney Miller, Terry Goodman, Jessica Poore, Jeff Belle, Daphne Durham, Vicky Griffith, Sarah Tomashek, Gabriella "Gabe" VandenHeuvel, Brooke Gilbert, Katy Ball, Nikki Sprinkle, Thom Kephart, Verena Betz, Jessie Hughes, and Jacque Ben-Zekry. To anyone I've inadvertently left out—my apologies!

I am incredibly lucky to have friends and family who are willing to read my manuscripts and give me honest, helpful feedback. My love and gratitude to Kay Bratt, Kay Ehlers, Geri Erickson, "Eagle Eye" Alice L. Kent, Charlie McQuestion, and Michelle San Juan.

To Roy Atkins, a note of appreciation for the use of your name and for providing my first taste of moonshine!

A big thank-you to my copyeditor, Anna Rosenwong, for saving me from myself many times over. Your work on the book is greatly appreciated.

My family helps me in so many ways. Greg, Charlie, Maria, and Jack McQuestion—I hope you know how much I love you.

Book bloggers are the unsung heroes of the publishing world. You are a powerful, insightful group and I've benefited greatly from your kind words. I'm sending virtual good wishes your way. Thank you!

Finally, I want to acknowledge the readers. Because of you, I've fulfilled my lifelong dream of writing novels for a living. As long as you keep reading, I'll keep writing.

And before I sign off, one final request: If you have enjoyed this book, and it's not too much trouble, a short review posted on Amazon or Goodreads would be appreciated. And if you'd like notification of my upcoming book releases, visit www.karenmcquestion.com and sign up for my newsletter. Thank you!

# ABOUT THE AUTHOR

Karen McQuestion writes books for all ages but has a special love for young adult fiction. She lives with her family in Hartland, Wisconsin.